A NOVEL OF SHATTERING SHOCK
WITH A STAR-STUDDED CAST

Marion Davies
Charlie Chaplin
Elinor Glyn
William S. Hart
Louella Parsons
Mack Sennett
William Randolph Hearst
and
Tom Ince,
the brilliant, ruthless, womanizing director whose strange death and even stranger life set a young reporter on a trail that led behind the scenes of Hollywood at its most dazzling and depraved—and into a labyrinth of shame, sin and scandal brought to light in the boldest novel ever written about the way it really was—

The Ince Affair

"A fascinating story about some of the most colorful, powerful people of the twenties. I've no idea if this is actually what happened, but I'm willing to believe it."
—VINCENT CANBY

SIGNET Bestsellers You'll Want to Read

THE INCE AFFAIR

A Novel by

Joe Morella
and Edward Z. Epstein

A SIGNET BOOK
NEW AMERICAN LIBRARY
TIMES MIRROR

NAL BOOKS ARE ALSO AVAILABLE AT DISCOUNTS IN BULK
QUANTITY FOR INDUSTRIAL OR SALES-PROMOTIONAL USE.
FOR DETAILS, WRITE TO PREMIUM MARKETING DIVISION,
NEW AMERICAN LIBRARY, INC., 1301 AVENUE OF THE
AMERICAS, NEW YORK, NEW YORK 10019.

SIGNET TRADEMARK REG. U.S. PAT. OFF. AND FOREIGN COUNTRIES
REGISTERED TRADEMARK—MARCA REGISTRADA
HECHO EN CHICAGO, U.S.A.

SIGNET, SIGNET CLASSICS, MENTOR, PLUME AND MERIDIAN BOOKS
are published by The New American Library, Inc.,
1301 Avenue of the Americas, New York, New York 10019

FIRST SIGNET PRINTING, JUNE, 1978

    1 2 3 4 5 6 7 8 9

PRINTED IN THE UNITED STATES OF AMERICA

In 1924, movie mogul Thomas Harper Ince died under mysterious circumstances. In THE INCE AFFAIR, all of the background information regarding nonfictitious characters is factual. Many of the events herein actually occurred.

What a mistake to suppose that the passions are strongest in youth. . . .

—Bulwer-Lytton

Prologue

"Hurry up. Let's get this over with."

The man spoke brusquely, a sharpness in his voice. Four men carefully hoisted the body onto the stretcher and silently transported their lifeless cargo over the polished mahogany deck of the yacht like ants carrying a prize grasshopper.

A small manservant, on deck running an errand for his famous employer, swiftly, silently stepped back into the shadows. He was relieved he hadn't been seen. As the group passed, a brisk night wind blew the sheet away from the face of the dead man. The servant stifled a gasp as he caught a glimpse of Thomas Ince, a bullet hole in his forehead.

The sheet was quickly pulled back over the corpse and the group continued with their stealthy work. As they lowered the stretcher onto the dinghy, fog closed in. The myriad of stars which had given life to the black sky vanished.

Two men held the body steady as two others briskly rowed toward shore. The splash of the oars cutting into the calm sea rhythmically broke the eerie silence. The lights of the gleaming white, 220-foot yacht receded and then disappeared completely. For a split second the corpse and its attendants were in a misty black void, a ghostly night world. The men exchanged nervous glances. Then, through the mist, a sign finally became visible. It was illuminated by two lonely electric light bulbs: "San Diego Harbor."

It was Thursday, November 20, 1924, 3:13 A.M.

Thursday, November 20

In Los Angeles it was still dark about 5:15 in the morning when Al Bradshaw's old Chevrolet—a 1912 model with a detachable rumble seat—came to a screeching halt in front of the staid, granite Los Angeles Tribune Building.

The sandy-haired, twenty-one-year-old Bradshaw was tall and athletic, brown from the sun. At the moment his collar and tie were askew, his blue eyes bloodshot. He brushed aside strands of hair hanging down over his forehead. Al was still tipsy, but not sleepy. "This is the last time I try it with college girls," he groaned to himself.

As Bradshaw entered the Tribune Building, he affectionately patted the bronze plaque which stated the newspaper's declaration of principles: *All the Truth, All the News*.

The young reporter made his way upstairs to the city room, where only a skeleton staff was on duty.

"Damn," he said, rummaging around impatiently at his desk. Then, in the far reaches of a drawer, he found the felt bag. "I've been saving you for a special occasion," he told it lovingly. He withdrew the precious pre-Volstead Act bottle of bourbon. There were only about two shots left. "Bottoms up." He smiled silently to himself, drinking directly from the bottle.

Thoughts of the earlier part of the evening caused him to scowl. "If not scoring in six hours doesn't drive a man to drink, nothing will. . . ." He hiccuped. "I

3

should have known better when she insisted I take her to a goddamn concert at the Hollywood Bowl!"

As the twelve-year-old liquid warmed his insides, Al growled with guttural satisfaction. "Nothing like the real thing." He grimaced, licking his lips. He tossed the bottle into a nearby wastebasket, grabbed his jacket, and walked out quickly, though a bit unevenly. Al took the shortcut, downstairs through the pressroom. The giant machines were grinding out the last edition of the morning paper. Bradshaw pulled a copy off the presses and tucked it under his arm.

As Al crossed Grand Street toward Vera's Place, his favorite diner, a sleek Packard zoomed unexpectedly down the deserted street. The car hit a puddle and splattered Al's trousers. "Screw you, you jerk!" he yelled. Dammit, he thought, wiping himself off, *nothing* was going to go right today.

But the bourbon and the warm, friendly atmosphere of Vera's soon restored his spirits. Al settled into a cozy booth and spread out the morning paper in front of him. He was struck by a headline: MOVIE MOGUL SHOT ON HEARST YACHT.

Bradshaw quickly scanned the short story:

San Diego, Nov. 20—Noted motion-picture producer Thomas Harper Ince was shot last night aboard the luxury yacht *Oneida* . . .

"Hot story, Al?" Al looked up as Vera Janowski placed a prune Danish and mug of coffee on his table.

"Oh, hi, sweetie." He winked. "Thanks," he said, motioning to the coffee and Danish, his regular order. But Al's eyes swiftly returned to the story.

. . . attending a boating party hosted by William Randolph Hearst, newspaper publisher and motion-picture producer, Mr. Ince . . .

"Good morning," said Vera tersely, aware she'd lost Al's attention. The slight annoyance in her voice and the bright glint in her green eyes confirmed that their relationship was considerably more than waitress-customer.

"I'm sorry, honey, forgive me." Al pushed the paper aside. "I had a rough night," he lamented, sipping his coffee.

"I can tell!" Vera's lips parted slightly into a smile. Al's rumpled clothes and bleary eyes clued her that he was not on his way to work but dragging himself home. "What's the matter, lover boy, technique slipping?"

Al laughed. He'd always admired Vera's uncanny perception. As he bit into the Danish, his concentration was split between Vera's chatter and his newspaper.

. . . details of shooting . . . film star Marion Davies aboard . . . Ince's condition . . .

Vera refilled his cup. "Those rumble seats will get you every time," she chided.

As the young woman ambled back to the kitchen, Al's eyes lingered on her curvy bottom. Vera glanced at him over her shoulder. "Insatiable, huh?"

"Let's say unsatisfied." He chuckled, shaking his head in dismay. Why, he asked himself, did he bother with young college stuff when the best was in his own backyard? Vera was a few years older than Bradshaw, but she was comely enough to garner any man's attention.

Her curly chestnut hair framed a pretty heart-shaped face. Her beautiful almond-shaped eyes, fringed with bristly lashes, were her most striking feature. She had healthy, clear skin. She wore makeup only on her pouty lips, which were always rouged a bright red in a facsimile of the fashionable cupid's bow. Today, a pair of imitation-pearl earrings dangled merrily from her ears.

As she waited on the few other customers, Al mar-

veled at her body. It was firm as any sixteen-year-old
flapper's. But it wasn't Vera's looks that Al and others
were drawn to. It was that direct manner, gutsy sense
of humor, and easygoing personality.

Bradshaw's thoughts returned to the newspaper. He
quickly leafed through to check if the three stories he'd
handed in late yesterday had made this edition. Only
one had.

Vera was back in a few minutes. "Haven't seen you
in a couple of days," she told him pointedly.

Al looked up again and smiled. He knew it was an
invitation. "How about tonight?" he asked.

She returned his knowing grin. "How about this afternoon? I knock off around three."

"At three I'll be at city hall covering the dumb
mayor. How about later on?"

"Hey, Vera!" screamed Rusty, the overworked
short-order cook, rudely interrupting their romantic
mood with a clatter of dishes.

Vera ignored Rusty and kept her sparkling eyes
riveted on Al. "How *about* later on?" She winked
seductively.

"Four-thirty?" asked Al.

"Four-thirty," she agreed.

"Vera!" Rusty screeched again.

"Keep your shirt on," she said laconically, walking
back to the kitchen.

As Al left the diner, Grand Street was still dozing la-
zily. Bradshaw loved these early-morning hours. Somehow watching the sleeping city stretch awake always
excited him.

Al dodged a trolley car and headed toward his room
a few blocks away. It was too late to catch any sleep.
After a quick shower and change of clothes, he walked
back to the *Tribune*.

By 7:30 the city room was bustling. The air, as always, was filled with smoke and charged with tension.

Phones were jangling, typewriters clacking, people arguing in loud voices.

"Hi, kid." "Good morning, Ace." "How ya doin', kiddo?" greeted Al as he walked through the musty, smoky room. This atmosphere was home to Bradshaw. He thrived on it. It was the only life-style he had ever known, having been engulfed in the tough, brash world of newspapers since his Seattle childhood.

"Always remember this, Al," his father had told him, " 'An honest man is respected by all parties.' " The famous Hazlitt quote was framed over the senior Bradshaw's desk. Al and his father—Ed Bradshaw was a widower, who lived for little more than his work and his son—often spoke of the "Bradshaw code": Find out the truth—and print it. But when Al was sixteen, he had the gut-wrenching experience of watching his father defend this philosophy. Plowed under when the newspaper syndicates invaded Seattle, Ed Bradshaw lost his small daily. Soon after, he died of a heart attack. He was only forty-four.

Al, lonely and disillusioned, odd-jobbed his way down the West Coast. Disgusted by the unethical practices of the growing, all-powerful newspaper chains, he tried to avoid the world of journalism. He told himself he didn't want to be a reporter. But by the time he landed in Los Angeles in 1920, he realized he'd never be happy as anything else.

There were at the time six Los Angeles newspapers: the staid Los Angeles *Times*; the *Examiner*, a flashy Hearst paper; the *Express;* the *Herald;* the *News;* and the *Tribune*. The *Trib* was a struggling family-owned affair. Its motto had struck a chord in Al. He wangled a job as a copyboy.

Al had worked his way up to reporter and for the last year he'd been covering the lighter side of city hall—the mayor's social schedule. Unimportant feature stories. Fillers. He was industrious and had broken several big stories. But each time, they'd been taken away from him and assigned to older reporters, and

Bradshaw was unhappy and restless. He felt the *Tribune* owed him the opportunity to cover important news with a regular byline. He'd been pushing Casey Clark, the city editor, for the last three months.

The mayor's press conference today at three was sure to be the usual uneventful nonsense. Bradshaw decided to make his biweekly pitch to Clark. He crossed the busy city room and stuck his head through Clark's open door.

"Casey, that mayor story is gonna be bull. What if I—"

"Hold it a second," barked the busy city editor without looking up from the story he was furiously red-penciling. Dubbed "Eagle Beak" because of his unusually pointed nose, the plump, balding, forty-seven-year-old Clark was famous for his gruff manner. He always spoke harshly, as if allowing a friendly tone to creep into his voice would mean the collapse of his authority. Clark completed editing. "Okay, kid, let's have that again."

Al knew Casey had heard him the first time. But he repeated, "That story on the mayor is going to be bull-shit. How about letting me go out and uncover something really big?"

"Like what?" demanded Clark angrily.

"I'll find something," said Al with confidence. He thought quickly. "How about a follow-up on the Ince shooting?"

The look of astonishment on Casey Clark's face pleased Al. Clark was a man who never showed any emotion other than anger. Al's suggestion had obviously touched a nerve. *Maybe the old fart's gonna go for it!* thought the reporter.

But there was a curious silence. The two men stared at each other until Al innocently asked, "Any new stuff come in on that, by the way?"

Casey reverted to his hard, businesslike self. He ignored Al's question and turned back to the papers he was shuffling and editing. Bradshaw waited quietly for a few seconds, then tried again. "Any more news on Ince?"

"Forget it!" Casey grunted, without looking up. "The story's been yanked."

"Yanked?" Al was incredulous.

"That's right," said Clark with finality.

Al would not be deterred. "How could it be yanked? It sounds like a big story."

Clark raised his head slowly and riveted his eyes on Bradshaw's. "I *said*, forget it. Your job is city hall, kid. You do your job, I'll do mine. Make sure we have that story on the mayor by five."

Their discussion was at an end. Al was dismissed by a wave of Casey's hand, as he returned to his editing. Bradshaw swallowed hard. He didn't know why a shrewd veteran like Casey Clark would pull a story that explosive. More important, Al was insulted that Clark would expect him—or any good reporter—to "forget it."

Bradshaw walked quickly to the wire desk. His reporter's instinct had taken over. He wanted to check what was coming in on the Ince-Hearst story. Al couldn't believe his eyes. "Jesus," he muttered aloud as he read the copy.

Bradshaw's favorite speakeasy was the Palm, in downtown Los Angeles. Though it was only a quarter of nine in the morning, inside the Palm it could have been any hour. Reporters liked the windowless restaurant-bar because hooch flowed freely, the food was passable, and information was easily exchanged. Night-shift newsmen stopped there before going home. Daytime reporters tarried to fortify themselves or to kill a couple of hours while they were researching a big story.

A gray-haired piano player pounded out current favorites on what seemed to be a one-hundred-year-old, tinny-sounding upright. A cup of "coffee" was permanently, precariously perched on the piano's ledge.

Al was relieved when he spotted his three best pals together at a table at the far end of the room. Sitting there was Mike Halloran, a veteran police reporter, a feisty gray-eyed man who always seemed to be chewing on a cigar. Halloran was a tough, self-educated man, a veteran of the Spanish-American War. He had pounded the pavements for many years tracking down countless leads on innumerable stories. Mike regarded Al as a surrogate son.

To his right was red-headed Patrick Taylor, who had been covering politics "since George Washington." Pat liked to remind people that "old George was as crooked a son of a bitch as any of 'em." Taylor was an amateur historian and considered himself "beyond cynicism." He wore a constant expression of quizzical amusement.

The senior member of the group was Vince Lewis. The black-haired, jowly, bushy-eyebrowed Lewis was a sharp-eyed wire-service reporter suspicious of everyone and everything. Vince was a native Los Angelino and had personally observed the sleepy little village of Hollywood turn into the Babylon of the New World. Lewis specialized in Hollywood-oriented stories. He was a backroom boy, a longtime observer of the powerful men who "fixed things" behind the scenes.

Although Halloran, Taylor, and Lewis were all twenty to twenty-five years older than Al Bradshaw, they shared an easy camaraderie with the younger man. Al was not regarded as a threat. In fact, each saw in Bradshaw some aspect of himself at that age.

To Holloran, Al represented the energy of youth, an energy beginning to wane in the old police reporter. Taylor saw in Al's eyes an idealism not yet beaten down by reality. And Vince Lewis was envious, but not jealous, of the integrity he sensed in young Bradshaw. Lewis would often tell the others, "That kid'll stand up for what's right, even though he's sure to get slapped down."

All three men were eager to offer "the kid" advice

on learning the trade, cutting corners, what team or horse to lay a sure bet on. And of course their expert advice on getting laid was always available.

But this morning, as Bradshaw stormed over to their table, dames and baseball obviously weren't on his mind. He was a man who had a spring coiled tight somewhere inside him.

"Hey, kid, cool off—you look like you're gonna have a heart attack!" Vince laughed.

"Some flapper give *you* the runaround for a change?" Mike joked.

Al ignored their jibes. "Did you guys read about the Ince business?" he asked excitedly.

"Hey, relax, kid," said Halloran, patting him on the back as he sat down. "You're too young for ulcers."

The men hadn't seen the morning *Tribune* and the story of Ince being shot. "It's morning?" Lewis asked, feigning surprise. But they all had read and discussed the other newspaper versions of the story.

"Did you read the *first* Hearst version?" Lewis asked Al.

"Yeah, I just saw it on the wire. That's the biggest load of bull I ever read."

"Let's see," mused Mike. "How did they phrase it? 'Special Car Rushes Stricken Man Home from Ranch.' That's a joke. Who ever heard of a ranch smack in the middle of the ocean? What I really liked were those fabulous Hearstian touches." He called over to the waiter. "Bill, bring us a copy of the *Examiner*."

Bill brought over the paper. "Not this one." Vince scowled. "The earlier edition."

Vince scoffed, reading the *Examiner*'s slogan aloud: " 'For People Who Think.' Hah!" Then he continued reading: " 'Ince, with his wife, Nell, and his two sons, had been visiting William Randolph Hearst at his upstate ranch for several days previous to the attack. When the illness came upon him suddenly, the film magnate, stricken unconscious, was removed to a special car attended by two specialists and three nurses and hurried back to his canyon home. His wife and sons, and his brothers, Ralph and John, were at his bedside when the end came.' "

Vince folded the paper.

"When they realized that that story wasn't going to wash, since too many people saw Ince board the boat, they came up with *this* beauty." Vince turned to the later edition of the *Examiner.* "Wait'll you hear this," he said, enjoying the rapt attention of his cronies.

" 'SUDDEN END ATTRIBUTED TO OVERWORK—Becomes Ill on Trip. Motion-picture circles and the entire business and social world of L.A. were shocked yesterday at the sudden death of Thomas H. Ince, nationally famous producer. On his way home from San Diego, where he had been on a business trip, Mr. Ince was seized with a severe heart attack.' "

"The *Examiner,*" Lewis exclaimed, "doesn't even *mention* anything else!"

"The *Times,* though," said Pat Taylor, picking up the Los Angeles *Times,* "does concede: 'Death was due to heart disease induced by an indigestion attack. Ince had gone to San Diego and became ill while aboard the yacht *Oneida,* owned by the International Film Corporation. The party aboard the yacht, it was said' "—Taylor allowed his voice to inject a note of sarcasm—" '*it was said*' " he repeated, " 'was given by William Randolph Hearst, publisher who controls the film corporation. Mr. Ince suffered an acute indigestion attack.' "

"Hah!" exclaimed Vince.

"Well," interjected Mike, "the *Times* man gives more information but I love the way the Hearst version tries for a touch of pathos." He read the tag of the *Examiner*'s story: " 'Ince was unconscious until a few minutes before he died. He smiled and tried to speak to his wife.' "

The men all continued to chuckle at the various versions of the story, comparing details in the *Times,* the *Tribune,* the *Examiner.*

"Hell, that's how history gets rewritten." Taylor smirked as he downed another beer.

"How the hell do they expect to get away with it?" wondered Al.

Halloran smiled benevolently at Al's naivete. "Well, they're smart, kid. They'll get away with the food-poisoning—indigestion angle. Ince did have ulcers and he was a big boozer. God knows this rotgut *we're* drinking"—Mike lifted his cup of bathtub gin—"is strong enough to kill any of us."

"You think they drink this cheap shit on the Hearst yacht?" retorted Vince. "They got the best Canadian Scotch."

"But the old man is a teetotaler," observed Pat Taylor.

"*He* is," confirmed Vince. "But that dame of his and their friends swill it down behind his back like there's no tomorrow."

"You think *she* bumped off Ince and the old man's covering up for her," asked Taylor.

Mike laughed. "Who knows? We'll never know the real story."

Al sat fascinated.

"Look," interjected Lewis, "however Ince went, you can be sure he had it good. Those Hollywood women were all over him. I saw it many times myself. Ince was probably making it with Marion Davies, and you know how jealous old man Hearst is."

"Who else was on the yacht besides Davies?" asked Al.

"Whoever was will say they weren't," noted Mike.

"Davies and a bunch of her pals were on the boat," Vince offered. "I'll bet Chaplin was there too."

The men continued their bawdy conjecturing of how Tom Ince died. But Al found no humor in the situation.

"I've waited four years for a story like this," said the young reporter fervently. "This could be my big chance. I can *feel* it. But that bastard Clark told me to stick to covering the shit-ass mayor."

"Hold your horses, kid," said Vince. "Even if Casey thought there *was* a story, he'd give it to McIntire anyway." Willard McIntire was the *Tribune*'s top reporter. Any *big* story was automatically assigned to him.

"If those jokers think I'm going to cover city hall and strawberry festivals forever, they're crazy," fumed Al. "I'm going to dig up what I can on this without telling Clark."

The three older men exchanged knowing glances. "Look, kid," soothed Halloran, "sure it's a big story, except don't you want to live to be a year older?" Mike wasn't fooling. The laughter stopped, and a somber mood descended over the table. "Someone like Hearst can have you followed, roughed up, have his papers print false items, investigate your private life, plant damaging evidence . . . and if that doesn't stop you—"

"Aw, bullshit," said Al, cutting him short. "What's everybody so afraid of?"

Vince turned to Pat Taylor. "Why don't you tell Al about your years in Chicago, Pat?"

Taylor smiled and ordered another beer. Then he launched into a harrowing recollection of his rough-and-tumble time working for Medill McCormick, Hearst's top competitor, who owned the fabulously successful Chicago *Tribune*. "That was back in 1910. Max and Moe Annenberg were Hearst's Chicago circulation managers then, and McCormick hired them away. It started the biggest circulation war the industry has ever seen, and I mean *war*. Hearst's paper, the Chicago *Examiner*, was selling for a penny, so McCormick droped the price of the *Trib* to a penny. The Annenbergs had been using a pack of cheap hoods to make sure that newsdealers in town sold more Hearst papers than any other.

"Naturally, when Max and Moe came over to the *Trib*, some of their boys—Walt Stevens, Red Connors"—he scanned his memory—"Mossy something or other . . . Anyway, they all came over with the Annenbergs. So Hearst's man, Andy Lawrence, then goes out and hires his own group of gunmen—Frankie McErlane and three brothers, Gus, Dutch, and Pete Gentlemen. 'The Gent Brothers,' we dubbed 'em.

"It was two years of hell for the newsdealers in Chicago, I'll tell you that. Both Hearst's and McCormick's thugs roamed the streets. There were a lot of overturned delivery trucks and shipments of papers thrown into the river. A lot of guys were beaten up if they weren't selling the 'right' paper. It went on for about two years, until the hoods finally began shootin' at each other. Dutch Gentlemen was sitting in a saloon when one of Annenberg's thugs walked in and shot him dead—"

"I never read anything like that!" Al's mouth was agape.

"Where the hell would you have read it?" retorted Taylor. "Neither paper printed anything about it, for chrissake. And those crooks who were running Chicago didn't give a damn what was happening. Both Hearst and McCormick had 'em in their pocket."

"Jesus!" exclaimed Al. "My dad went through circulation wars back in Seattle, but it never got that rough. No one was murdered."

"Well," lamented Pat, "it got real rough in Chicago. If the hoods had only gunned each other, it would have been all right. But almost thirty innocent guys were beaten or shot to death. And it really got shitty toward the end. Not only were Hearst and McCormick threatening the newsdealers, they began threatening ordinary people! I remember once, one of Hearst's gangsters was on a trolley car and he got pissed because the passengers weren't reading Hearst's *Examiner*. So he fired six shots into the ceiling of the streetcar, to shake everyone up. He told them to remember which paper to buy next time they plunked down their pennies."

"Well, who won?" asked Al.

"In the final analysis, I suppose McCormick won.

The *Trib*'s circulation went up, the *Examiner*'s down. I'll tell you, what's going on in Chicago now ain't nothin' new. In fact," Pat conjectured, "if anybody's responsible for Chicago being the gangster capital of the world today it's men like McCormick and Hearst. Those bastards stop at *nothing*."

There was a silence. Vince Lewis turned to Al. "Forget the story, kid. Besides the fact that you might get your arms broken, don't you realize no one will give you any dope anyway? Everybody's afraid of Hearst blowin' the whistle on them. Hearst's too big. Nobody can touch him."

"No one's that big," Al persisted.

"You're wrong, kid." Vince chuckled sadly. "Leave it alone."

"Look, fellas," Al said with finality, "I'm not gonna leave it alone. We all know there's a story here—probably the biggest goddamn story of the year. And I'm going to get it."

"So where do you propose to start?" asked Pat Taylor. "Gonna call Mr. Hearst and ask him why the discrepancies in his story?"

The men guffawed. Al remained silent. He was disillusioned with his buddies, and it was easy for them to sense his loss of respect. Each began rationalizing his position.

"It's a fool's quest," said Taylor.

"You don't have a Chinaman's chance," declared Halloran.

"It's a waste of time," Lewis added.

But the look of frustration and determination on Al's face told all three hardened newsmen that no amount of cajoling or logic would dissuade him.

Vince Lewis was the first to soften. "Well, if the kid is going to go ahead with this," he told the others, "we might as well help him all we can."

Al brightened, like a child whose faith in Santa Claus had been restored. He eagerly pulled his chair forward. "Well, what do you guys know about Ince?" he asked.

All three began rattling off names of people who knew the famed producer-director, men and women who might talk to Al. It wasn't necessary to advise the kid to play it cagey with anyone who'd see him.

"You think anyone hated Ince enough to shoot him?"

"Sure," said Mike Halloran. "A lot of people hated Ince's guts. Bill Hart for one. Find out if Hart was on that cruise."

"Yeah," concurred Taylor. "Hart and Ince had a big row a few years back."

William S. Hart. A smile crossed Al's face at the mention of the famed cowboy star. Bradshaw's mind clicked ahead. Sure, sure—Hart and Ince, Ince and Hart. Al remembered the many title cards he had seen on nickelodeon screens, and on posters, which read: "Thomas H. Ince presents William S. Hart . . ."

Talking to Hart might be the beginning of Al's piecing together this whole story. "I can get through to Hart," enthused Bradshaw. "A publicity man at Paramount owes me a favor."

The reporter bounded up and headed for the pay phone outside the john.

"Loo-o-ok, Sophieee," whined a man using the phone, slurring his words. "Thish is a verrry important story and I cannot come home right away. An old woman murdered her husband and . . . What? Dammit, Sophie, would I l-l-lie to you? . . ."

Al paced impatiently. As he thought of William S. Hart, many memories sprang to mind. When he was young, Bradshaw had idolized Hart. He was the biggest cowboy star in films. Al had seen dozens of Hart westerns, as had millions. The star made an indelible impression on the entire nation. Everyone was familiar with his long, lean, intense face, piercing eyes, towering stetson, and his famous quick draw.

"Hello? Helll-ooo?" Disgruntled, the man using the

pay phone slammed down the receiver. "It's all yours, pal," he told Al, weaving away.

Bradshaw glanced at his pocket watch—9:30. Barney should be at the studio by now. Al pulled a crumpled piece of yellow paper from his wallet, deciphered Barney's scribbling, deposited a nickel, and gave the operator the private number. The call went straight through.

"Yes?" answered a gruff, unfriendly voice.

"Barney? Al Bradshaw, the *Tribune*."

The publicist's attitude changed abruptly. "Oh, yeah, yeah." The voice was friendly now. "How are ya, kid?"

Almost two years ago the young reporter had helped Barney by withholding a potentially scandalous story about Paramount star Wallace Reid, a fresh-faced young actor billed as "The All-American Boy." Reid, whacked out on morphine, was wandering around downtown Los Angeles late one night and had stumbled into Vera's. She recognized him immediately and telephoned Al at the *Tribune*. Al and Vera cajoled Reid into a quiet booth and spent half an hour humoring him until Barney and a couple of the boys from Paramount came down to pick Reid up.

Barney Henderson had never forgotten "the kid on the *Tribune*." In gratitude for not exposing Reid, Henderson saw to it that Al was invited to press parties. On occasion Barney even sent Al and Vera invitations to premieres. At these functions Barney always gave Al a big hello, and even gave "the kid" his private number: "Anytime you ever need *anything*, just call."

This early-morning telephone call was the first Henderson had ever received from the reporter.

"Barney, I have to talk to William S. Hart. Can you arrange it?"

Barney was relieved the request was so simple. "Sure, kid, I can fix it up. When do you want to see him?"

"Today."

"Today?" He seemed surprised. "Well, I don't

know, kid. They're filming out in the valley today. The picture's running behind schedule and they've been shooting all week."

If Hart was working all week, he couldn't have been on the cruise. That was one detail out of the way, thought Al.

"How about seeing Hart sometime next week?" asked the publicity man.

"No, Barney. It's got to be today."

"Hang on." In a few seconds Barney was back on the line. "Okay. I can arrange it. They break late for lunch. How about two-thirty?"

"Two-thirty is fine. I'll need more than a few minutes with him, though. This is more than a movie-star interview."

"Oh, Jesus. You're not gonna try to sell him a script, are ya? He *hates* that."

"No, no, I promise. Nothing like that. Just want some background information."

"Okay, don't worry about it, then. Take all the time you need. I'm sending a messenger up to the set so Bill'll know you're a personal friend of mine."

An excited Bradshaw returned to the table. "Hart can see me at two-thirty. But . . ." He suddenly remembered. "Oh, Christ, I'll never be able to cover the mayor at three."

"I'll cover for ya, kid," volunteered Mike Halloran. "Phone me around four and I'll read you the story."

"Whaddya gonna do till then, Al, waste time?" asked Vince. "Why don't you go out to Inceville or to Ince's studio in Culver City? Maybe you can pick up some information there."

"Yeah," agreed Pat. "If you're really hot to follow this up, do it right. Make a list of your leads. Talk to everybody you can who knew Ince and the other people on that yacht. If you're gonna stick your neck out, don't do it half-assed."

An early-morning dose of philosophy burst forth from Taylor. He raised his cup: "Idealism is a wonderful luxury, my boy—the one luxury only the young can afford."

"Good luck, kid," said Lewis.

The four men clicked glasses.

Al had scribbled down notes of people to see, questions to ask, places to go. As he placed the scraps of paper in his breast pocket and rose to leave, Halloran offered a final suggestion: "Why don't you also stop at the studio where Marion Davies is shooting her new picture?"

United Artists Studios, in Hollywood, where Marion Davies was shooting *Zander the Great*, was a pleasant assemblage of Spanish-style buildings on a square block of tree-lined Santa Monica Boulevard.

Bradshaw hadn't had much contact with the film industry, aside from the occasional parties to which Henderson had invited him. Al was surprised that the UA Studios were so unimposing in appearance. Unlike Universal or the Ince Studios, there was no vast backlot. At UA, everything was contained within one city block.

Bradshaw knew that United Artists had been formed by the most powerful stars and directors in the business—Mary Pickford, Douglas Fairbanks, Charles Chaplin, and D. W. Griffith. Even though their salaries had been in the millions, the quartet had decided to produce and release their own films in order to keep *all* the profits. Their former employers at the established film companies countered with the slur, "Now the inmates have taken over the asylum." But in five short years United Artists was as successful as the leading studios, Paramount, Pathé, and First National.

Bradshaw parked his car about a block from the studio gate. He had no idea whom he might get to see or what information he might learn. But he had to start somewhere.

"Hi. I'm Al Bradshaw, Los Angeles *Tribune*." He smiled and showed his press card to the gateman. "I'm

new on the paper and they sent me up to meet some of
the people in publicity," he lied.

The gateman had a friendly, cherubic face and responded to Al's warmth. "Ned Gargan's in charge of
publicity," he said. "His office is in that building over
there. He may not be in, though. I'll call."

"Thanks." Just then Al spotted a familiar figure
walking across a path. "Grace!" he called out. The
woman turned and stared at them.

"Oh, do you know Miss Kingsley?" asked the
gateman.

"Of course." Al smiled. "We're old friends."

Grace Kingsley walked toward them. She was a
pretty woman, feminine, a successful cinema corre-
spondent for a number of papers, including the New
York *News*. Al knew her casually, as most Los Angeles reporters knew each other.

"Hel-lo," said Grace, smiling at Al. "What brings
you here?" she asked in a cheery voice. "The mayor
coming or something?"

Al laughed. "How about showing me around?" He
turned to the gateman. "Is that okay?"

"Sure. There's no answer in the Gargan office. But if
you're a friend of Miss Kingsley, I know you're okay."

"Well, thank you, Bill." Grace smiled. As she and
Al walked onto the lot, Grace asked coquettishly,
"Trying to get into the movies, dear? You're handsome
enough, Lord knows!"

Al got right to the point. "Actually, Grace, I'd like
to interview Marion Davies."

Grace turned somber. "Not today, Al. Haven't you
heard? There's been a tragedy. Tom Ince is dead."

"I know. That's why I want to talk to Davies. I
thought she could give me some background stuff."

"Well, she's not here. And the publicity boys aren't
around either. But," said Grace, spotting a pert
brunette, "see that girl over there?"

Al saw her. She was quite a looker. Her legs were
particularly shapely, and she was bending over smooth-

ing a stocking while chatting with a costumed extra outside the makeup building.

"She's working on Marion's picture," said Grace. "Her name's Mona something-or-other. She might know when Marion is coming back." Grace grew quizzical. "You on the movie desk of the *Tribune* now, dear?"

"No, Grace. It's just some city-room stuff." Al quickly changed the subject. He could see Grace was dressed for an important occasion. "What are *you* doing here today, looking like the prettiest flapper in town?"

The flattery was successful. "I'm interviewing Doug Fairbanks, darling," she said, fluffing her hair. "He, Mary, and I are all having lunch together," she revealed in awe.

"Gee-e-e," said Al, duly impressed. He glanced over and noticed that the leggy brunette had finished her conversation and was heading toward one of the bungalows.

"See you later Grace," Al said, pecking her on the cheek. "Thanks, and give my best to Doug and Mary." He waved, jogging toward the brunette.

He caught up to her quickly. "Excuse me, Miss Moore?" he asked a trifle breathlessly, tapping her on the shoulder. The girl turned around. Al pushed back his sandy hair, clicked on the charm, and smiled at her dazzlingly. She stared at him blankly. "Miss Moore?" he repeated.

"Who?" she asked, her high-pitched voice betraying a nasal Brooklyn twang.

"Aren't you Colleen Moore?"

The girl preened. "Well, no." She giggled. "My name's Mona Petersen. Lotsa people *think* I'm Colleen Moore. From a distance."

"Well, you are in the movies, aren't you?"

"Not yet," she said disappointedly. "I'm an actress, but right now I'm working in the wardrobe department."

"I knew you were an actress." Al smiled. "In my business, you learn to recognize people."

"What's your business?"

"I'm a reporter." He flashed his press card. "Al Bradshaw. L. A. *Tribune*. Just making the rounds of studios on general assignment. Talking with stars and aspiring actresses."

Mona was hooked. Her brown eyes sparkled as she asked, "No kiddin'?"

"Do you know many stars?"

"Well, right now I'm workin' with Marion Davies."

Al nodded, impressed. "What's she like?"

"She's sweet," said Mona. "This is the first picture she's makin' in Hollywood. Metro's gonna release it. But there wasn't any room on the Metro lot. That's why we hadda rent space here."

Al was amused at Mona's use of the pronoun *we*, as though she had a vote on the board of directors of Hearst's Cosmopolitan Pictures.

"Marion's generous, too," Mona continued. "I hear she gave Bill, the gateman, a case of Scotch—*real* Scotch." She lowered her voice to a confidential tone. "It's probably because Bill signals her when Mr. Hearst is on his way to the set." Mona's hand shot up to her mouth. "Hey, you ain't gonna print any of that, are ya?"

"Nah. I'd like a good case of Scotch myself!"

Mona smiled, and winked. "You know, you're good-lookin' enough to be an actor yourself."

"Thanks! But it's a wonder they haven't put *you* in the movies."

"Yeah, ain't it the truth," said Mona disgustedly. "Mr. Ince was gonna put me in the movies."

"You knew Thomas Ince?" This was more than Al had bargained for. But he remembered that "You'll usually get information from people who don't realize they're giving it to you!" had been one of his father's basic tenets.

Al took a crumpled pack of Luckies from his pocket and offered Mona a cigarette.

"Knew 'im? Ince was around here all the time. He was gonna take over Miss Davies' career. And mine."

"Wow," Al said. There was a brief pause. They were walking along slowly, side by side. Mona remained silent. Al ventured, "It's a shame what happened on that cruise."

"Yeah," said Mona, anger rising in her voice. She puffed on her cigarette. "I had a *feelin'* somethin' bad was gonna happen, though. I don't think they really wanted to go on that trip."

"No?"

"Nah. When Louella Parsons and Charlie Chaplin came by the other day to pick up Miss Davies, there was a . . . a whaddya call it? A *tension* between 'em."

"A tension between Miss Davies and them?" he asked.

"Not exactly. Elinor Glyn was going on the cruise too, and they all . . ."

Suddenly Mona realized she was talking too much again. She stopped in mid-sentence and concentrated on her cigarette. A pair of costumed extras passed and waved. They provided a neat opportunity for Al to change the subject so that Mona wouldn't clam up.

"This is the first time I've ever been on a movie lot. Gee, back in Seattle, where I'm from, they don't make movies. And to think that *you* really know Charlie Chaplin! Wait'll I tell the guys back in Seattle that I met somebody who knows Chaplin!"

Al's charm had wooed her back into chattering. "Liss-en," she confided. "Chaplin don't look *nothin'* like he does on screen. He don't have a mustache. He's got curly hair, sort of salt-and-pepper gray, not black. He's not funny-lookin'. He's good-lookin'. Sexy."

"Hey, Mona!" yelled a woman from a second-story window. "They're waitin' for that costume!"

"Jesus, I gotta go." Mona fluttered, grinding out her Lucky.

"Can I call you?" asked Al.

"Sure, I'm at the Studio Club. Call anytime, hand-some. Your name's Al, right?"

It had turned into the kind of gorgeous Southern California day that the natives bragged about. The sky was clear, the air crisp, and the magnificent green Hollywood Hills loomed off to the right. Bradshaw's Chevy chugged along leisurely. He turned left onto Robertson Boulevard toward Culver City and the Ince studio.

He gathered his thoughts. What a story this could be! Almost unprecedented in scope and intensity. If he could uncover what might be the greatest cover-up since the Teapot Dome, he'd be *made*. *He'd* be like Rocky Rochlen of the *Times*, or Willard McIntire of the *Trib*, reporters that all the big stories were assigned to. And, more important, if he could bring the story off, his success would be a small but sweet victory for all people—like his dad—who had been victims of a Hearstian kind of power.

The principals in the Ince affair were famous, flamboyant, wealthy, powerful. Incredibly so.

Bradshaw had seen Thomas Ince once—three years ago—when Al was a cub reporter on the *Tribune*.

". . . And so, Mr. Ince, we take pride in giving you this award, not only for your genius but for your belief in the wonderful industry which has risen to such heights in so short a time, thanks to men like yourself . . ."

Ince was beaming. It was a special luncheon at the Hollywood Hotel, where representatives of the city of Los Angeles had presented him with a gold key in recognition of his services to the film industry. All the movie moguls, and many big stars, were there. It was obvious that Ince was highly respected and deserving of the award. Along with C. B. De Mille and Griffith, Ince was responsible for making Los Angeles the new home of the motion-picture business, which now ranked first among California's thirty-five leading industries.

"Wizard of the Westerns" was D. W. Griffith's apt description of Thomas Ince as a moviemaker. As a man, Ince was magnetic. He exuded enormous energy—it was almost a visible aura surrounding him. He was ruggedly handsome and manly, very Irish in appearance, with arresting light blue eyes and curly, close-cropped brown hair, graying at the temples.

He was an easy smiler, a ladies' man, suave and lighthearted. But he revealed passionate convictions even in casual conversation. Al Bradshaw saw how every woman's eyes at the gathering had followed Ince's movements.

Bradshaw also noticed an obvious change in Ince's attitude when it came to discussing business. He was more than merely assertive. When necessary, a toughness rose to the surface. Observing Ince deep in discussion with Adolph Zukor, Al watched how Ince wielded persuasive charm with force and intelligence. In contrast to the other moguls, like Zukor, B. P. Schulberg, and Jesse Lasky, who were businesslike and asexual, Ince was intensely sensual, a dynamo, a man who drew both men and women into his orbit.

At the luncheon Ince was lauded as being the first moviemaker to make the grueling trip to Los Angeles, back in 1911. His terrific talent was for putting together stories that *men* would like. Outdoor western adventures, tales of cowboys and Indians. "Ince has got the energy of a cyclone," marveled producer Carl Laemmle, who was the founder of Universal Pictures. Laemmle had hired Ince back in New York after a meeting at which Ince was as subtle as a battering ram: "I can make the kind of pictures that'll make you the richest man in town."

That kind of thinking articulated what Laemmle had in mind. *Custer's Last Fight* and *War on the Plains* were Ince's cinematic contributions to Laemmle's bank account. Both pictures were big hits.

Ince took his share of the profits and leased land in California: "That's where the big money is." He took an option on 20,000 acres, which eventually became known as Inceville. The total cost was $35,000, a lot of money in those days. However, Ince was soon worth a couple of million dollars—on paper, at least. But no one could point an accusing finger at him for making money off the sweat of others. He was supercharged with nervous energy and had worked round the clock like a madman for every penny.

At the time of the Ince luncheon, Marion Davies and William Randolph Hearst were still making their "flickers" in New York. It was only this year that Hearst had decided to move his film enterprises west.

Bradshaw had first seen Marion Davies only a month ago, when Cosmopolitan Pictures threw a big bash celebrating her arrival in Hollywood. Most of the reporters in Los Angeles had been invited, and Bradshaw's pal Barney Henderson saw to it that Al was on the list.

Al had of course seen Marion Davies on screen. *When Knighthood Was in Flower* and *Little Old New York* were his favorites. Both had been enormous successes and among the top ten films of the year. In the flickers Marion seemed somehow petite and childlike. Obviously, in films, Hearst wanted Marion to look like another Mary Pickford. All the important female stars were physically tiny: Pickford, Gloria Swanson, Lillian Gish. If Davies was to be a big star, she'd better appear tiny too, was typical Hollywood thinking.

In person, however, Bradshaw was surprised that Marion was tall, at least five feet five inches. And not childlike at all.

Marion in the flesh was an alluring combination of hoyden and aristocrat. She was like a blond butterfly, bursting with vitality and a sense of fun in a totally feminine, animated manner.

Her skin was flawless, porcelainlike. She was slim,

sensual, stylish—tastefully flashy. Spectacular jewels glittered from her hair, fingers, wrists, ears. Even Al's untutored fashion sense picked up on the perfection of her ensemble, a pastel blue something-or-other that flowed with her movements and brought out the blue of her eyes. Even from a distance those eyes flashed and sparkled, like two aquamarines with tiny lights behind them.

Though the general public might be unaware of it, Bradshaw, like everyone else in the newspaper business, knew that Marion Davies was the personal property of William Randolph Hearst. He had literally picked her out of the chorus, fallen madly in love with her, and made her a star. As simple as that.

At the Cosmopolitan Pictures party, Marion was not the only star. The glamorous Talmadge sisters, Norma and Constance, held court, along with Alma Rubens and the dazzling Barbara Lamarr. And the moguls, of course, attended in force—De Mille, Lasky, Louis B. Mayer, Goldwyn . . . and Thomas Ince. But none of the glittering assemblage outshone the party's host, William Randolph Hearst.

Al was truly fascinated to finally observe the legendary Hearst in person. He was very tall and formidable, with patrician features set off by a head of distinguished gray hair. Hearst's one physical flaw was a high-pitched voice, almost ridiculously incongruous in a man his size.

He was constantly surrounded by hangers-on buzzing around like bees around a honey pot. It seemed as though everyone who spoke with Hearst wore the expression of a puppy dog anxious to please his master. A sense of power emanated from the man like electrical energy. Hearst was *feared*.

Bradshaw's thoughts concentrated on the infamous publisher. W.R.—"The Chief"—the most powerful private citizen in the world. His immense fortune was estimated at $400 million. It was mostly in real estate, stocks, and business holdings. The enigmatic, unpredictable Hearst was accountable to no one. Fifty-eight years old, he had for years controlled a force even more powerful than his incredible wealth—public opinion. His awesome journalistic empire—twenty-two daily papers, fifteen Sunday papers, seven magazines—had the largest number of readers in the country. Hearst could influence, often sway, the American public. Everyone knew that he had single-handedly been responsible for America's involvement in the Spanish-American War. His editorials, often in bold headlines on the front pages of his papers, had inflamed the country.

"He gives the people the kind of stories they want, and they worship him for it," someone had said. One thing was certain: the Hearst papers and the public had been remarkably in step.

By 1920 Hearst had turned his attentions from his newspapers and political ambitions to Marion Davies and her career.

For the last few years he had seemed to enjoy playing the role of starmaker. And he made an effort to enjoy Marion's friends and newfound life-style. But for the most part Hearst's socializing with actors was equivalent to a feudal lord deigning to cavort with court jesters.

Al and several others at the Cosmopolitan party were shocked when the old man got out on the dance floor and did a rousing Charleston with one of the professional dancers. While Hearst's body was sort of pear-shaped, he was not ungraceful in his movements. There was a naturalness in his manner, and Al noticed the old boy never seemed uncomfortable.

Throughout the party Hearst kept a friendly smile on his face, but his blue eyes were cold, distant, unreachable, and constantly keeping watch over Marion Davies.

Hearst could hardly have missed the gay conversation Marion and Thomas Ince engaged in throughout most of the proceedings. Naturally she had chatted with and smiled gaily at almost all the famous men present, including Tommy Meighan, John Barrymore, and John Gilbert.

Actually she seemed to flirt with *every* handsome man. Any fool could easily understand how Tom Ince and Marion Davies would gravitate toward each other. And Hearst was hardly a fool.

Is that what happened? speculated Bradshaw, motoring along in the Chevrolet. Had Davies and Ince been carrying on, and had Hearst finally found out about them? Was Hearst a jealous man? He had displayed no jealousy that night Bradshaw saw him together with Marion. In fact, a special expression came over Hearst's face every time Marion stood next to him. His features softened. He was, unmistakably, a man in love.

As Al pulled onto Washington Boulevard in Culver City, the massive Ince Studios came into view. Production would certainly be shut down here today. But Al was hoping the offices would be open. Vince Lewis had told Al to be sure to get to see Clifford Spencer, Ince's chief writer: "He'll be able to tell you plenty."

The Chevy sputtered along, and soon the imposing white facade of the main building, a grand, pillared edifice, loomed ahead. It appeared to be the main house of a Southern plantation. Al was impressed. He presented the gateman with his press pass and asked to see Mr. Spencer.

"I'll see if he's in," said the guard. To Bradshaw's surprise, he *was* in. Al was instructed to take the stairs to the second floor and walk to the far end of the building. "You'll find Mr. Spencer waiting in his office."

Al walked slowly down the long, expansive corridor, gazing at the elaborately framed photographs which lined the walls. Each of Ince's top stars had posed with "The Boss"—H. B. Warner, Lewis Stone, Mary Boland, Billie Burke, Charles Ray. There were framed scene blow-ups from Ince's films, and one entire wall was devoted to stills from his latest epic, *Anna Christie*, starring Blanche Sweet.

At the end of the hallway, Bradshaw saw that the door to Spencer's office was open. Al stood silently in the entranceway. Clifford Spencer was seated in a comfortable, deep, high-backed leather chair. He was staring out the window. The man's even features, calm demeanor, and conservative manner of dress reminded Al more of a college professor than a hotshot movie writer.

A pleasant aroma from Spencer's brierwood pipe filled the mahogany-paneled room. Spencer finally turned, half-smiled, rose, and walked slowly over to greet Al. Bradshaw, sensing the man was slightly dazed, noticed an open, almost empty whiskey decanter on the desk. "If my best friend had just been killed, I'd go on a binge too," reflected Al.

The men exchanged the usual amenities. Then Spencer asked, "How can I help you?"

"I'd appreciate anything you can tell me about Mr. Ince's background."

Spencer would be delighted to do so, he said. "Tom and I were together from the start, you know. Twelve of the best years of my life," intoned the writer. He proceeded to relate general information, most of which Al remembered from the luncheon—that Ince was born in Newport, Rhode Island, on November 16, 1882. He had two brothers, John and Ralph. "The Inces were a theatrical family, you know, so I suppose it was inevitable the boys would be in show business too. Tom acted in various stock companies back east. It was during the run of *For Love's Sweet Sake* that he met—and married—Elinor. Elinor Kershaw, that is."

Spencer smiled. "Here's a typical Tom Ince story. Around 1910, Ince was out of work in New York. He went over to the IMP studios and they hired him as an actor for five dollars a day. Then Biograph offered him ten dollars and old Tom got 'em up to fifteen." Spencer

chuckled. "He bounced back and forth between IMP
and Biograph, whichever would pay him more. And he
learned the business. In those days, you know, all
movies had to do was move. There was no plot, no
story, no writer. So Ince did just about everything. He
acted, wrote, directed, produced.

"Then, with his wife in the lead, he made *Little
Nell's Tobacco*. Ever see it? No, you were a kid. Nell's
his wife's nickname, you know. Well, it was a big hit.
Let's see, that was still around 1910. Tom always
bragged how he showed the film to Carl Laemmle and
sat there, pointing out to Laemmle, scene by scene,
what a great director he was!"

Spencer sighed and paused to relight his pipe. Al
could tell the writer had deep affection for the dead
man.

"When Tom and I came out here, back in 1911, we
had a successful meeting with the famous Miller Brothers' 101 Ranch Wild West Show.

"Tom told them, 'I'm gonna make wild-west movies,
boys, but I'm going to have to have professional per-
formers. I'll pay your troop twenty-five hundred dollars
a week and they can do their stuff in front of the
cameras.'

" 'You've got a deal,' the Millers said. We all shook
hands, and I could have croaked right on the spot!
Christ, where were we going to get twenty-five hundred
bucks a week? We couldn't scrape up a hundred between us! But then Tom wired Kessel and Bauman and
other distributors in New York telling 'em we fought
hard, outbidding everybody, to get Miller for only four
thousand a week. And Kessel and Bauman came
through. We made *War on the Plains*. A big hit. And it
was the first time real Indians were ever used in a
movie. Up till then they used Mexicans disguised as
Indians."

Spencer obviously enjoyed reliving the good old
days. He poured himself another Scotch, and offered
one to Al.

"By 1913, we were rolling along. De Mille's *The Squaw Man* was a big hit that year. But our *Battle of Gettysburg* was even bigger! Ince and I wrote it. Tommy directed it. You know, along with De Mille, Ince is"—Spencer paused sadly and corrected himself—"was a master of the 'spectacle western.'

"Do you realize we began with one little stage out in Santa Inez Canyon? Then, almost overnight, Inceville was a thriving community. Seven hundred and fifty permanent residents! Ten production units working simultaneously. Our biggest step, of course, came in 1915. With Griffith and Sennett as partners, Ince formed Triangle Productions.

"I remember the day they signed the contracts," recalled Spencer. "It was quite a move forward for the industry. Tom made *Civilization* for that company. God, that was a wonderful movie. . . ."

As Spencer continued relating details of Ince's career, Al thought of questions he'd *really* like to ask: What did Clifford Spencer know about the rumor that Ince was shot? Why did Ince go on this yachting trip in the first place? Did Hearst and Ince argue a lot? Was Ince having an affair with Marion Davies?

But Bradshaw had learned from long experience he dared not ask this type of question; he'd find himself out the studio gates instantaneously. Al knew he'd have to bide his time, hoping Spencer would inadvertently reveal some information enabling him to find out what kind of man Ince really was and if anyone would really want to kill him.

Al's mind wandered momentarily as he gazed out the window and surveyed the studio's grounds—the rows of white frame buildings, the now empty stages and quiet streets of the city within a city. Then Al's thoughts quickly turned back to Spencer, who was saying: ". . . He was the only producer I ever met who did not want to be surrounded with yes-men. You could tell him that his picture was the most putrid, hopeless mess you ever saw in your life, and he would smile and ask, 'Any suggestions on how to fix it?' And he passed instant and fair-minded verdicts upon your suggestions."

According to Spencer, no other producer who ever lived had ever worked in such a whirlwind of nervous energy as Tommy Ince. "He helped write all the stories, selected all the actors, cut and edited all the pictures personally, and wrote most of the titles.

"His scenario conferences were lessons in dramatic construction. Sometimes he used to hold the meetings out at his magnificent home in Benedict Canyon. He would sit curled up on a big couch like a little boy, looking from one face to another as the other writers and I outlined our opinions. Then suddenly he would bound into the middle of the floor, and talking so fast that it was sometimes hard to follow him, he would outline it all into a striking play.

"He could never remember the names of the characters, so as he went along he used to christen them with the most amazing names. He would say—his eager face hot with excitement—'Now, you see, here comes Mr. Step-and-Fetch-It, and he meets Mary Pickles, and this Snupples kid . . .'

"To see Tom at his best, though, was to sit with him in a projection room," reminisced Spencer. "He always insisted on having the most artistic and beautiful projection room in the business. It depressed him to work in ugly surroundings.

"While the picture was running, he would sit back in his wicker chair, feverishly smoking cigarettes and watching the screen narrowly. Suddenly he would punch the bell to stop the film, and with one bound he would be in the middle of the floor—acting, gesturing with both hands, his face sputtering out subtitles. He would have driven an ordinary film cutter to suicide!"

Spencer glowed as he recalled, "Ince was the master cutter of the world. His equal never lived.

"I remember once," Spencer went on, "Ince took a movie so bad that it seemed a hopeless mess and he made one of the great box-office successes of the year out of it. He reorganized all the footage and wrote all new titles, and it worked."

Al interrupted. He wanted some hard information "I hear he was a tough guy to work for," he said. "That he argued a lot with his workers."

Clifford Spencer was reflective for a moment. Then he admitted, "Yes, I guess you could say Tom did supervise everything with an iron hand. 'Action, we need action!' he would always yell when he visited the sets. 'Ride that damn horse till its feet fall off,' he once told director Fred Niblo.

"But underneath it all, Mr. Bradshaw, Tom was a softie. The Ince Studios were the easiest place in Hollywood to find a job. When there was a shabby, scared little girl biting her nails in the waiting room, Tom's quick Irish imagination was always ready to see in her the next great scenario writer of the world!

"And Ince was a starmaker," Spencer said with relish. "He was responsible for making Sessue Hayakawa a star back in 1914. And, of course, Charlie Ray. Charlie was one of our biggest stars. Yes, Tom was *the* starmaker. He brought William S. Hart to the screen, you know. Those films, the ones he did with Bill Hart, were some of Ince's greatest successes."

"But all his stars left him," Al pointed out.

"Yes, that's true," the writer conceded. "He wouldn't pay them what they wanted, so they got it somewhere else."

Ince's frugality was almost legend. Spencer related the well-known story of Ince's meeting with members of the Sioux and Blackfeet Indian tribes, who were toiling in Ince productions. They wanted a raise, from two to three dollars a day.

" 'I'm sorry,' Tommy told them. 'I'd like to give you the money, but I can't. There just isn't that much profit in pictures.'

"The Indians puffed on their pipes. One of the old

Indians said, 'Mr. Ince, we must tell you that we all feel admiration for you.'

"Tom began to glow with a warm feeling of self-satisfaction. The old Indian continued, 'You are the first man here early in the morning, you are an industrious man. You never lose your temper and become abusive; you are a patient, kind man. You always lead the way into all dangers—you go on your big horse. You never say like other directors, "Go here." You take the most dangerous position and say to us, "Come on." You are a man of high courage . . .'

"Tommy was bursting with pride. 'Mr. Ince,' the Indian added, 'with this industry, this patience, this kindness, this high courage—with all those qualities— if you can't make enough money out of your pictures to give us three dollars a day, then you'd better find some other business.'

"Ince gave them their three dollars." Spencer laughed. "He was cheap with salaries, but he would never stint on production. Often an entire picture, in those early days, wouldn't cost more than twenty thousand dollars. But one time, for a picture called *Lying Lips*, Ince invested forty-two thousand dollars just to build a ship for a key sequence.

"The ship was moored off the San Pedro breakwater, but when a storm came up it began to drift toward the pile of rocks that protects the harbor. The cast remained on board, and the cameras continued to grind. Reggie Barker and Harry Schenck, who were in charge, realized that loss of the ship before completion of the sequence would mean a serious financial loss for Tom. So they continued working.

"But Tommy was out there in the harbor on his own boat. He saw the crash was imminent. He took a small boat and rowed out through the breakers.

" 'Get off that ship,' he yelled to the crew. 'The life of one actor is worth more than any goddamn picture. Get back immediately!' "

Al Bradshaw realized that on such stories of romantic daring the larger-than-life he-man image of Thomas Ince had been built.

"When Inceville was reaching its peak, in 1915, we built these new studios in Culver City," related Spencer.

"On New Year's Eve, Tommy threw the most spectacular party Hollywood had ever seen. 'Let's open the new studio with the new year and open it with a *bang*,' he said.

"Tom always did things in a big way—the *biggest* way. *Everybody* came to the party. Everyone from Inceville. All the industry big shots. Griffith. Sennett. Lasky. The great stage actors, Sir Herbert Beerbohm Tree, DeWolf Hopper. Even the L.A. chief of police, Snively, and the district attorney, Woolwine, dropped by.

"It was a helluva night to remember, all right. A thousand people were here. There was no Prohibition then, and we had fountains of the finest champagne. Late in the evening there was a grand march. We were all in costume. At the stroke of midnight there was a show. One of our old character actors, Walt Whitman—he's gone now, too—Walt was costumed as 1915. Our child star, Thelma Slater, was diapered as 1916—the new year. . . ."

Recalling the heyday of Inceville and the opening of the studio had put Clifford Spencer in a warm, philosophical mood. Al sat back as the writer waxed poetic.

"They say that every man is like some animal," Spencer said, puffing on his pipe. "Some are like bulls. Others like horses. Tom always made me think of a clean, fastidious white bull terrier. He had the same eager interest in life, the same courage, the same cheerful willingness to give you either affection and warm sympathy or a fight—whichever your temperament demanded."

The writer insisted on talking Al on a tour of the studio. "This place is his monument," said Spencer somberly, and he began a monologue of tribute.

"Thomas Ince was a great man, you know. No one ever worked as hard as Tom Ince. After all the rest of us had dragged our weary feet home, Tommy would send for his lawyer and the distribution people and plunge right into a whole other series of problems and business deals!"

All the information was interesting. But Al was disappointed. He hadn't found out any startling facts or clues.

By now Spencer and Al were seated on canvas chairs in one of the vast, empty clapboard stages. Al felt he could comfortably pursue a couple of potentially touchy subjects.

Al sensed that direct questions would irritate Clifford Spencer. So he resorted to his innocent-youngman approach. "Golly, Mr. Spencer," he said, surveying the vast, deserted stage. "Is this where William S. Hart made his films? When I was a kid, Hart was my favorite star. He was my hero."

"Yes, Hart was really something, wasn't he?" Spencer fell back into another reverie. "He was Mr. Ince's greatest success. No, the films weren't made here. Most of the Hart films were made back in Inceville."

Al settled back as Spencer continued.

"You see, Hart came out to Hollywood in 1914 to make two-reel westerns for us. As the feature film proved itself, Bill began to extend the length of his pictures. He was a writer, you know, and that was important to his rise. So was the fact that he was over forty when he entered pictures and therefore had to create a character suitable to himself. But"—Spencer chuckled—"the old boy was capable of doing it."

Generally, Hart played "the good 'old' man." He would start out as a desperado of some kind and then a set of circumstances—or a good woman—would put him on the right track. "One of his titles, *Selfish Yates*, is an outline, in two words, of his type of picture," said Spencer.

"Before Bill Hart, westerns had consisted of little more than a few scenes—mainly hero with heroine, hero with villain shooting it out. Hart was the first to write explicit details into his scripts."

"Why did Hart and Mr. Ince have a falling-out?" Al asked quietly, hoping to sneak the question by. But the inquiry jarred Spencer out of his mood.

He studied Bradshaw, and puffed on his pipe. "Let's say artistic differences, mostly."

"You've told me so much already, Mr. Spencer, and I appreciate it. Would it be asking too much to ask you to say a little more about the 'artistic differences'?"

Clifford Spencer rose abruptly. He began walking toward the studio gate. Al swiftly followed. He caught up to Spencer and the writer told him, "I believe we've spent quite a bit of time together, and I've done that in memory of my friend Thomas Ince. I hope that your story will reflect his contribution to the industry," he said coldly.

Al had nothing to lose now. "Newspaper reports are saying that Mr. Ince was on a business trip when he died. Was it motion-picture business?"

Spencer remained silent.

Al quickly added, "This is off the record, of course."

As they continued strolling through the lot, Al waited for a response.

Finally Spencer replied: "Now that Tom is dead, I suppose it won't matter if I tell you. Yes, it was picture business. Mr. Hearst is looking for a new distributor for Miss Davies' films. The thought was that Mr. Ince would direct her pictures as well."

"Were there any violent arguments between Ince and Hearst?"

Spencer was shocked at the question. "No, Mr. Bradshaw," he blurted out almost angrily. "What ever gave you that idea?"

Al began babbling a response, but Spencer was no longer hearing the young reporter's words. Spencer's thoughts had careened back to the explosive scene that had occurred only two weeks ago at the fabulous dinner party.

Even Clifford Spencer, a veteran of Hollywood's gilded excesses, had been impressed. He had found a solid gold favor wrapped in his napkin, as had all the guests. The food was incomparable, the surroundings incredible. Throughout the mansion, works of art abounded. But none of this was the cause for Spencer's awe. What impressed him was that he, Clifford Spencer, a former-actor-turned-writer from Binghamton, New York, was here as the personal guest of America's uncrowned emperor and his mistress.

Walls, lined floor-to-ceiling with mirrors, made the enormous dining room seem even larger. They enabled the fifty dinner guests, a glittering assemblage of moviedom's elite, to admire their own reflections.

All Hollywood eagerly sought invitations to these huge dinner parties Marion Davies threw twice, sometimes three times a week. This was the first one to which Clifford Spencer had been invited. He was hoping that the negotiations between Ince and Hearst would prove successful. It would mean frequent travel in this charmed circle.

"Let's go into the library. We'll have our coffee and cigars in there," William Randolph Hearst said quietly to Thomas Harper Ince, who was seated to his right. But before rising, Hearst waited until he caught Marion's eye. She was seated at the other end of the long dinner table.

Hearst smiled and nodded to her. She laughed gaily, winked, and waved back to him. Then Hearst rose, and Ince followed.

As the two men got up from the table, there was a brief moment of concern among the other guests. Conversation quieted as all looked over to see what Marion would do. But she remained seated, continuing her animated chatter with John Gilbert, Elinor Glyn, and Clifford Spencer. So the others acknowledged Hearst's departure but resumed their dinner conversation.

John Gilbert's eyes surveyed the room. "Marion, I simply can't believe it. How ever did they get it all done in time? Where did this room come from?"

Marion giggled. "W-w-well, I wanted to surprise W.R. and throw a really *big* dinner party to welcome him back to Los Angeles."

Elinor Glyn turned to Clifford Spencer. "Think of it, dear boy. Marion not only had this room built in two days, but she had it decorated and electrified! And," the practical Elinor added, "to think it's only a rented house!"

Marion roared with laughter. "Well, W.R.'s so good to me," she said. "And he does enjoy these parties so."

Everyone knew that Hearst was good to her. The new $75,000 emerald ring on her right hand was the latest token of his affection.

"Y-y-you all have fun," Marion said to the assemblage, pushing her chair back. "I'll be back as soon as I can."

As she passed Spencer's chair, she tapped him on the shoulder. "C-c-come join us in the library," she whispered to him. "W-w-we want your opinion too."

The mahogany-paneled library was a warm and luxurious setting. A fire glowed in the massive fieldstone fireplace. When Marion and Spencer entered, Hearst and Ince, seated in deep leather chairs, quickly rose.

"M-m-may I offer you gentlemen some brandy?" Marion asked. She caught Hearst's scowl and coquettishly waved away his objections. "I'm sure the m-m-men would like an after-dinner drink, W.R."

"Thank you, yes," Tom Ince said quickly and heartily. The one-cocktail-only dinner had been an ordeal for the hard-drinking Irishman.

Marion strode over to a section of the book-lined wall. Two of the panels were fake, concealing doors to a magnificently stocked mirror-lined liquor cabinet.

Spencer saw her pour three drinks. She finished one

herself, behind Hearst's back, before returning with a brandy snifter in each hand. She handed one to Ince and one to Spencer, then daintily sat on a leather hassock at Hearst's feet.

After inconsequential chatter among the men, Marion interjected, "Tom, wh-wh-what would you think of me doing *A Woman in Command?*"

Ince's face lit up at the mention of the popular novel. "It's *perfect* for you, Marion. Why didn't I think of that?"

Hearst's mouth fell open as Ince spoke enthusiastically about how wonderful the story was, what a great change of pace it would be for Marion, how she was ready to play a liberated woman who took charge of situations and made things happen in her life. In a matter of seconds, Ince, Spencer, and Marion were acting out adaptations and variations of a scenario.

All of a sudden Hearst rose with such force that his leather chair toppled backward and crashed onto the polished mahogany floor. The noise stunned the others into silence.

"How could you even consider Marion for a part like that?" ranted Hearst, his voice rising to almost soprano range.

"I think it's a good change of pace for her," said Ince.

"She doesn't need a change of pace," countered Hearst angrily.

Ince remained unruffled, and firmly contended: "It would give some range and dimension to her instead of keeping her trapped in little-girl roles."

"You're *wrong*. I should have realized it would be a mistake to deal with a man who makes two-bit westerns!" Hearst screamed.

Ince was astonished. "No man talks to me like that," he fumed, his Irish temper flaring. "Who do you think you are—Caesar?" Ince slammed his brandy snifter down on the mahogany desk with such force that the liquid splashed out. "Come on, Cliff, we're getting out of here."

But before Ince could leave, Hearst had stormed out of the room, slamming the door behind him.

Ince stood flabbergasted. Then he bolted for the door, but Marion grabbed his arm. "Wait, Tom. Please. Wait here for a minute."

She quickly exited. Ince went back over to the bar and filled another brandy snifter. "I should have known better than to trust anyone who doesn't drink," he snorted, and downed the brandy.

Spencer knew enough to keep his mouth shut, and quietly picked up the overturned chair.

Hearst reappeared in a moment. Though Ince's face was flushed with anger, the veins at his temples throbbing visibly, Hearst behaved as though nothing had occurred.

"What's the matter, Tom?" he asked innocently.

Ince was in control of himself now. "I'm not used to being yelled at," he said.

Hearst was not a man to say he was sorry. But Ince was shrewd enough to recognize an unspoken apology.

"Let's sit down and talk," Hearst said, motioning Ince and Spencer toward chairs.

Spencer sat. Ince remained standing.

"You see, Tom," Hearst explained, "Marion respects your opinion. *A Woman in Command* is not exactly the kind of script I want Marion to do. I've bought *The Red Mill* for her, and I was hoping you'd see it as her next vehicle. Frances Marion is doing the adaptation, and it's much more suitable in terms of how the public likes to see Marion."

Ince and Spencer both knew that Hearst was saying it was how *he* liked to see Marion, as a young waif who escapes from her humdrum existence by finding true love. Since Hearst was paying the piper, he expected to call the tune.

As if by cue, Marion reentered. "Have you t-t-two shaken hands yet?" She smiled brightly. Hearst extended his hand to Ince. Ince extended his. "Let's not talk business anymore tonight," said Hearst. "Let's join the others. After all, this is a party."

Marion beamed, linked her left arm in Hearst's, her right in Ince's, and, with Spencer trailing behind, they rejoined the group.

The memory of Hearst's frightening, volatile personality—from rage to gentle diplomacy in minutes—and the vision of Tom Ince's stifled fury were foremost in Spencer's mind as he repeated his answer to Al Bradshaw's question.

"No, no," Spencer said slowly. "There were never any arguments between Mr. Hearst and Mr. Ince. No disagreements of any kind." Spencer's manner softened. He smiled impishly and added, "Few people disagree with Mr. Hearst."

Spencer had certainly overreacted to the question about Hearst, confirming Al's suspicions. But the writer hadn't provided Al with any new leads. Bradshaw was hoping Hart would reveal a lot more.

Al pulled out of the Culver City lot and headed up toward the San Fernando Valley for his meeting with the cowboy star. His stomach began grumbling and he realized he had become so engrossed in the Ince story that he had forgotten to eat.

Spotting a gas station and a sign that said "Eats," he pulled off the road.

"Fill 'er up, and what do you have that won't poison me?" Al smiled. The proprietor, a squat, ugly man with a head shiny as a billiard ball, didn't appreciate the humor.

"Whaddya want?" he snarled back.

"A hot dog, I guess. And a cup of mud. Got a phone?"

"Got a nickel?"

Al threw a dime on the counter. "Here, it's long distance. Downtown, L.A.," he said sarcastically.

The proprietor took the phone from behind the counter and handed it to Al, who grimaced at the poker-face when his back was turned.

The Palm's line rang. And rang.

Finally: "Yeah?"

"Harry? Al Bradshaw. Mike Halloran there?"

"Hang on."

Al glanced at a clock on the wall. It was almost two P.M.

In a couple of minutes, Al heard the familiar voice. "Halloran here."

"Just checking in, Mike. You going to cover that mayor's meeting for me?"

"Oh, Al, it's you. Sure I will. What time is it?"

"It's about two. Mayor's meeting is at three."

"Okay, don't worry, kid. I'll be there. Meet me after four, I'll have the story. How's it going, anyway?"

"Not much. I'll see you at the Palm about four-thirty."

Al munched his hot dog, sauntered outside, and yelled over to the attendant, "Don't forget to fill up the radiator, too."

Al checked his watch. He had to be at the Paramount ranch by 2:30.

"That'll be eighty-five cents for the gas, a dime for the hot dog. You want that coffee?" asked the proprietor.

"No. I don't have time."

Al jumped in the Chevy and headed toward the valley. His stomach grumbled—now courtesy of the hot dog. Bradshaw's thoughts turned to the other members of the fatal yachting party.

Elinor Glyn. "The Leopard Lady." The snazziest female novelist in Hollywood. She'd been written up in the *Trib*'s Sunday roto section a month ago, and Al remembered she seemed like quite a character. She was British-born, which gave her extra snob appeal. "Racy" novels were her specialty, but she wrote them with "class." The leading characters in her controversial best-seller *Three Weeks* elegantly screwed on leopard-skin rugs in front of open fires. Leopard thereafter became Glyn's trademark. She was in demand to write scripts at the best studios, at top prices.

Al had an idea of what she looked like from her photographs. But photos could be deceiving. It was apparent she was no kid, wore plenty of makeup, expensive jewelry, and smart clothes. She actually had a rather matronly look, and wouldn't have been at all flattered to know that she reminded Al of his Aunt Hattie in Denver.

But Glyn was one of *the* Hollywood social leaders. She had even boasted, in the roto piece, that she had introduced Marion Davies to Charlie Chaplin.

Charles Chaplin. "The Little Tramp." The most beloved, and phenomenally successful, comedian in motion pictures. What role did he have in all this? Was he carrying on with Marion Davies? He seemed to prefer very young girls, considerably younger than twenty-four-year-old Marion. Wasn't Charlie currently involved with sixteen-year-old Lita Grey, who was starring opposite him in *The Gold Rush*, the film he was shooting now?

The boys at the Palm often joked about Chaplin's preference for "chicken," and to some extent it was public knowledge. About six years ago Chaplin had had to marry an underage actress, Mildred Harris, when she claimed she was pregnant. It turned out she wasn't, and eventually Chaplin divorced her. But not before a lot of unpleasant publicity. One interesting note: Mildred's mother was the wardrobe mistress at the Ince studio. Ironic, thought Al, how all these lives intertwined. Hollywood was a very small town, after all. And, reasoned Al, as with all small towns, there were lots of skeletons in everyone's closets. And lots of people eager to expose them.

The sun was beating down unmercifully as Al approached the Paramount ranch in the San Fernando Valley. A few cars and a chuckwagon were parked where a group was breaking for lunch. Bradshaw pulled the Chevy over and asked a young man where he could find William S. Hart.

"They're filming down the road about a mile," said the lad.

Al began to feel anxious. He was about to encounter, face-to-face, one of his idols. William S. Hart! "Jesus," he muttered, "I hope I don't screw this up."

As he drove up to the site, the company was still shooting. The film was *The Son of Draw Egan*. Hart was astride his famous pinto, Fritz.

"Let's shoot one more, Bill," called director Lambert Hillyer.

Bradshaw was mesmerized as Hart galloped along the plain, shooting at a band of Indians.

A young Paramount publicity man, Billy Griffin, introduced himself to Bradshaw. "Mr. Hart will be here soon. They'll be breaking for lunch. Mr. Hart doesn't drink, but there'll be lemonade. If you want me to spike yours, I have a flask," he added confidentially.

Al smiled. "That's okay, kid, thanks. Lemonade'll be good enough."

"Cut!" yelled director Hillyer. Hart dismounted and slowly approached the group where Al was standing. Bradshaw was surprised, indeed shocked, at how old Hart appeared close up. Even under heavy makeup he looked his age, which was close to fifty-five.

Hart's steely, close-set blue eyes were penetrating. He was not a person who encouraged friendliness. It was obvious that he was as humorless offscreen as he was onscreen.

"You the guy Barney Henderson asked me to talk with?"

"Yes, sir."

Hart sat down slowly, as though his bones ached, and motioned Al to sit too. "Shoot," he said, as he began munching on a sandwich.

"Well, I'd like to know about Tom Ince."

Hart stopped chewing and stared at Al. "Off the record?"

"Yes, of course."

"What do you want to know about the cocky bastard?"

Wow! thought Al. He hadn't expected such a ready response. But he was relieved. Smiling back at Spencer all morning had been tiring. Thank God he wouldn't have to put on a charm act for Hart.

"Tell me when you met." The questions spilled out: "What kind of person was he, why did so many people hate his guts, why did you two break up?"

The stone-faced Hart almost smiled. "That's a lot of questions, boy. Well, let's see. . . . We met in 1905. Ince was an actor then. We trouped together in a bunch of plays, I can't remember most of them. I was a Shakespearean actor back east, you know," he said with a note of pride. Al was surprised. "But I'd grown up with Indians and trail herders, and I even toured in a wild-west show," the actor continued.

"I got here a few years after Ince. Tom was already a big shot. But he was just throwing pictures together. I wanted to do something *worthwhile*."

Hart paused, to let the meaning of the word sink in. Then he turned to the young Paramount publicist. "Leave us alone, Billy. This fella and I will get along fine."

Billy reluctantly departed. Hart turned back to Al, and in a low voice confided, "This'll be my last movie for Paramount. They don't want good stories anymore, just action. I'm working on my own project. *Tumbleweeds*. Great story."

Al was thrilled Hart was confiding so freely.

"The only good thing about working with that bastard Ince was finding Fritz." Al lit up at the mention of the famous pinto, the "wonder horse" who had as many fans as any star in Hollywood.

"Yeah, we had fun those first couple of years," mused Hart.

"You and Ince?"

"Me and Fritz," Hart corrected him. "The minute I saw Fritz, I knew he was something special. I even wrote a poem about him, *Pinto Ben*. I used to direct my own pictures, and I made a flicker based on my poem."

"*Pinto Ben!* I saw it!" exclaimed Al, genuinely enthusiastic. "I remember it very well!"

"Well, then you know Fritz was no ordinary horse. But Ince hated him."

"Why?" asked Al.

"Because he liked to take credit for everything, and since he hadn't discovered Fritz, the horse couldn't be any good. Well, Ince had this property, *The Narrow Trail*. All of a sudden he comes to me and says, 'Bill, let's not use Fritz in this.' 'Not use Fritz?' I said. 'Christ, Tom, the horse is incredible. People will react to him like he's a person.' 'Look, Bill,' he says, 'I run this studio, and, to be frank, you look like a jerk riding that horse. He's too goddamn small. Your legs almost touch the ground, for chrissake.' Well, I had to control myself. I wanted to flatten Ince then and there. So I said, 'No Fritz, no Bill Hart.'

" 'No Bill Hart then,' said that . . . Well, I lost my temper and smacked him on the jaw. 'Get the hell outta here,' he bellowed. But I heard from him later that day. We sort of made a truce, and he said I could use the horse. I did, and *The Narrow Trail* was the biggest moneymaker of the year. Fritz became a star. He began getting more fan mail than I did. Ince came to me and said, 'Well, you were right, Bill. Now you can use Fritz in all your pictures.' I looked him in the eye and said, 'Screw you. I'm not usin' Fritz in *any* of the pictures I do for you.' My contract called for about fifteen more pictures, and I didn't use Fritz in one of 'em.

"Then I left Ince. I wanted to buy Fritz and take him with me. But Ince wouldn't sell him to me. Said the horse was too valuable. What a load of bull! That bastard wouldn't have cared if they had made glue out of Fritz. But finally I did buy Fritz, for forty-two thousand dollars. Ince thought he was getting his revenge, by chargin' me that. But the joke was on him. I would have paid a million."

Hart gulped down some lemonade.

"Wasn't there some sort of lawsuit between you and Ince?" asked Al.

Hart frowned. "That's right. When I left him to join Paramount, the bastard sued me for breach of contract. He had made over six million bucks on my films and was paying me peanuts. Ince was a pretty square guy when we first met. But I guess Hollywood, and all the money, went to his head. He sure turned into one of the most unethical bastards I've ever known. I've told you the Fritz story. Any man who thinks animals are stupid creatures, any man who has no feeling for animals, what can you expect?"

"What about Ince's personal life? Did he run around on his wife?"

For the first time Hart hesitated. "The man's dead," he said, "and I usually don't like to talk about the dead. But the man had no morals," Hart said heatedly. "Always had two or three women on the side. Was sure he could talk himself into—or out of—anything. In his house, he had a specially constructed . . . Well, never mind. All I'll say is that it was the most disgusting thing I'd ever encountered."

"What was it?" asked Al, intrigued.

"That's all I'll say," said Hart, the subject obviously closed. He'd finished his lunch and rose to return to work.

"One last question," Al persisted. "Did Ince have a lot of enemies? Did a lot of people dislike him?"

"Well, son, let me put it this way. In this town, we've *all* got enemies. A man doesn't become as successful as Tom Ince, Griffith, De Mille, Sennett—or me—without making a lot of enemies."

Bradshaw quietly asked, "Do you think anyone could hate Mr. Ince enough to shoot him?"

Hart was surprised. "Shoot him? I haven't heard that he was shot. Where did you hear that?"

"That's what some people think."

"I see, I see." Hart pondered a moment. "Well . . . knowing Tom Ince, I would have to say there might be some people who would *want* to shoot him. But we knew the same people, and I can't think of one who would have the guts."

Bradshaw had certainly received extreme views on Ince. The reverence with which Spencer spoke of him contrasted sharply to William S. Hart's bitterness and anger. Whichever was closer to the mark, Ince obviously was a man who evoked deep emotions from the people who knew him.

After learning so much about the famed mogul, the young reporter suddenly had an urge to see Inceville, the once-bustling capital of the director's vast empire. Before heading back to the Palm to get the mayor's story from Mike, Al drove west.

As Bradshaw entered the verdant valley of Santa Inez, he realized he might be lost. He spotted a group of kids picking oranges in a grove. He slowed down, honked his horn, and yelled over, "Hey, you guys, where's Inceville?"

"Turn right at the next dirt road."

In a few minutes Al came upon a startling sight. A ghost town. There were outdoor stages and platforms. Replicas of western towns. Corrals. Barns. A general store. A single horse was tethered to a pole in front of one building. The sign on the plate-glass window read "Saloon."

Bradshaw stopped his car, hopped out, and bounded up several steps onto the wooden sidewalk. The place was eerily silent. As he strode through the door of the saloon, he had to stop short to keep from falling. The building was only a facade, and on the other side of the door there was a drop of several feet to a field below.

But that horse over there was real, thought Al. Someone must be here.

The reporter walked cautiously down the creaky wooden sidewalk, past the general store, the funeral parlor, the hotel. All were facades. Then he saw that across the street, smoke was coming from the chimney of a brick structure marked "The Jail."

Al slowly crossed the dirt road and approached the building. When he reached the door, he rapped on it lightly.

No answer. He turned the knob.

"Who's there?" a raspy voice suddenly bellowed.

Al jumped. "I'm a reporter for the L.A. *Tribune,*" he answered quickly.

The voice became softer and friendlier. "Ain't no more movie stars here."

Al relaxed when an old man stepped into view. He looked like one who'd be cast as an old watchman—shaggy, scraggly beard, long gray hair. A corncob pipe was clenched between what was left of decaying teeth.

Al offered his hand. "My name is Al Bradshaw."

"Howdy. My name's Abraham Lincoln Farnsworth, but call me Pop. Everybody does." His handshake was like an iron vise.

Al excused himself for barging in. "It didn't look like there was anyone here," he explained.

"Nope. Most everybody moved to Culver City 'bout ten years ago. Then, after the fire this year, *everybody* moved. All that's left here is a few buildings, a coupla horses . . . an' me."

"The fire," said Al. "I remember reading about that."

"Yep. It was horrible. Horrible." Pop expectorated with perfect aim into a nearby spittoon. "Guess you're here to talk about Tom Ince," he said.

Al hadn't expected such an abrupt change of subject. The old coot was perceptive.

"Well," Al conceded, "I thought you might be able to tell me a few things."

"Sure can. Been here since 1912, when he founded the place."

Al settled into a rocking chair. Obviously the old man was grateful for a visitor and welcomed the opportunity to talk. Al wouldn't have to pry—just listen.

"Wanna drink?" asked the septuagenarian, cocking his thumb, indicating a jug that was probably moonshine.

"Sure," said Al. He took a hefty swig. The liquid burned his throat, blood rushed to his head, and he felt his eyes were going to pop.

"Shouldn'ta took so much," said the old man, his expression unchanged.

Al coughed convulsively for a couple of moments. His eyes began tearing. Finally he could talk again. "How . . . long . . . did you know Ince?" He took out his handkerchief to wipe the tears from his eyes.

"Ever since he got here."

Much of the information the old man had to offer was repetitious of what Al had already learned. But the old boy spoke in much grittier terms.

"He was a tough son of a bitch, all right," Pop declared. With gusto he related a tale of one sweltering day in Inceville a dozen summers ago. . . .

The blistering sun was baking the ground, and the cowboy actors were trudging around in heavy costumes, sweating profusely. "Okay, start that camera!" screamed Ince, as a posse began thundering down the dusty road.

Ince became furious when an extra hesitated in picking up the cue. "You're supposed to be chasing an outlaw, you dumb bastard."

Instead of heeding Ince's command, the extra pulled the horse up short and yelled back, "*You* move him, you stupid son of a bitch. I'm sick and tired of you screaming directions!" He dismounted and shouted angrily, "I quit."

"Get back up there," directed Ince. "You can't quit until I fire you."

A bloody fistfight ensued.

"But Tom could take care of himself," the old-timer recalled. "Except for a black eye every now and then, he always came out ahead. Ince had this town by the balls. Made more movies—and more money—faster than anyone else. Shoulda stuck to westerns, though."

Pop's opinion was that Ince got into financial trouble when he stopped making westerns and attempted "all that arty stuff"—like *Anna Christie* and *Human Wreckage*.

"One thing I'll say for him," the old man continued. "He never made excuses. He used to say, 'Judge by the boxoffice. My films are good if people pay to see 'em. If they don't, I know I'm doin' something wrong.' "

The old man again offered Bradshaw the jug. "Want another drink?"

"Thanks, no," said Al, stroking his throat. "Do you make that stuff yourself?"

"Yup. Don't trust anybody else. Newspapers say that that's what killed Tom Ince, bad liquor."

Al grabbed the opportunity. "Some people say he was shot."

"Could be," said the old man, unruffled. "Known a lotta husbands that would have liked to shoot him."

"A real ladies' man, huh?"

"Let's put it this way. There wasn't a woman Tom couldn'ta had, if he wanted her. He used to come and visit us here at Inceville every month or so, just to look the place over, and he always had a pretty filly on his arm."

"Was there any special lady friend?" Al asked.

"Well, the last coupla times he was here with a cute little girl. Diane Enright. Feisty little thing."

"Diane Enright. Where is she? Where can I find her?"

"Don't know. You might ask in Culver City."

It was a little after 4:30 when Al got back to the Palm. He grabbed a beer and headed for the back room, hoping Mike hadn't let him down. There he was, good old Mike, fortified with five shots—the empty glasses were neatly lined up on the table—pounding out the mayor's conference story.

Halloran sensed Al reading over his shoulder. "Same old bull, kid," he said, without striking a wrong key. "I'm stretching it to four pages to make you look good. Get me another drink, will ya?"

Al ordered two from the bar.

"How did it go?"

"The only real news is that Ince had a steady dame. Diane Enright. Ever hear of her?"

"Nah."

"One other thing. Hart talked about some special, strange feature at Ince's house in Benedict Canyon. Know anything?"

"Nothing much," answered Mike. "Except I knew he used to throw a big party every weekend. They got pretty wild. Vince would have more dope on that. Did you stop at United Artists?"

"Yeah. I met a cute little skirt who probably knows more than she's telling. Says Chaplin, Elinor Glyn, Louella Parsons, were some of the people on the cruise."

"Louella Parsons?"

"Yeah. Why the surprise?"

"Look at this." Halloran handed him a newspaper. Louella Parsons' column was datelined New York.

"New York? How could she possibly have gotten back to New York already?"

"Who knows where she is, kid? I told you this wasn't going to be easy."

Mike gulped down a shot of rye and ripped the story

out of the typewriter. "Here, you better get over to the paper with this, or Eagle Beak will have your ass."

. As Al began to scan the story, Mike said, "Don't bother. I wrote it like I was you. Oh, by the way," he said, gesturing to the five empty glasses, "I charged these to you."

"Where the hell ya been, Bradshaw?" Casey was angry.

"Here's the story, boss, here's the story," Al said placatingly. "Page one, banner headline," he joked feebly, knowing the piece was of little interest and would be buried.

"Don't be a wise-ass, kid."

"Sorry. Hey, Casey, have you seen Barry Farr?"

"He should be in the composing room, working on a Sunday piece."

Al mock-saluted and walked quickly through the city room, down two flights of stairs to the composing room. The presses were grinding, and Barry was approving a layout. Farr had been the *Tribune*'s entertainment editor, and was now features editor for the paper's Sunday roto section.

"Barry, got a minute?"

The editor glanced up, peeved. "Yeah, kid, what is it? I've gotta finish this damn Sunday piece before midnight!"

"Barry, it's important. Just give me a few minutes."

Farr saw Bradshaw was troubled. "Okay, what is it?"

"Give me some dope on Louella Parsons."

Farr thought this a strange request coming from a guy like Al. "Why the interest in a movie reporter?"

Al could hardly tell Barry the truth, and to answer his question he hedged: "I'm just trying to get some background on the Hollywood crowd."

Bradshaw was certain Louella Parsons had been on that cruise. The cute brunette at United Artists had unwittingly confirmed that fact for him. But now Parsons and Hearst, by datelining her column New York, were trying to establish that she wasn't even in California. Why?

From Farr Al learned some fascinating unpublicized facts about Louella Parsons, the popular gossip columnist who was already being syndicated nationwide. Although she was a romantic and a moralist in her columns, her own personal life was stormy and somewhat mysterious. Her first husband had been a reporter, John Parsons, who later went into real estate and left Louella and their daughter when he fell in love with his secretary.

Louella married again—a riverboat captain, a handsome Irishman named Jack McCaffrey. They moved to Chicago, where Louella wrote scenarios for the Essanay film studios. When she lost that job, she became a gossip columnist for the Chicago *Record Herald*. After the *Herald* was absorbed by Hearst's *Chicago American*. Parsons was out of work again. But she headed for New York loaded down with letters of introduction and job prospects.

Richard Watts, movie editor at the *Morning Telegraph*, had been drafted into the Great War. It was a break for Louella. She got Watts's job.

A forty-year-old woman with an unswervable career direction in mind, Parsons began continually plugging Marion Davies and her films. From 1918 to 1922 the columnist gave so much coverage to Marion that Louella's line, "Marion Davies never looked lovelier," was already on its way to becoming a cliché. But the calculated mountains of praise eventually paid off handsomely.

"About a year ago," Barry Farr related, "Louella moved over from the *Telegraph* to become motion-picture editor of Hearst's New York *American*. And now she's dedicated as hell to the old man."

The picture Farr had painted of Louella Parsons was that of a relentlessly driven, ambitious woman. She was full of charm but was a cagey observer whose reputation had built to the point where now everyone in the movie business knew "she'd double-cross you for a headline."

"I guess you could sum her up," Farr concluded, "by saying she's a lousy writer but a good reporter."

A good reporter! What kind of reporter could she be, scoffed Al to himself, if she was on board that yacht when Ince was shot and she's sitting on the story?

Farr had turned his full attention back to his layouts. But Al had more questions.

"What can you tell me about Tom Ince?"

"Aw, c'mon, kid, you've gotta be kidding!" Farr looked up from his work. "We could be here all night!"

Al's voice now displayed the urgency he had held in check. "I've *got* to find out all I can about Tom Ince!"

"Why?" asked Farr. "The bum's dead."

"Then just tell me this. What do you know about Hearst and Ince's business dealings? Weren't they getting together?"

"I suppose," said Farr blandly, as though it should be general knowledge, "they were joining forces because Hearst has millions to spend and in the last couple of years Ince's pictures weren't doing too well. Ince had the know-how and Hearst has the money. It seemed like a natural partnership."

Al had a dozen more queries. Farr was like an encyclopedia. His mind retained every detail of every important story that had ever hit Hollywood.

"What's up, anyway?" asked Farr with growing annoyance and curiosity.

"I'm just trying to get background," Al repeated lamely. He knew Farr wasn't buying it. but didn't want to reveal any more.

"Talk to me tomorrow, kid, I'll have the time."

"I can't wait!"

At that moment the head makeup man charged

over, holding a proof page. "It's gonna take about ten minutes more, Mr. Farr."

Farr turned to Bradshaw and took him by the arm. "Come with me."

They strode briskly to his office. Farr's cubicle contained a desk stacked with papers, books, and magazines. He reached under the desk and came out with a huge scrapbook. "Here," he said, dropping the heavy volume into Al's arms. "Enjoy it," he said sarcastically.

Al settled into Farr's chair and began leafing through the voluminous text, which consisted of many hundreds of press clippings. In the past four years scandal had reared its ugly head on many occasions in the paradise known as Hollywood.

There was the Olive Thomas tragedy. Miss Thomas was considered the most beautiful of all the fabled Ziegfeld showgirls. The ivory-skinned brunette seemed to be the girl who had everything—even a perfect marriage, to screen star Jack Pickford, brother of America's Sweetheart, Mary Pickford.

Before coming to Hollywood, Olive had been the toast of New York. Publisher Condé Nast fell in love with her and saw to it that his fashion magazine, *Vogue*, featured her prominently. Ziegfeld convinced Olive to pose in the nude for a brilliant rising young Peruvian artist, Alberto Vargas. The painting was a sensation and she became the most famous "Vargas Girl."

Sixteen-year-old Olive was signed for films by Myron Selznick, who billed her as "The Ideal American Girl." Her pictures were hits, and her marriage to "Ideal American Boy" Jack Pickford made them filmdom's most glamorous and "Ideal" young couple. It came as an incredible shock to the world when, in 1920, twenty-year-old Olive committed suicide in the elegant Crillon Hotel in Paris. After much investigation it was revealed she had been involved with leading drug dealers on the continent. Olive had unsuccessfully tried to secure a large amount of heroin, allegedly intended for her husband. This allegation was furiously denied by the Pickford family. After Olive's suicide, Jack Pickford, "in a state of nervous collapse," was committed to a hospital. But the tabloids went to town, with typical headlines screaming: OLIVE THOMAS A DOPE FIEND!

The Thomas scandal was followed by an equally shocking case involving beloved screen comedian Roscoe "Fatty" Arbuckle. It was exactly one year later, to the day—September 10, 1921—that this second scandal broke. Fatty, a "fun-loving butterball," had started as a five-dollar-a-day comedian for Mack Sennett back in 1913, and in four short years he was earning five thousand dollars a week. Twenty percent of his income went to his agent, Lou Anger, who in turn kept his rotund client's sexual peccadilloes out of the press. Fatty liked his girls *very* young and voluptuous, and enjoyed group orgies.

In 1921, to celebrate his new multimillion-dollar contract with Paramount, Fatty took a group of fun-loving friends up to San Francisco's posh St. Francis Hotel. The bootleg booze flowed freely. Arbuckle's attentions were focused on young starlet Virginia Rappe. As the festivities got wilder, Virginia and Fatty adjourned to a bedroom. Soon afterward, a piercing scream rang out—Virginia was hemorrhaging.

What was fascinating to Bradshaw about the Arbuckle case was that obviously there had been a failed attempt at a cover-up. Virginia Rappe had been taken to a private hospital on Pine Street, but five days later she died. Arbuckle might have gotten away with it except that the deputy coroner of San Francisco had received an "anonymous phone call" about conducting a postmortem. When the coroner investigated, it was revealed that Virginia's bladder had been ruptured by some form of violence. The coroner called for a police investigation. Arbuckle was indicted for murder. The charge was later changed to manslaughter. But the insinuations were hideous. Had Fatty violated the girl with a bottle? Or was it a jagged piece of ice? Or had he flattened her with his massive weight?

Al noted with distaste that the seamiest details regarding the sexual side of the case were avidly reported—where else?—in the Hearst papers. Their moralistic attitude continued unabated right through Arbuckle's trials.

There had been three trials, with two hung juries, before the comedian was finally acquitted, for lack of specific evidence or reliable witnesses. But Fatty's career was over, and the entire episode was a black mark for Hollywood.

While Arbuckle was still on trial, yet another scandal broke. Director William Desmond Taylor was found murdered. Again, there was an attempt at a cover-up. The body was discovered in Taylor's home in the posh Westlake section of Hollywood. Before police arrived on the scene, Paramount executives were already there, a fire blazing in the fireplace, burning up incriminating evidence.

There were two bullets through Taylor's heart. It came to light that not only had he been having affairs with top actresses Mabel Normand and Mary Miles Minter, but also with Miss Minter's mother, Charlotte Shelby.

Further investigation proved that William Desmond Taylor had abandoned a wife and daughter years earlier, and that Sands, Taylor's butler, was in reality his brother, a forger who was wanted by the law. Even more scandalous than this was the revelation that Taylor had been a dope addict and frequented opium dens. He owned a formidable collection of pornography and collected "undies" and lingerie from his lady friends, each tagged with the date and their initials. When a pink nightie embroidered "MMM" was allegedly found, the career of Mary Miles Minter—famous for playing virginal roles—was ruined, despite the fact she had committed no crime. Taylor's murderer was never found.

Al saw that at the height of the Taylor-Minter scandal, some of the Hearst papers had published as many as thirteen editions a day! In the scrapbook, Barry Farr had noted that this exposé had sold more newspapers than any other Hollywood-oriented story.

After these stories rocked Hollywood, it came as no surprise when, the following month, March, 1922, motion-picture producers and distributors banded together. They realized they had better censor themselves before the government got around to it, and formed a self-censoring association, which they named the MPPDA—Motion Picture Producers and Distributors Association. Highly respected and well-connected former U.S. Postmaster General Will Hays was hired to administer it.

Al read on. Later in 1922, however, even blacker headlines hit the stands with the disclosure of popular star Wallace Reid's drug addiction. Al fleetingly thought of the night he and Vera had salvaged Reid from bad publicity.

Alongside the *Tribune*'s story of Reid's death, Farr had pasted ads and reviews of the film *Human Wreckage*. It starred Reid's wife, Dorothy Davenport, billed in huge type as "Mrs. Wallace Reid," and detailed the perils of drug addiction. The film's producer and distributor: Thomas Ince.

Reid had died, in a padded cell, six months before the film's release. Al recalled that the rumor on the street was that since neither his family nor his studio could control him any longer, in desperation Reid had quietly been "put to sleep."

Al closed the scrapbook and sat deep in thought. Farr's collection consisted of scandals that had reached such proportions they could no longer be suppressed. And yet in all these cases there had been attempted cover-ups. The studios used their wealth and power to protect their box-office stars.

William Randolph Hearst's fortune and influence made even the mightiest studio mogul's seem puny. It was inconceivable that Hearst would *not* attempt to cover up a situation that could be ruinous to the career of Marion Davies, the one person in the world he seemed to really care about.

Bradshaw scribbled "Thanks, Barry" on a piece of yellow paper and placed it on top of the scrapbook. Heading back to the city room, he was intercepted by Johnny Brackin, the sixteen-year-old copyboy.

"Hey, Al . . . I just answered your phone. It's some dame. She's holding on. She sounds cute. I think it's the same flapper who's been tryin' to reach ya all afternoon."

"I can't be bothered now," said Al. It was probably Shirley, last night's washout. "I'm too busy."

"Then set *me* up with her if you don't want her," Johnny pleaded.

"If it's Shirley, you can have her!"

Casey Clark passed by. "Listen, you two horny bastards, this ain't no social club!"

"Can't help it if I'm popular." Al smiled, walking over to his desk. He picked up the receiver. "Hello, honey, what can I do for you?"

The caller came right to the point. "They tell me you're asking questions about Tom Ince's death." The woman's voice seemed anxious, distant, but definitely sexy.

"Yeah, that's right. Who is this?"

"Never mind," the voice purred. Al sensed that she might be drunk. "If you believe that story about Ince having a heart attack, you're a lousy reporter," she said.

Was he hearing right? He kept silent.

"Did you hear me?"

"I think I heard you."

"Don't buy that story that Ince had a heart attack."

The line clicked dead.

"It's got to be that dame Diane Enright!" said Bradshaw excitedly, gulping down his gin. Even the soothing atmosphere of the Palm couldn't calm him. "Vince, who the hell else could it be?"

"How do you figure it's her?"

"The old man at Inceville. Who else would know I'm interested in the story?"

"What about Hart and the people over at Paramount?"

"I didn't think of that."

"And you were at United Artists nosing around too."

"True."

"Or it could be some crank."

Al wouldn't buy that. "Vince, do you realize that it was an anonymous phone call that started that whole Fatty Arbuckle investigation? I think this Enright dame's got information for me. If she was Ince's current chippy, then she probably was on the cruise too."

"Then why didn't she call the police?"

"Maybe she has!"

"Kid, listen to me," cautioned the old veteran. "The only chance you have of cracking this story is to stick to hard facts. Don't get sidetracked with jealous lovesick dames."

Al swallowed the remainder of his gin. "Jesus, this hooch is awful!"

"It's good for back rubs, kid." Vince signaled the proprietor of the Palm. "Hey, Harry. You seen Frank Fairfield?"

"Nope."

"Fairfield?" Al had seen his byline. "Doesn't he work for the Long Beach rag?"

"Yep. It was the only job he could get when he came out here from New York. He can give you a lot of dope on Hearst. He hates his guts." Vince lit up a cigar. "I've asked him to meet us here. You can pick his brains and see if you can't piece together a story."

While waiting, the men ordered a couple of steaks and beers.

"Did you see that blurb in today's *Examiner*?" asked Vince. "Christ, I almost choked. 'Miss Davies Postpones Ball Out of Respect.' " Lewis picked up a copy of the *Examiner* and read: " 'In deference to the memory of Thomas Harper Ince, Marion Davies announced the indefinite postponement of a ball she had planned for Miss Norma Talmadge on Saturday evening. The affair was to have been a Hawaiian costume party at the Hotel Ambassador. Over 200 invitations had been sent.' "

"Those poor people," clucked Al. "What will they do with their Saturday night?" He brought Vince up to date on his meeting with Hart. "Geez, he isn't at all like I remember him in the movies. He's an old man. He's really bitter about Ince, too. He let slip something about some 'disgusting' aspect in Ince's house, but then he wouldn't talk about it. And he sure as hell didn't think much of Ince's moral character."

"Hah!" exclaimed Vince. "Who's Hart to talk? That old bastard. You know the story about him, don't you?"

Al shook his head.

Vince arched an eyebrow. "Hart lives with his maiden sister, Mary."

"I thought he was married," Al said.

"Yeah, he got married. He was at least thirty years older than his pretty bride, too. Her name is Winnie Westover. Real cute little girl. My kid sister ran around in the same gang as Winnie. Anyway, after Winnie married Hart and moved into his house, when she took her place at the head of the dinner table, Hart flew into a rage, screaming that his sister would continue to sit there because Mary was still the head of the house!"

"Didn't Hart and his wife have a kid?"

"Yeah, a boy. But I hear Hart refuses to see the kid, even when Winnie sends him over to the studio."

"But I thought he was a good family man!"

"Hah!" Vince laughed. "The son of a bitch used to give Winnie 'love pinches' "—Vince demonstrated with his thumb and index finger on Al's arm, and Al yelped—"pinches like that that would leave her black and blue. Winnie kept quiet about it, but everyone knew Hart beat her. Eventually the poor little thing left him and went back to her mother."

Vince seemed amused at Al's astonishment. "What's the matter, kid, you thought he was the hero you saw on the silver screen? Don't you realize most of these Hollywood people aren't anything like what their publicity makes 'em out to be? Who the hell would believe that half of 'em are shootin' up with cocaine? Or that some of 'em enjoy screwin' with dogs, for chrissake! Or that some pure-lookin' little flappers who play coeds in films got their training in stag flickers? Jesus Christ, half of the men like men better than they like women! And half the women don't care, 'cause they like women too! I even hear that a lot of stars get their kicks by bein' chained to walls and beaten with whips!"

Al blanched. He had heard stories about the Hollywood crowd being "weird." But he found it difficult to believe many of Vince's allegations. Then again, nothing was impossible, and he found himself asking, "Do you think Ince had a dungeon or something in his house?"

"Who knows? It's worth checking into."

The steaks and beers arrived just as Frank Fairfield entered the Palm.

Fairfield spotted Vince and ambled over. He looked to Al like a man who would be at home managing a warehouse. Heavyset, balding, potbellied, with a blotchy red face and a red nose, he had sharp, intelligent blue eyes. Frank pulled up a chair.

"Want a steak?" asked Vince.

"No thanks." Fairfield smiled. "What's new, Vince? This your friend?"

"Frank Fairfield, meet Al Bradshaw."

The men shook hands. Al offered Fairfield a cigarette. He declined. Vince, puffing on a cigar, looked over to the bar and snapped his fingers. It was a prearranged signal for Harry to bring over a bottle of rye and three shot glasses.

Harry poured the first drink, then left the bottle. Fairfield downed a shot, then poured himself another. Al and Vince began eating their dinner, and the three men sat in relative silence. Fairfield stared intently at Bradshaw. Surprisingly, Al didn't feel uncomfortable under the man's scrutinizing gaze.

After several minutes Fairfield seemed satisfied that he had found whatever it was he was searching for in the young man's face. He poured another drink, relaxed, and asked, "Well, what is it you want to know, kid?"

"Anything you can tell me," said Al. "I don't know much about Hearst."

At first Fairfield spoke impassively. He restlessly shifted his weight several times. His conversation hit one or two unrelated points about Hearst's life, but then suddenly he seemed to find a comfortable position and his story began taking shape. "Well," he said, "we all know a lot of shit has been written about Hearst and his family, but these are the *facts*. It was W.R.'s father, George Hearst, who made all the dough. George was a tough, shrewd mining engineer who trudged out west from Missouri around the time of the gold rush. He, shall we say, stepped over a few dead bodies and found himself with the deed to the Comstock silver lode. He bought up most of California and a lot of Mexico. Most of Hearst's money today doesn't come from his newspapers, you know. They're only the tip of the iceberg.

"Anyway, after old George struck it rich, he went back home and married a young girl from a well-to-do family. Phoebe Apperson was twenty years younger than George. They were a good-looking couple but a sort of beauty-and-the-beast combination. He was a rough outdoors character—'uncouth,' some people called him—and she was schoolmarm proper.

"Even after he brought her back to San Francisco and their son, William Randolph, was born, George Hearst would go off for two and three months at a time looking for new mines. So Phoebe brought up the boy from the beginning. That was fine with old George. He was more interested in increasing the family fortunes, and little Willie became his mama's darling."

Al was surprised. "William Randolph Hearst, a mama's boy?"

"And how, although all three of them, father, mother, and son, were pretty close. But the time came when Papa Hearst was afraid Billy Buster—that was his Mother's pet name for him—might turn into a mama's boy in more ways than one. Little Billy had gone to Europe with Mama. She educated him in the world of art, and he became as interested in 'beautiful objects' as his mother. Old George Hearst was afraid the kid wasn't interested in girls. William Randolph had a high-pitched voice to boot, which didn't please his father either."

Frank took a gulp of whiskey. His face flushed even redder as the liquid traveled to his stomach.

"Don't stop now, Frank!" Al implored.

"Don't worry, kid. This is a pleasure, telling someone all this crap. Okay, where were we? Old man Hearst was worried that his kid might be a sissy. So he told him, 'I'm going to give you a big allowance, and you can spend it on as many pretty girls as you like.' As things worked out, the kid *liked* to spend it on dames. And Mama Phoebe didn't dare interfere, because even her friends had said she was turning her son into a mama's boy.

"Well, the kid took to broads like type to paper. Did you ever hear of Pussy Soule?" Fairfield noted Al's blank expression and continued, "Nah, that was before your time. Katherine 'Pussy' Soule. She was the daughter of Senator Frank Soule. William Randolph was only a teenager. 'Puppy love,' they called it. It didn't work out.

"Then Hearst fell for Sybil Sanderson, but his mother broke that up because the girl was a couple of years older than he. Besides, she was a singer. You ever hear of her? She went to Paris and became an opera star. Massenet even wrote stuff for her, for chrissake!"

"He went for show-business types even then," observed Vince.

"Obviously. Then there was Eleanor Calhoun, who also wanted to be on the stage. Phoebe put a stop to that affair too. She shipped Billy Buster off to Harvard, figuring he'd be out of the clutches of the dames in San Francisco."

"Well, there couldn't have been much female distraction at an all-male school," noted Al.

"Oh, yeah?" Frank smirked. "Well, she didn't count on the waitresses in the dining room. Hearst fell for this cute little skirt, Tessie Powers."

"Did Hearst graduate from Harvard?"

"Nah, he was kicked out. But wait a minute, don't get ahead of yourself. So he fell for this waitress and took her to Europe with him. They even got as far as Egypt."

"He wasn't stingy, was he?" exclaimed Vince.

"That's one thing no one can accuse him of. Then he took her back to San Francisco with him. By this time old man Hearst was a U.S. senator from California. So he and Phoebe moved to Washington."

"I didn't know George Hearst was a senator," said Al.

"With that kind of money, you can buy almost anything. Anyway, Phoebe and Hearst were off to Washington playing politics while William Randolph was with Tessie back in San Francisco playing newspapers. Papa had given him the San Francisco *Examiner* as a gift."

A sharp look of disgust came over Fairfield's face. "Can you imagine that? His father gave him the *Examiner*, like my father gave me a baseball glove!" Fairfield belched. "Son of a bitch. Some goddamn people have all the luck. . . ." Fairfield was about to launch into a lament on his bad luck. Vince, to avoid it, asked, "Tell us more about Tessie Powers."

"Tessie. Oh, the waitress. Yeah," Frank continued. "W.R. kept her with him for about eight years. Eight years! But he would never marry her. Meanwhile, old George died, but instead of leaving his fortune to his son, he left it all to Phoebe. Not that W.R. needed any money. He already had plenty, *and* the *Examiner*. Boy, can you imagine if we owned our own newspaper?"

This time fifteen minutes of rambling conversation, regarding newspapers and the "wonderful days" back in New York before the war, was unavoidable. Fairfield's memory seemed to mix reality with desire. But his account of "the good old days" faded, like a flickering light bulb, and soon he resumed his story of his hated former employer.

"Eventually, Willie boy got the political bug himself. He started badgering his mother into advancing him enough money to buy more newspapers. But Phoebe drove a hard bargain. She didn't like the fact that her son was living with a waitress. So she paid Tessie a little visit and offered her a fortune—I hear it was a hundred and fifty thousand dollars—if she'd blow town and leave Sonny alone.

"W.R. was depressed for a whole year after Tessie left him. I guess he didn't trust women after that. But Mama placated him by selling her interest in the Anaconda Copper Mine for seven million bucks and giving Willie the money so he could play newspaper big shot.

"Then," said Fairfield expansively, "came the business years. Hearst realized early on that the man who influences public opinion is more powerful than the one who owns a bank. Hearst had quite a talent for writing, and knowing good writing, and newspapers are the obvious molders of public opinion."

"Who were the women after Tessie?" asked Al.

"He fooled around with a lot of showgirls. But nothing serious. Until he met Millicent."

"Mrs. Hearst?"

"Yeah. Today she sits in her palaces like the Queen of Sheba, more proper than old Phoebe ever was. She's a snob who makes most snobs seem like ordinary garage mechanics."

"She sounds lovely." Al laughed.

"She's a cold cookie to most people. And freezes out anyone who remembers her very un-society beginnings, kiddo. You know how she met Hearst?"

Al shook his head.

"She was a tap dancer! Elegant old Millie and her sister Anita were hoofers. Hearst caught their act in a show, *The Girl from Paris*. He introduced himself to them after the show, and he fell for Millie. One thing about William Randolph. When he likes a dame, that includes her whole family, regardless. He took the whole goddamn Willson brood to Europe. Back in New York, after the theater, at nights Millie would go with him to the newspaper plant. She'd pick daintily at a supper he had sent in, while he'd work on the layout for the front page. Wrote the editorials himself, too. And they were damn good."

"Yeah, he was quite a newspaperman in those days," recalled Vince.

"When did they marry?" asked Al.

"Around 1903, I think. He was about forty. She was in her early twenties."

"How did his mother take it?"

"He never asked Phoebe's permission. Just told her he was getting married. When the old lady heard the girl was a stage dancer, she nearly croaked. But Sonny Boy had made up his mind, and that was that. But Millie eventually won the old dame over. In fact, she became more society than Phoebe. And gave Hearst five sons along the way, including the twins."

Al had stopped eating a while back. Half his steak

remained on the plate. He was caught up in the story Fairfield was relating so vividly.

"Even with all his money, Hearst found out it wasn't as easy as in his father's day to buy a governorship or a Senate seat," continued Fairfield. "He always seemed to back the wrong candidates and the wrong causes, anyway. For a while, during the big war, people *hated* Hearst. Right in the middle of the war, in 1915, Hearst went to Germany and had himself photographed smiling with the Kaiser!"

"Christ!" exclaimed Al.

"You said it," Fairfield agreed. "Everyone seems to have forgotten about that now. But Hearst was pro-German and anti-British. His papers kept telling people we should either stay out of the war completely or join on the side of Germany. After a while, the U.S. Senate began an investigation of Hearst and his pro-German attitudes. The government even planted a spy who posed as a butler in his house.

"People burned Hearst newspapers. In movie houses so many people hissed the Hearst Pathé newsreel, the company had to drop the Hearst name and just call it the Pathé news.

"Of course," Fairfield continued sarcastically, "after we did join the Allies, nobody could have been more American than Mr. Hearst. He even changed the name of some of his papers and included the word *American*. He even made his little newsboys wear American-flag pins.

"But people didn't forget so easily. There was a big donnybrook after the war, when that idiot Mayor Hylan appointed Hearst New York's official greeter for the returning troops. Of course, everybody knew that Hylan was in Hearst's pocket and the poor slob had to do what Hearst told him to do. But Christ, what a furor. Teddy Roosevelt himself got off his deathbed to lead a group to oppose Hylan.

"That time it looked like old Hearst had gone too far. There were even threats on his life. And everybody figured the soldiers getting off the ships would throw bricks at him. But the old man wouldn't back down. I'll say this for him—Hearst's no coward. The pressure on him was unbelievable. Everybody wanted him to resign from that committee. He laughed. He wouldn't buckle under. Even though bricks might have been thrown at him, he went to the docks to meet the troops. He defied all the big politicians, from Al Smith on down, and that took care of any chance Hearst had of running for governor."

At this moment, however, Al Bradshaw wasn't interested in Hearst's war record or political ambitions. It was Hearst's personal life that might give Al some clue to the Ince Affair.

"When did Hearst meet Marion Davies?" Al asked.

Fairfield smiled. "Around 1916. By then Hearst was bored to death with Millie. She had become so proper, he couldn't stand her. He always went for young ones anyway, and Millie was an old broad of thirty-five. When he first saw Marion, she was sixteen and a knockout. He found her just as he had found dozens of others—on a stage. She was one of those show dames, dressed in satins and plumes, who just stood there and looked beautiful. I guess they couldn't give her any dialogue because of her stutter."

"She stutters?"

"And how!"

"Hearst discovered her in the Ziegfeld Follies," stated Vince Lewis.

"It was *before* the Follies, pal," Fairfield corrected him. "Marion was in some show called *Stop! Look! Listen!* At the time, Davies was the chippy of another rich old geezer, Paul Block, a friend of Hearst's. Block's a publisher, too. The Brooklyn *Eagle* and the Toledo *Blade*.

"As a matter of fact, Hearst first saw Davies when he went to the show with Block."

"Don't tell me it was that old stage-door-johnny shit, waiting for her outside the theater!" Al scoffed.

"Nah, they do things with class in New York, kid. After the show, Block would squire Marion to the penthouse apartment of Frank Crowninshield, the classy magazine publisher. I was sweet on a dame— Peggy Morrison—who was in the same show. Peggy knew that whole Crowninshield setup. Crowninshield's little bashes were the perfect place for wealthy johns to meet showgirls and models.

"Peggy told me the situation between Marion, Hearst, and Block was tricky at first. Like I said, Marion was Block's girl."

"Then how did she wind up with Hearst?"

"What's there to say? Hearst and Block were both old geezers to a young kid like Marion. They both had dough and they could both show her a good time. But Marion's a shrewd operator. Hearst is the loyal type. Don't forget, he kept Tessie Powers for eight years! Since Hearst promised a longer run, Marion eased Block out."

"You're making her sound like a female Machiavelli, with a stutter!"

"Not bad, kid. That's not far off target, either, but the funny thing is, I like her. You'd like her, too. I suppose it's not her fault she was bred to be a gold digger. When the Dourases—"

"Dourases?"

"Douras is her real name. When the Douras family saw Marion had a big fish on the hook, they weren't about to let her let him get away. Not too many people knew it, but Marion's sister Reine—and their mother, Rose—masterminded the kid's career. Both on"—he paused for emphasis—"and *off*stage."

"That Reine's quite a character, too," noted Vince. "I knew her myself, years back. Reine's a nickname for Irene. And she's the one who picked the name Davies off a real-estate sign, I think. Anyhow, she married that producer, George Lederer, and then moved her whole family in. That's how they all got into show business in the first place, through Lederer."

Fairfield agreed. "Peggy told me one story that'll curl your hair." He smirked. "After Davies dumped Block and switched to Hearst, there was some important unfinished business. It seems Marion had been stupid enough to write Block some letters, real hot stuff. Reine was afraid Block would blow the whistle on Marion. Hearst would find out about the letters somehow. Block might even show Hearst the letters himself and say, 'Look, this kid's just another chippy, don't make a fool of yourself.'

"Reine was no dummy. She figured if that happened, Hearst would drop Marion like a hot potato. Even though the old bird was already telling people he was deeply in love with Marion, if he found out about the letters, he'd be humiliated—there's no fool like an old fool, right?

"So Reine and a girlfriend, Frances, went up to Block's one night, see? They sat around and had a few drinks. The old guy figured he was gonna lay one of them, if not both. Frances said, 'Where's the loo?' She steals off to the other room while Reine butters up to Block.

"Reine's whispering sweet nothin's in Block's withered old ear while Frances is in the bedroom rummaging around. She finds the letters, plus a couple of photos, and tucks 'em in her girdle.

"Back in the parlor, Block's getting hot under the collar. The old bird's almost coming in his pants. He's about to pin Reine down when Frances comes out just in the nick of time, like the cavalry saving the fort. . . ."

Fairfield, using a falsetto voice, played the part of Frances. " 'I'm not feeling well, we'll have to go!' " The men laughed. Fairfield continued.

"Block was really pissed, see? But Frances just winked at 'em and promised, 'We'll get together next time.' Then the two girls scuttled down the stairs, Frances pattin' her girdle where she's got the goods stashed.

"The showgirls on the street were buzzin' about that one for weeks!" Frank added. After a pause, he lamented, "Boy, those rich bastards have it easy. Listen, kid, you and I wanna get a dame in the sack, what can we do, buy her a beer? Take her to the beach? The movies? A show? Maybe if we've saved a coupla bucks we'd spring for a trinket or something. But guys like Hearst and Block do it different. They can show off for her.

"If Block got into Marion's pants by giving her a diamond ring or something, so what's a diamond ring? Any guy with money could buy her that. Hearst took a different route. He'd show her what he could do for her career. He tells Vic Watson, editor of the New York *American*, to feature her in the Sunday supplement. She's just a broad in the Follies then, nothing special, no star. Then all of a sudden Watson sends her up to Campbell's Photography Studio and she's treated like an important Ziegfeld Girl, like she was Lilyan Tashman or somebody.

"But everybody knew the score," he scoffed, "because who's there at Campbell's to oversee things— quietly, mind you, in the background, but *there*—but the Chief himself. They gave Marion's photograph a whole page in the *American,* and it was just the beginning.

"At the time, everyone figures, 'Well, Hearst's wife is pregnant but after she has the kid he'll drop the showgirl.' But Marion was a little smart, too. After Hearst's wife has the twins, the family goes to Florida. Marion followed them down to Palm Beach. You know Gene Buck, the songwriter for Ziegfeld?"

Neither Al nor Vince knew him.

"Well, he was there too. He knew Marion and invited her to go bike riding. Gene realized Marion was Hearst's girl, and he didn't want any trouble. What Buck *didn't* know was that the Hearsts were in Palm Beach.

"One day Marion and Buck are pedaling along on

their bikes. Buck looks and sees a maroon Cadillac coming toward them. 'Looks like Hearst's car,' he joked. Marion almost pissed in her pants. Her bike swerved and she ran into the curb. She fell off the bike and her legs were up in the air, her bloomers showing.

"Buck rushed over to help her as Hearst's car came to a screeching halt. The old man leaped out and rushed to help Marion too."

Now Fairfield imitated Hearst's voice. " 'May I help you with this accident?' He's real formal, see, pretending he doesn't know either of them.

"Marion and Buck didn't know what the hell was going on—until they spotted Millie Hearst in the car, taking in the whole scene. Now comes the kicker! *Hearst insisted that Marion get in the car with him and his wife.* Hearst said he wanted to take Marion to a doctor. He and his chauffeur put her bike in the trunk. 'Good-bye,' Hearst says to Buck, leaving him alone on the road.

"Buck never knew what the hell happened after that, but Marion had to be a pretty good actress to carry off *that* scene!"

As he finished the anecdote, Frank Fairfield shook the empty bottle of rye over his glass, so the few remaining drops wouldn't be wasted. Al immediately signaled the waiter to bring another bottle. When it arrived, Fairfield poured himself a fresh shot, as though the evening were just beginning.

Frank complained bitterly that for the last couple of years he had tried to move from the Long Beach paper up to one of the Los Angeles dailies. But somehow or other his attempts were always thwarted. When he spoke of Hearst, a strong current of emotion seemed to surge through him.

"You want to know why I hate the son of a bitch?" he asked intensely. "I was one hell of a reporter. The New York *Tribune* never had a better one. I beat Hearst's paper out every time. You wanna know what Hearst's got that we all want? Money. Even Howey couldn't resist. Hearst gave him thirty-five thousand dollars a year. That's a big jump from eight thousand, wouldn't you say?" Al and Vince knew Fairfield was referring to Walter Howey, the Chicago *Tribune*'s famous crack city editor, who had been lured into the Hearst camp.

"Well, I'm no different from Howey, see? Hearst offers me four times what I'm making on the *Trib* to move over to the *Journal*. My pals all warned me, 'Frank, don't be an asshole.' But I went over for the dough. Who wouldn't?

"But I'm a reporter, I'm no yes-man. With Hearst's editors, they're all kissing his ass. Everybody calls him the Chief, and they talk to him by saying things like, 'Mr. Hearst, may I be so bold as to suggest . . .' And crap like 'With the greatest respect, may I say . . .' Well, screw that shit. I report the news. And the truth, too."

Fairfield took a long swallow of liquor, then delivered the inevitable postscript to that kind of thinking: "I lasted a year. Nobody bucks the Chief."

It was impossible not to notice the derision in Fairfield's voice when he used the words "the Chief."

"They wouldn't take me back at the *Tribune*, and I didn't blame 'em," lamented Fairfield. "I hadda come out here and start all over again."

The three men sat in silence, staring at their glasses. The vitality Fairfield had displayed in the last hour had suddenly vanished. The fire had passed from his eyes. Al realized Frank Fairfield was a defeated man.

Although Fairfield had consumed at least a quart of alcohol, the old warhorse could never be drunk enough to lose his newspaperman's instinct. "You got something big on Hearst, kid?"

Al hedged and tried to con Fairfield that he was just interested in background information.

"Don't shit me," said Fairfield. He hadn't missed the glances Lewis and Bradshaw had been exchanging.

"I'm not tryin' to steal your thunder, kid. I'm too

are, either. Those people don't really 'preciate
the ship, anyway. It's wasted on 'em."
ve you ever been on the boat?"
e never been on it, but I've talked to most every-
ho works on it. What's your interest, anyway?"
m a reporter for the *Tribune* and I'm doing a
s of stories on famous yachts."
ha! Then you should talk to some of the boys
work on 'em."
Where would I find them?"
'About three blocks down there's an eatin' and
nkin' place where all the sailors spend time. It's the
ack up the road. Says 'Bait' outside. The *Oneida*
here now, ya know. But one young squirt some-
s stays in port t' get laid." She exploded into a
terous laugh. "Little squirt's cute, too. I saw 'im to-
. Ask for Jerry. Tell 'im Lou sent ya."
l thanked her. He hurried back to his car. The
ys had found the cap and filled the radiator. Al
iled. "Great job," he said, handing the leader an-
er quarter.
He drove the four blocks to the waterfront dive. The
ary, damp area was dark and deserted. Al had
rd of dudes wandering into this part of town and
er coming out. The "Bait" shack's foreboding ap-
rance didn't welcome outsiders.
As Bradshaw studied the shack he realized he was
inappropriately dressed. He yanked off his tie and
jacket and threw them in the car. He rumpled his shirt,
mussed his hair, and put on an old dirty sweater he
kept under the driver's seat. Still he looked like an ex-
high school athlete.
"Yeah?" spoke a threatening voice the moment Al
crossed the threshold.
"Is Jerry around?"
"Who wants to know?"
"I want to know."
"Who are you? And who sent ya?"
"Lou sent me."

old, too goddamn tired to be interested in goin' after
whatever it is you're on to. But I'll give you a really
good piece of advice. If you're tangling with Hearst—
watch your ass."

Al felt queasy walking toward his automobile. He
realized he had had too much booze trying to keep up
with Frank and Vince. At least the evening air was
cool and would help sober him.

Still, his brain felt clouded. He was getting too much
information, too fast. He needed time to sort it all out.
Maybe a drive down to Long Beach would clear his
head.

He didn't even know if the Hearst yacht was back
yet at the Wilmington docks. It might still be moored
in San Diego. But it was certainly worth a trip to try to
talk to people at the waterfront.

"No doubt about it," he said aloud to himself as he
drove along, finding the sound of his voice reassuring.
"Old man Hearst is crazy about Davies." The question,
thought Al, remained: Is he crazy enough to kill for
her? Or did Marion kill Ince and was Hearst covering
up for *her*? And what about Diane Enright?

Christ, there were a dozen people on the yacht and
at least thirty more crew members. There must be
someone who'll tell the true story.

Al was traveling at about twenty miles an hour and
the flow of cool air against his face was soothing. But
abruptly his thoughts were interrupted. The radiator
cap hissed loudly, then shot off with an explosion. The
car had been overheating, and Al, preoccupied, hadn't
noticed. He cursed, braking the Chevy to a cranky
halt. It was the third time this had happened in a week.
Luckily, he was only half a mile from the beach.

He trudged down Santa Monica Boulevard and came
across a group of four boys in their early teens, playing
ball on the sand.

"Hey, fellas. Anyone wanna make a quarter?"
They bounded over.

"That's my car over there." He pointed. "Here's a quarter now, and I'll give you another one when I get back, if you guys'll fill my radiator with water and find the cap. It blew off back there."

The leader of the group, a towheaded ruffian who reminded Al of himself as a kid, pocketed the money. "You got a deal, mister."

"I'm looking for someone who can tell me something about these yachts," said Al.

"See that shack over there?" The boy pointed to a wooden shanty about a hundred yards away. "Lou practically lives there. Sells clams and shrimps and knows everything about everybody."

Al smiled, reached in his pocket, and gave the kid a dime. "Thanks."

"Hey, Georgie . . . let's get started," ordered the towhead as Al strode over to the shanty.

Up close, Bradshaw saw the shack was actually a roadside stand. The counter smelled of fish. An old oil lamp, hanging in one corner, illuminated the crude hand-lettered sign: CLAMS. Al squinted. Inside he could make out the silhouette of a hefty, crusty old sailor breathing heavily, moving bushels of clams and huge hunks of melting ice.

"Lou?" called Al.

"Yeah?" answered a gruff voice. "I'm closing," Lou added, without looking around.

"Don't want any clams," Al assured him. "I just want to talk."

"What about?" Straightening up and turning around, Lou was massive, all right, but to Al's surprise, he was a *she*, an old woman, her huge breasts sagging almost to her waist. She wore a black turtleneck sweater. A woolen cap was pulled over her matted hair. In the lantern light Al could make out a mole on the right side of her nose. She was chomping on what looked to Al like a small cigar.

"Lou's short for Louise," she said in answer to Al's unasked question. "And I've got no time for talk."

"I understand that William R[...] his yacht down here. Can you te[...] anyone who works on it?"

Al had touched upon Lou's passi[...] next few minutes she rhapsodized [...] was an old sailor at heart, the daugh[...] tain. She had been brought up on ships[...] Lou was ten, she had sailed around the H[...] per helmed by her father. After Papa r[...] loted the ferry from San Pedro to Catalina I[...]

It took Al a while to steer Lou away fr[...] story and back to the information he wanted.[...]

"The *Oneida*? Beeee-u-tiful boat! But it's[...] of the ships Hearst owns, you know. The *Bucc[...]* beauty too. A hundred-thirty-eight-footer. It's[...] steamer, with a steel hull. The Navy even used[...] durin' the Spanish-American War. But it's his ot[...] yacht, the *Hirondelle*, that's the real prize. He boug[...] it from the Prince of Monaco, some little country ove[...] there in Europe. I hear tell it's got a bottom made [...] glass, can you imagine that? They say that when y[...] press a button, the wood floor just slides away a[...] you can see the fish and everything! Keeps it in t[...] East. Never brings it out here."

"But it's the *Oneida* that comes out here a lot," [...] noted.

"Sure does. The *Oneida*'s a steamer too—396 t[...] Built back east around the turn of the century. [...] owner was the old German Kaiser. Hearst picked [...] for a song after the war. Yeah, of all his ship[...] *Oneida*'s the only one that comes out here. 'C[...] nowadays," reminisced Lou, "they don't have to[...] around the Horn. They can bring it up here fro[...] York through the Panama Canal. The *Oneid[...]* hundred twen'y feet of the most seaworthy ves[...] docked here!"

Al wanted information about goings-on a[...] *Oneida*.

"Don't know nothin' about what goes on [...]

old, too goddamn tired to be interested in goin' after whatever it is you're on to. But I'll give you a really good piece of advice. If you're tangling with Hearst—watch your ass."

Al felt queasy walking toward his automobile. He realized he had had too much booze trying to keep up with Frank and Vince. At least the evening air was cool and would help sober him.

Still, his brain felt clouded. He was getting too much information, too fast. He needed time to sort it all out. Maybe a drive down to Long Beach would clear his head.

He didn't even know if the Hearst yacht was back yet at the Wilmington docks. It might still be moored in San Diego. But it was certainly worth a trip to try to talk to people at the waterfront.

"No doubt about it," he said aloud to himself as he drove along, finding the sound of his voice reassuring. "Old man Hearst is crazy about Davies." The question, thought Al, remained: Is he crazy enough to kill for her? Or did Marion kill Ince and was Hearst covering up for *her*? And what about Diane Enright?

Christ, there were a dozen people on the yacht and at least thirty more crew members. There must be *someone* who'll tell the true story.

Al was traveling at about twenty miles an hour and the flow of cool air against his face was soothing. But abruptly his thoughts were interrupted. The radiator cap hissed loudly, then shot off with an explosion. The car had been overheating, and Al, preoccupied, hadn't noticed. He cursed, braking the Chevy to a cranky halt. It was the third time this had happened in a week. Luckily, he was only half a mile from the beach.

He trudged down Santa Monica Boulevard and came across a group of four boys in their early teens, playing ball on the sand.

"Hey, fellas. Anyone wanna make a quarter?"

They bounded over.

"That's my car over there." He pointed. "Here's a quarter now, and I'll give you another one when I get back, if you guys'll fill my radiator with water and find the cap. It blew off back there."

The leader of the group, a towheaded ruffian who reminded Al of himself as a kid, pocketed the money. "You got a deal, mister."

"I'm looking for someone who can tell me something about these yachts," said Al.

"See that shack over there?" The boy pointed to a wooden shanty about a hundred yards away. "Lou practically lives there. Sells clams and shrimps and knows everything about everybody."

Al smiled, reached in his pocket, and gave the kid a dime. "Thanks."

"Hey, Georgie . . . let's get started," ordered the towhead as Al strode over to the shanty.

Up close, Bradshaw saw the shack was actually a roadside stand. The counter smelled of fish. An old oil lamp, hanging in one corner, illuminated the crude hand-lettered sign: CLAMS. Al squinted. Inside he could make out the silhouette of a hefty, crusty old sailor breathing heavily, moving bushels of clams and huge hunks of melting ice.

"Lou?" called Al.

"Yeah?" answered a gruff voice. "I'm closing," Lou added, without looking around.

"Don't want any clams," Al assured him. "I just want to talk."

"What about?" Straightening up and turning around, Lou was massive, all right, but to Al's surprise, he was a *she*, an old woman, her huge breasts sagging almost to her waist. She wore a black turtleneck sweater. A woolen cap was pulled over her matted hair. In the lantern light Al could make out a mole on the right side of her nose. She was chomping on what looked to Al like a small cigar.

"Lou's short for Louise," she said in answer to Al's unasked question. "And I've got no time for talk."

"I understand that William Randolph Hearst keeps his yacht down here. Can you tell me where to find anyone who works on it?"

Al had touched upon Lou's passion. Ships. For the next few minutes she rhapsodized about them. She was an old sailor at heart, the daughter of a sea captain. She had been brought up on ships. In 1870, when Lou was ten, she had sailed around the Horn on a clipper helmed by her father. After Papa retired, he piloted the ferry from San Pedro to Catalina Island.

It took Al a while to steer Lou away from her life story and back to the information he wanted.

"The *Oneida*? Beeee-u-tiful boat! But it's only one of the ships Hearst owns, you know. The *Buccaneer* beauty too. A hundred-thirty-eight-footer. It's steamer, with a steel hull. The Navy even used durin' the Spanish-American War. But it's his ot yacht, the *Hirondelle*, that's the real prize. He bou it from the Prince of Monaco, some little country ove there in Europe. I hear tell it's got a bottom made glass, can you imagine that? They say that when yo press a button, the wood floor just slides away a you can see the fish and everything! Keeps it in t East. Never brings it out here."

"But it's the *Oneida* that comes out here a lot," noted.

"Sure does. The *Oneida*'s a steamer too—396 t Built back east around the turn of the century. owner was the old German Kaiser. Hearst picked for a song after the war. Yeah, of all his shi *Oneida*'s the only one that comes out here. 'O nowadays," reminisced Lou, "they don't have to around the Horn. They can bring it up here fro York through the Panama Canal. The *Oneid* hundred twen'y feet of the most seaworthy ves docked here!"

Al wanted information about goings-on al *Oneida*.

"Don't know nothin' about what goes on

Don't care, either. Those people don't really 'preciate or enjoy the ship, anyway. It's wasted on 'em."

"Have you ever been on the boat?"

"I've never been on it, but I've talked to most every-one who works on it. What's your interest, anyway?"

"I'm a reporter for the *Tribune* and I'm doing a series of stories on famous yachts."

"Aha! Then you should talk to some of the boys who *work* on 'em."

"Where would I find them?"

"About three blocks down there's an eatin' and drinkin' place where all the sailors spend time. It's the shack up the road. Says 'Bait' outside. The *Oneida* here now, ya know. But one young squirt some- s stays in port t' get laid." She exploded into a terous laugh. "Little squirt's cute, too. I saw 'im to- Ask for Jerry. Tell 'im Lou sent ya."

l thanked her. He hurried back to his car. The ys had found the cap and filled the radiator. Al iled. "Great job," he said, handing the leader an- er quarter.

He drove the four blocks to the waterfront dive. The ary, damp area was dark and deserted. Al had rd of dudes wandering into this part of town and ver coming out. The "Bait" shack's foreboding ap- rance didn't welcome outsiders.

As Bradshaw studied the shack he realized he was inappropriately dressed. He yanked off his tie and jacket and threw them in the car. He rumpled his shirt, mussed his hair, and put on an old dirty sweater he kept under the driver's seat. Still he looked like an ex-high school athlete.

"Yeah?" spoke a threatening voice the moment Al rossed the threshold.

"Is Jerry around?"

"Who wants to know?"

"I want to know."

"Who are you? And who sent ya?"

"Lou sent me."

From the shadows a tough-looking heavyset man emerged. "You a friend of Lou's?"

"Yeah, I'm her friend. She said you'd direct me to Jerry."

"You a cop?"

"No."

The tough old ox hesitated momentarily. "He's back there," the man said, pointing to a wooden door at the rear of the shack. Al walked toward it. As he put his hand on the door handle, Bradshaw felt a hard object poking into his back. The man had silently slid up behind him. "You better not be a cop, mister, or you're gonna be in big trouble."

With a sweaty palm Al turned the latch. The stench of fish burned his nostrils and it took a few seconds before his eyes adjusted to the darkened, smoke-filled interior. Groups of sailors congregated in shadows at various corners of the room.

"That's Jerry," said the bouncer, indicating a skinny young sailor seated at a table at the far end of the room.

Al walked over. Bradshaw guessed that Jerry was about twenty. The boy had beady black eyes that darted around nervously, like those of a bird searching frantically for a worm. He had curly black hair and a slight build. He would probably look twenty years old for many years.

"Jerry? Lou sent me over," Al said in a friendly manner.

Jerry looked up. "Sent you for what?" he asked suspiciously. A young oriental girl was unsuccessfully trying to engage the young sailor in conversation. But Jerry was obviously uninterested.

"Can I buy you a drink?" Al asked him.

"Beat it, mister."

Al sat down anyway. There was a tense silence. The two young men stared at each other until the bartender came over. The bruiser glowered over them. Bradshaw proffered a five-dollar bill. "A bottle of whiskey," he ordered. Al was trying to remain calm, but he could feel perspiration forming on his forehead. The bartender remained threateningly still. He looked over to the sailor. When Jerry nodded in assent, the bartender snatched the bill and disappeared back into the shadows.

At the sight of Al's money, the oriental girl's attentions now focused on Bradshaw. "You wanna good time, mister?" Her accent was strictly Los Angeles, no trace of Hong Kong.

"Not tonight, sweetie." Al turned to Jerry. "Here's another fin for you if we can talk. Alone."

Jerry pocketed the five. "Beat it," he said to the girl. After she left, Jerry stared at Bradshaw. "Cop? Or reporter?"

"Reporter."

"I thought so."

"You work on the *Oneida*?"

"Sometimes."

"How come you're not on it now?"

"I take off five, six days a month."

"How long you been working on the ship?"

"Two, three years."

"Sign on here?"

"No. New York."

"Nice work?"

"Some...es."

"Bet you been a lot of fancy places."

"Whaddya really wanna know, mister?"

"Just some background. What's it like working for the old man?"

The bartender returned with the whiskey. He put down the bottle and two shot glasses, then left. Al poured the drinks. The stuff seared his throat as though it were rubbing alcohol. Until now, Bradshaw had never appreciated the Palm's hooch.

Jerry smirked at Al's discomfort. "This is stuff for *real* men, mister," he said, throwing back his head and swallowing the whiskey in a single gulp.

"Have another," said Al.

The sailor seemed to relax after the third shot. "Whaddya *really* wanna know?" The word was ominously emphasized.

Al wouldn't be intimidated. "Background, mostly," he lied. "What's it like?"

"Hard work, for people like us," Jerry said with bitterness. "*Th*ey all have fun. Booze. Sunbathing. The women showin' their tits, sometimes when they don't know we're lookin'. And especially when they know we are."

Jerry droned on about superficial aspects of his work, but Al saw he was bright and observant. After several more whiskeys, the boy finally loosened up and Al learned Jerry had run away from home because his mother, a schoolteacher, didn't want him to become a sailor.

He had first worked aboard the *Oneida* in the fall of 1921. He remembered the passengers on that cruise: Hearst, Marion, her mother, Rose, and sister Ethel, and people involved with Marion's movie *Enchantment*: director William LeBaron, writer Luther Reed, set designer Joseph Urban and his daughter Gretl, and other friends.

It was intended to be just a short sail, for a day or two, a yachting party on which they would screen Marion's new picture.

But then, on an impulse, Hearst decided: "Let's sail on to Mexico. I have business there. We can *all* go and have a great time."

"We can't, protested Ethel Davies. "None of us have brought enough clothes."

"Don't worry about that," replied Hearst. "We'll stop in Baltimore." When the ship docked in Baltimore, Hearst passed out cash to all his guests. "Please get anything you need. Let's all really have a good time."

The entire group then sailed on to Mexico, remaining there for six weeks.

"Six weeks?" exclaimed Al. "What did you guys do?"

"Just took care of the ship," recalled Jerry. "And waited. Took out some pretty Mexican girls. A couple of guys caught the clap!" He laughed noisily at that recollection.

Jerry also remembered, "Old man Hearst had a private train, which went down to Mexico to meet the group. The train took the whole damn boatload of people on a tour of the country."

Al knew that Hearst owned a great deal of land in Mexico, and he remembered reading that on this trip Hearst and Marion had had a private audience with the President of Mexico.

"I heard later," Jerry revealed, "that old lady Hearst was really pissed about the Mexican trip."

"Is it true that the old man doesn't drink?"

"He don't drink. But, Jesus Maria, everyone else who comes aboard does. Especially the Davies family. I had a backache for a week unloading the cases of Scotch we picked up in Vancouver. But if the old man ever caught anyone drunk, you were washed up. Hearst had this bodyguard—that's what they called 'im, but he was really around to keep an eye on the dame. A fun-lovin' kind of tough guy. But he can't handle his liquor. The old man fired him."

"What was his name?"

"Fletcher," said Jerry. "Grady Fletcher."

"What happened to him?"

"Who knows? Still in town somewhere, I guess."

"One more question . . ." Jerry was drunk now, slobbering and eyeing a big-breasted brunette who had joined the crowd at the bar. "Would you know anything about old man Hearst's being an antivivisectionist?"

"Nah," said Jerry vehemently. "That ain't true. I don't care what they say. He ain't a queer."

"No," said Al. "What I mean is, is he against killing animals?"

"I ain't heard nothin' about that."

"Does he keep any guns on board?"

"Oh, sure," said Jerry, pouring out the last of the whiskey. "Brags about how he grew up on a ranch. He's a mean shot, too. Carries a silver gun with a pearl handle. Holster style, like Tom Mix. I've even seen ol' man Hearst shoot a seagull from fifty yards from a hip position."

It was past midnight when Al arrived home. His tiny, stuffy room was cluttered with more newspapers, magazines, and books than ever. Surveying the sorry mess, Bradshaw pushed a pile of *Tribune*s out of his way so he could open the bathroom door.

His stomach was churning from the cheap booze. As he mixed a bromo, a single thought, like wheels clicking against railroal tracks, kept steadily repeating: "Hearst can hit a seagull with a single shot from fifty yards!"

Al felt sweaty. He stripped and stepped into the shower. Bradshaw's head cleared a bit with the rush of cold water on his face. But he was too keyed up to relax.

He toweled himself off, flopped on his bed, and clasped his hands behind his head. "What a goddamn story this could be," he said to himself. But he was totally frustrated. "If I turn over what I know to the paper, they'll give the damn story to McIntire," he reasoned. "If I don't, I'm working in the dark."

He had a sudden thought. He had given his last five dollars to the sailor. Bradshaw scrounged through his trouser pockets. He counted a total of $1.77, all in change. Payday was a week away. He knew he would probably have to pay for more information. Without telling Casey why, he could never get an advance on his salary.

Al couldn't clear his mind of the story. It was hopeless to try to sleep. He popped out of bed, dressed quickly, and raced the three blocks to the *Tribune*. The presses were humming. The morning's edition was coming out. He glanced at the paper to see if they had used his—Mike's—story on the mayor. There it was, cut considerably and buried on page three.

Al went up to the morgue on the fourth floor and dug out all the clippings on Ince, Hearst, Davies, Hart.

First he went through the files on Ince. There were pictures of the famed producer with Mack Sennett and D. W. Griffith, the three partners in the "newly formed Triangle Corporation" in 1915, now defunct. Al knew that at the time of his death, Ince was still good friends with Griffith, but not Sennett. Perhaps Sennett, the King of Comedy—a notorious womanizer himself—might be willing to tell Al more than Hart had concerning Ince's lady friends and "that disgusting feature" in Ince's house.

How, though, would he get through to Mack Sennett? Maybe Barney Henderson again, or Vince or Farr—he'd get through somehow. On a scrap of paper, Al began jotting the names of all the people he'd better call first thing in the morning.

He turned back to the clips. There were numerous photographs of Ince aboard his stately yacht, pictures and stories about Ince and his wife, Nell, photos of the mogul with the great screen stars: the Talmadges, Pickford and Fairbanks, William S. Hart, of course, and western writer Buck Connors. There was even a shot of the handsome Ince with President Woodrow Wilson.

Al searched for a photograph or at least a mention of the actress Diane Enright. There was none. How deeply involved in all this was Enright? he wondered, recalling the sultry voice on the telephone. How did she fit into the story? Was she a woman scorned because she hadn't been invited on the cruise? Or had she been on the yacht? On his scrap of paper, Al noted, "Find Enright."

The clips on Ince were not illuminating, but Al discovered surprising facts he hadn't known about

William Randolph Hearst. In the file on Hearst Al found many editorial cartoons depicting the tycoon. Hearst was often portrayed as a bear or an octopus. Most of the Hearst clips concentrated on the man's political ambitions.

There were stories about Hearst attending the Republican and Democratic conventions in 1920 and 1924. The gist of these pieces was that, since the days of the great war, the old man had really lost much of his political clout.

But the old boy was still in there pitching. Just this summer, during the Democratic convention in New York, Hearst had thrown a huge soiree for more than six hundred delegates. He had taken over the entire ground floor of the Ritz Carlton Hotel and had it transformed into a palm-filled garden. With a smiling Mrs. Hearst by his side, W.R. had welcomed a bevy of political notables, including Mr. and Mrs. Franklin Delano Roosevelt, New York Mayor and Mrs. Hylan, former presidential candidate William Jennings Bryan, William McAdoo, Mr. and Mrs. James A. Farley.

Hearst had even hired the Paul Whiteman Orchestra for entertainment on this occasion, and at an intimate midnight gala for his guests, Will Rogers, Jimmy Savo, Clifton Webb, and the legendary French chanteuse Mistinguett performed.

Though the delegates obviously enjoyed Hearst's lavish hospitality, when it came time for the voting at Madison Square Garden, they turned their backs on his candidate. Hearst had supported Senator Walsh of Montana as the Democratic candidate for president. The delegates voted in John W. Davis. The publisher then promised to back Davis if in return Davis would appoint Hearst secretary of the navy when he won. Davis refused, and an angry Hearst sent a directive to his editors that the Hearst newspapers would support neither candidate.

As Al flipped through earlier clips detailing Hearst's political ambitions, he was able to piece together a frightening story. In 1920, Hearst had supported Senator Hiram Johnson of California for the Republican presidential nomination. Many people feared that Johnson, if he won, would be Hearst's man in Washington.

But Warren Harding received the nomination, and Johnson was offered the second spot. He—and Hearst—declined, and the nod for vice-president went to an obscure politician from Vermont. The Republicans won that year, and when President Harding died in office, the little-known vice-president, Calvin Coolidge, was catapulted into the most powerful office in the world. Now Coolidge had just won reelection for another four years by beating Davis.

If Hearst and Johnson had decided to take the second spot on the ticket with Harding, Hiram Johnson would be president today! And Hearst would be controlling the country. The thought was mind-boggling.

Al lit his last cigarette, and tackled the remaining two files.

Marion's file was movie-star stuff. Al sifted through dozens of clippings displaying her in the role of celebrity—arriving in Hollywood to make her first film; the glittering all-star premier of Marion's *Yolanda*. There were countless stories on Cosmopolitan Pictures, Hearst's film corporation, distributing first through Select, later Paramount, and most recently the Goldwyn Corporation.

The last file contained clips on Marion and Hearst. These were stories which had made the front pages, not merely the movie pages. Bradshaw realized he had read most of the articles when they had initially appeared, but he had forgotten the details. It was obvious to Al that just reading an occasional story which referred to Hearst and Marion had made little impression on him. But now, with the batch of clippings before him, Bradshaw was able to assemble facts. A clear picture began to emerge.

The first point which impressed Al was that in the last few years there had been frequent and unflattering reports about the multimillionaire publisher and his young girlfriend.

A scandal had erupted when, in the fall of 1922, Marion, still living in New York, attended a party at her sister Reine's home. Constance Talmadge, Victor Moore, Leo Carillo, and most of the Douras family, including Marion's father, "Judge" Douras, were present. The scandal revolved around one of the guests, Peter Marvin, and his wife. The Marvins fell into an argument over the attentions Peter was paying "a blond movie star"—obviously Marion. Marvin happened to be carrying a gun, and when the Marvin couple fought, Marvin was shot—not fatally, but he suffered a neck wound.

The police—and tabloid reporters—arrived on the scene quickly.

As Al scanned the stories, he saw that all accounts mentioned that Reine Lederer's party had been in honor of her sister, Marion Davies. All accounts, that is, except those in Hearst's papers. His papers omitted mentioning Marion's name.

Successive newspaper accounts reported that Marion Davies' lawyer had phoned each New York newspaper to say that Marion *hadn't* been present. The stories continued for a week. Bradshaw had to smile at some of the headlines: MARION DAVIES SAYS SHE WASN'T THERE. MARION'S FRIENDS SAY SHE WASN'T THERE. SPECULATION ON MARION REACHES HEIGHTS—WAS SHE THERE? Marion subsequently sued the *Daily News* and the *Telegram*.

Bradshaw sifted through another stack of stories until he was hit by the most startling headlines about Hearst and Marion. They heralded and reported the infamous trial of William J. Fallon, the noted New York lawyer. Earlier this year Fallon had been accused of bribing a juror. He eluded police but was indicted *in absentia* while in hiding at his mistress's apartment.

One of Hearst's New York papers, the *American*, had run on the front page a mock-up "Wanted" poster which read: WANTED. FUGITIVE FROM JUSTICE. WANTED BY THE U.S. GOVERNMENT.

When Fallon was finally arrested and taken to trial, the Hearst papers downplayed their coverage. Al could tell why from articles in non-Hearst papers. Fallon claimed Hearst was out to get him because Hearst knew that he, Fallon, had in his possession birth certificates of the illegitimate children of "a certain blond moving-picture actress."

Another article noted that the jurors were each asked if they knew of a motion-picture actress named Marion Davies.

Could it be, wondered Al in amazement, that Davies had actually had illegitimate children? He'd have to check Barry Farr on that whopper.

And here was another provocative clipping. Just two years ago, there had been another tragic accident during one of Hearst's junkets. Guy Barham, publisher of the Los Angeles *Herald*, had sold his paper to Hearst. In celebration, Mr. and Mrs. Barham took a trip to Europe with W.R. and Millicent. Piecing together these and other clips, Al realized that Marion was in London at the same time. She had sailed in May 1922, the voyage widely touted as her first trip to the Continent.

In London Barham was stricken with abdominal pains—the same story as with Ince, thought Al—and Barham died within hours. Was there a cover-up there? Could they be repeating this food-poisoning angle for the Ince story?

Bradshaw's eyes were beginning to smart, and his body ached from the uncomfortable cane-backed chair. He stretched and yawned, knocking over a batch of papers.

"Dammit," he muttered, as he reached to retrieve them. He spotted a clip by his friend Grace Kingsley.

Dated only three days ago, it read:

Charlie Chaplin continues to pay ardent attention to Marion Davies. He spent the evening at Montmartre dining and dancing with the fair Marion the other night. There was a lovely young dancer entertaining that evening. And Chaplin applauded, but with his back turned. He never took his eyes off Marion's blond beauty. Miss Davies wore a powder-blue dinner dress and small blue hat and looked very fetching indeed.

Marion and Chaplin? Al would have to check Grace Kingsley on this one!

Friday, November 21

"What'd you do, sleep here?" The abrasive, sandpaper voice was Johnny Brackin's. The copyboy had found Al slumped over the reader's table in the morgue.

Al slowly opened his eyes. "What time is it?"

"Boy, you look like hell!"

Bradshaw lifted his head and stretched his neck. There was a sour taste in his mouth, a queasy feeling in his stomach. "What time is it?" repeated Al, as he rubbed his eyes.

"Six-thirty," Johnny answered.

Al stood up and almost fell. "Christ, what a hangover," he said. "That rotten hooch from the waterfront speakeasy. . . ." He fell back into his chair. "Bring me some water, kid, will ya?"

Through somewhat blurred vision Bradshaw saw the table in the morgue was littered with the files he had dragged out last night. When Brackin returned with a cup of water, Al asked: "Be a pal, Johnny. Put these away for me."

"Aw, c'mon, Al," the boy complained.

"Be a sport," Al persisted. "I'll fix you up with that blond down in circulation."

Johnny's attitude brightened. "For fair?"

"Sure, kid, I promise. I'll even let you use my jalopy."

Bradshaw slowly and painfully made his way down the three flights of stairs. Outside, the bright morning sun almost blinded him. He quickly shaded his eyes with his hand. He realized he'd never be able to make it back to his room to change. From his growing feeling of nausea he also knew he'd better get some food in his stomach. Luckily there was little traffic on the street as he staggered across to Vera's.

Al brushed past a couple of customers, their paper hats signaling their profession as *Tribune* pressmen, and made his way to his usual booth.

"What the hell hit you?"

With great effort he looked up. It was Vera, staring down at him as though he were from another planet.

"Bring me some coffee, honey. And maybe you'd better spike it."

Instead of spiked coffee, Vera brought him a bromide. "Bottoms up," she said sarcastically as she stood over him, hands on her hips, until he downed it.

He crossed his arms on the table and buried his head in them. He groaned quietly, until Vera returned with coffee and scrambled eggs. But the smell of food almost made him upchuck. Vera took away the eggs and reappeared in a few minutes with several slices of toast.

"Here," she said, throwing the plate down in front of him. "You've gotta have something to sop up all that alcohol." Vera waited until he swallowed some toast and took a sip of coffee. Then she asked, "Was she worth it?"

"Who?"

"The little chippy from last night."

"It was business." He coughed, almost retching.

Vera quickly pointed him to the john.

When he returned to his table, he called over, "Gimme some cigarettes, will you?" She threw him a pack of Camels from across the counter.

Al was surprised at her attitude. She was usually sympathetic when he had a hangover. Then it hit him. "Oh, God! We had a date yesterday afternoon!"

Vera acknowledged his statement with an icy stare.

"Vera, honey. I'm sorry. I got tied up."

"You mean you tied one on, don't you?" She refilled his cup.

"No kidding, Vera. I'm onto the hottest story that's ever hit this town."

"Sure, sure." Vera had heard this excuse before. But Al grew angry when she misunderstood. He took hold of her arm in a tight grip. His sincerity was authentic. "I'm not kidding, Vera. I swear."

A couple of tables away a man was reading the morning *Times*. Al spotted the bold headline: INCE FUNERAL TODAY.

"Shit!" Al released Vera's arm, bounded up, and grabbed a copy of the morning paper lying on the counter. He scanned the story.

"What's up?" Vera asked.

"I've gotta go to this funeral!"

"They way you look right now, they'd mistake you for the corpse."

"That bad, huh?"

She went behind the counter, grabbed a bunch of keys, and threw them at him. "Go on up," she told him.

Still queasy, Al climbed the back stairs up to Vera's apartment. It was a bright three-room layout with frilly drapes and other feminine furnishings. Al found it refreshing to take a shower in a clean bathroom for a change. There was a pleasant feminine scent on everything. He wondered why Vera's shower curtain wasn't grimy like his. "This place isn't like my shithouse." He smiled, soaping himself.

The ice-cold water revived him. He stepped out of the shower, toweled himself off, and studied his face in the bathroom mirror. He needed a shave. In the medicine chest was his razor-away-from-home. He lathered up his face. But his mind was on the Ince affair, and while shaving he nicked himself a couple of times.

"Feel better?" Vera was picking up his socks and shorts, and Al was surprised to see her when he walked back into the bedroom.

"Who's minding the store?"

"Rusty can handle it for a while." She fetched him a clean shirt from a dresser drawer. "Here," she said.

"Thanks, baby. What would I do without you?"

They kissed. He threw the shirt on a chair and guided her toward the bed. Just then there was a heavy banging from downstairs. "I gotta go," Vera said reluctantly.

"Aw, come on. Wait ten minutes." Al was naked and his body revealed that for the moment his mind definitely wasn't on the Ince story.

"Yesterday I had all afternoon set aside for you," Vera said pointedly.

"Ah, come on Vera, please. I wasn't with another dame." He pressed himself against her.

She broke away. "Put your clothes on." She smiled. "I'll be here later."

It was 7:30 when Al walked back into the city room. His stomach was still upset, but after a quart of orange juice, four cups of coffee, and half a pack of Camels, he was alert.

"Hey, Bradshaw," Casey called loudly. When Al went into the city editor's office, Casey thrust some papers at him. "I need a rewrite on these by noon." Clark pretended not to notice Al's look of disgust.

Bradshaw trudged back to his desk and looked over the stories. They were dull. Board of Education rulings, the mayor's social schedule for the following week, and a story about a phony faith healer. Al threw them aside for the moment. The Ince story was gnawing at him.

He looked at the latest edition of the *Examiner*. It contained front-page testimonials by the movie greats about the passing of their peer, Thomas Ince. Marcus Loew, owner of one of the country's largest theater chains, said: "The shock of T. H. Ince's death leaves me at a loss for words. . . ."

From Joseph Schenck, head of United Artists, came

these words: "T. H. Ince's death comes as a staggering blow to all of us. . . . He had perhaps more friends than any other man in the motion-picture industry. . . ."

Hal Roach, Cecil B. De Mille, Irving Thalberg, Norma Talmadge—all had glowing words of praise for the departed mogul.

"Hey, Johnny." Al beckoned. He lowered his tone of voice and said in a confidential whisper, "I gotta go out. Cover for me. Don't let 'em know I've left the office."

"Sure, Al."

"I'll be back at eleven-thirty."

A crowd was already beginning to congregate outside the small, elegant chapel on the grounds of the beautifully landscaped Hollywood cemetery. The chapel was well guarded. There was no way that Al Bradshaw could wangle his way inside without one of the special printed passes that had been issued. Even with his L. A. *Tribune* press card, Al had been turned away.

Bradshaw spotted Pete Turner, one of his friends on the police force. Turner waved and smiled as Al approached. Pete was red-nosed, overweight, and prematurely gray, with a deeply furrowed brow.

"Any chance of getting me through, Pete?"

"No chance, Al." The uniformed patrolman wore a worried frown and gestured toward the chapel. "This one's tighter than a drum."

There were hundreds of people milling about. Many were obviously fans hoping to catch a glimpse of celebrities. Others were extras from Ince's Culver City studios, gossiping about what would happen to the studio now. The crowd was growing in size, a fact ominously noted by Turner.

"Nelson's here," remarked Pete, referring to his immediate superior. "And so's Kallmeyer."

"Kallmeyer?" Al was duly impressed. Kallmeyer was a detective lieutenant.

"There are eight dicks here too," noted Pete.

"Is that Scott over there?" asked Al. Ralph Scott was the chief of the Los Angeles fire department. He was entering the chapel with a small detail of city firemen.

"Yeah," said Pete. "Seems Ince was a member of the International Association of Fire Chiefs."

"Ince was a popular guy, huh?"

"Had everything. Seems a shame, don't it? Leavin' three young kids, too."

As additional mourners began arriving at the chapel, a sense of excitement was building. This was a funeral, a solemn occasion, but to the public it meant the appearance of Hollywood idols. Fans were eager to pay tribute.

The pushing and shoving increased as the crowd began inching forward. Cries of "Watch it!" "Stop shoving!" "You're stepping on my feet!" "I can't see!" were heard as people struggled for vantage points.

One woman, carrying a package wrapped with string, yelped when the string broke and the contents of her parcel—two peaches, a napkin, and several photographs of stars—emptied onto the sidewalk. From another part of the crowd a man shouted, "Here comes someone, here comes someone!"

The people surged forward, and Pete Turner stiffened. "Uh-oh. See ya later, Al, gotta go to work. Norma Talmadge's limo just arrived."

"Hey, watch it, buddy!" snapped Al angrily as he collided with members of the crowd. Bradshaw tried to reach into his pocket for his pad and pencil. He wanted to note how many of the people who were supposedly on the cruise would attend the funeral.

He pushed through the noisy throng and managed to wangle a decent vantage point. Dozens of celebrities had turned out to pay their respects to Ince: Pickford and Fairbanks; Harold Lloyd; Mack Sennett; Charles Ray and his wife. Sam Goldwyn. Sid Graumann.

But not William Randolph Hearst. Not Louella Parsons. Not Elinor Glyn. No one from the cruise except Marion Davies and, a few minutes later, Charlie Chaplin. The comic actor's appearance created pandemonium.

Among the non-notables, Bradshaw recognized Clifford Spencer. And Pop, the old man from Inceville. Al wondered if Diane Enright was here. He cursed the crowd. If he could get through to Pop, perhaps the old man would be able to point her out. But Pop, along with a dozen or so others from Ince's studio, had disappeared into the chapel. It was futile for Al to buck the mob.

Bradshaw managed to push his way back through the crush, and headed around to the rear of the building.

There, miraculously, there was no crowd at all. Two hearses from Day and Strother, the morticians, stood ready.

"Where's Ince going to be buried?" Al casually asked one of the drivers.

"These cars ain't for the body," answered the man gruffly. "They're for the flowers."

"Burying Ince here, then?"

"He ain't gonna be buried. He's gonna be cremated."

Cremated! Al felt a sudden sinking feeling in the pit of his still-queasy stomach. Any doubts that Ince hadn't died an unnatural death instantly vanished.

As Bradshaw stood stunned, a weak-featured, pale-faced man in a black suit walked over to him.

"Is there anything I can do for you, sir?" There was an offensive undertone in the man's voice.

"Are you handling the funeral?" Al inquired.

"Yes. Can I be of assistance?

"You certainly can." Bradshaw showed his press card and identified himself.

The man stared vacantly at Al.

"Why is Mr. Ince being cremated?"

"Those are his wife's wishes," the man answered icily.

"What did he die from?"

"You'll have to ask the coroner." With that statement, the man turned on his heel and swiftly walked away.

"Cremated!" exclaimed Vince.

"How d'ya like that," commented Mike Halloran with an air of resignation. "That way they can't exhume the body to perform an autopsy."

"I'm gonna go to Casey with this," declared Al, an intensity vibrating in his voice.

"Don't be an ass, kid," advised Vince, motioning him to calm down. "You don't have any evidence."

"I can *feel* I'm onto something." Al punched his hand into his fist. "I can *feel* it."

Mike cut in. "Look, kid, if you're gonna do this thing, do it right. You gotta catch the fish, not scare it away. If you create a lot of noise, with nothing to back it up, they'll come down on you and come down hard. You gotta be quiet about it—until you've got 'em *nailed*."

"He's right, Al," agreed Vince. "Casey'll throw you out of his office if you go in telling him that because a man's been cremated it's proof he's been murdered!"

Al knew they were both right. His emotions were running high. He gulped down his beer and took out the notes he had made at the funeral.

"Look, Vince, I saw Sennett at the funeral this morning. I thought he hated Ince."

"He does, as far as I know."

"Can you get me through to him?"

"I think so. Mack's a pretty right guy. But I don't know how much real dirt he'll give you. You see how this Hollywood bunch closes ranks when they're in trouble. I'll see if I can set something up, though."

"I checked Farr on the possibility of Marion Davies having had a couple of bastard kids," related Al. "Farr said it was just an ugly rumor, but who the hell knows? What do you guys think?"

"Well," remarked Halloran, "anything's possible. But don't get sidetracked. The story you've got to keep in mind is Ince. Was Ince murdered, and if so, why?"

They ordered another round of beers just as Johnny Brackin rushed into the Palm. The copyboy was breathless. "Al! I knew you'd be here. Casey's *screamin'* for you!"

"Great," said Al, throwing up his hands. "Just what I need."

Casey was seething. Al saw his anger was genuine. "Where the hell are those stories?" demanded the editor, his eyes boring into Bradshaw.

Al began sweating. He could feel drops of perspiration traveling down his armpits. "You'll have 'em in two minutes!" he answered quickly.

He banged out the rewrites. "By the time these are printed, they'll only be a paragraph each, anyway," he grumbled. He wondered if now was the time to tell Casey he was investigating Ince's death.

Handing in the rewrites, he decided to level with Clark. "Casey?" he asked cautiously.

"Yeah?"

"Who's covering the Ince story?"

Casey, perusing Al's material, didn't look up. "Farr covered the funeral."

"No. I mean the Ince *story*."

"What Ince story? We ran that two days ago. He's dead! Jesus Christ," he said, red-penciling furiously. "You better lay off the booze, kid. This stuff is crap."

Al leaned forward and placed both of his hands on Casey's desk. "Give me a story I can get my teeth into, instead of this bullshit," he said angrily.

Al's tone of voice forced Casey to glance up momentarily. "Like what?"

"Like the cover-up on Ince's murder."

Casey's red pencil stopped in mid-sentence. He stared at Al. "Who says he was murdered?"

"I say it. At least he *might* have been murdered. Our first story said he was shot, remember? Then the story was yanked, and today Ince is cremated. Doesn't that all seem too pat to you?"

"Look, the story was yanked because it was *wrong*. We can't open the paper up to a libel suit."

"How do you know the story was wrong?"

"Some two-bit, half-loaded stringer from San Diego phones it in, and the rewrite man takes it down verbatim. He didn't ask any questions, didn't ask for evidence. Some hotshot here figures we can make the late edition and rushed the story to press before checking it out."

"Who's the San Diego man?"

"Never mind. Just forget it, kid. Ince died of a heart attack."

Casey turned and yelled to a reporter outside, "Hey, Bill! Get your ass over here." Al knew his audience with the city editor was over. But as he stalked away, Casey called after him: "And don't disappear again all afternoon, Bradshaw. There just might be some *real* big story that has to be covered."

Al went back to his desk. He called Johnny over and handed him a quarter. "Go over to Vera's and get me a coffee and Danish, will you?"

"Sure." Johnny handed Al a stack of papers. "More rewrites, Al."

"Dammit." Bradshaw put a fresh sheet in the typewriter and began pounding out the new stories. Then, suddenly, he stopped. The hell with this shit, he thought.

He took out his notes on the Ince story. He had made a list of the names of people the various news accounts listed as being on the cruise.

Marion Davies, her sisters Ethel and Reine, Elinor Glyn, Samuel Balenkoff, Dr. Daniel Carson Goodman.

Al had also made a list of other people not *officially* on the cruise: Chaplin, Louella Parsons, Diane Enright.

Al grabbed the phone book and flipped through it for the listing of Hearst's film company.

The switchboard promptly answered after one ring. "Cosmopolitan Pictures, International Film Corporation."

"Dr. Goodman, please."

Daniel Carson Goodman was the man who headed Hearst's film enterprises. It was common knowledge that Goodman was an M.D. and the lover of Alma Rubens, Hearst's other major star. Talk on the street was that Alma was a drug addict and Goodman provided her with more than love and advice.

"Dr. Goodman's office," said a lilting feminine voice.

"Dr. Goodman, please," repeated Al.

"Who's calling?"

"Al Bradshaw, Los Angeles *Tribune*." Al didn't actually expect to get through to Goodman and was a bit surprised when a male voice came on the phone almost immediately.

"Yes?" The voice was controlled and smooth.

"Dr. Goodman, I'm doing a follow-up story on the death of Thomas Ince," Al lied, "and I'd like to speak with you, if I may."

"Mr. Ince's death was a terrible tragedy," said Goodman. "I'll be glad to answer any questions you have. I've already given all the facts, but if there's anything you'd like cleared up, just ask."

Al was suspicious of Goodman's availability and eagerness to please. "Would you just tell me, in your own words, what happened?"

"Surely." Coolly and precisely, Goodman related his tale: "Last Saturday, which was the fifteenth, I took the *Oneida,* which belongs to International Film Corporation, with a party on board, to San Diego. Mr. Ince was to have been one of the party but he was unable to leave on Saturday. He had to work, but he said he would join us on Sunday morning. . . ."

Al was scribbling furiously. Already Goodman's story wasn't jibing. Al knew from the girl at United Artists that the group hadn't left on the cruise until Tuesday!

Goodman continued: "When Mr. Ince arrived on board, he complained of nothing. Just being tired. During the day we discussed details of his agreement with International Film Corporation to produce pictures in combination. Mr. Ince seemed well. He ate a hearty dinner, and retired early.

"The next morning he and I arose early, before any of the other guests, to return to Los Angeles. Mr. Ince complained that during the night he had had an attack of indigestion, and still felt bad. On the way to the station he complained of a pain in his heart. We boarded the train, but at Del Mar Mr. Ince had a heart attack. I thought it best to take him off the train and insisted upon his resting in a hotel.

"I telephoned Mrs. Ince immediately and told her her husband was not feeling well. I called in another physician and remained myself until the afternoon, when I continued on to Los Angeles.

"Mr. Ince told me that he had had similar attacks before, but that they had not amounted to anything. Mr. Ince gave no evidence of having had any liquor of any kind. There was no liquor on board the *Oneida*. My knowledge as a physician enabled me to diagnose the case as one of acute indigestion."

Al was shocked. He hadn't asked Goodman anything about liquor being on board. And yet Goodman had already denied it! It seemed to Al that Goodman might be reading from a prepared statement.

"When did Mr. Ince die?" Al persisted.

"I left Mr. Ince in Del Mar," said Goodman. "You'll have to get the rest of the story from Mrs. Ince. I do hope I've been of some help to you," he said smoothly.

"What was the name of the hotel in Del Mar that you stopped at?"

Goodman hesitated a moment. "Just a minute," he

said. There was a long pause. Goodman came back on the line: "It was the Stratford Inn."

"Thank you, doctor."

"Anything to help."

The Stratford Inn. Al would check that out.

He hung up the phone and perused the notes he had taken while speaking to Goodman: Ince had indigestion . . . no liquor on board . . . they left for the cruise last Saturday . . . Ince joined them on Sunday. None of this information jelled. Everyone involved with this case had a different story, different dates.

Bradshaw checked his notes from last night: Call Grace Kingsley. He did. Grace was out covering a story. Barry Farr wasn't around either.

Then Al phoned the *Examiner* and got through to Walt Edwards, a rewrite man and an old friend of his father's. "Walt, settle a bet for me," asked Al. "A friend of mine says he saw Louella Parsons last night, but her column is datelined New York. Is she in town or isn't she?"

"Let's see, she was in the office on Tuesday. . . . I suppose she could have left then and she'd be in New York now. Even if she were on her way to New York, they'd dateline her column there."

"She was definitely here this week, though?"

"Oh, yeah. I saw her myself. She came into the office Monday and Tuesday."

"Thanks, Walt."

Al jotted down: Louella definitely in town. May have left Tuesday or not.

Unfortunately Al hadn't been able to take notes last night when talking to the sailor. But Bradshaw remembered that the kid had mentioned the name of a bodyguard who had been fired by Hearst. Grady was the name—the first name. "Fletcher!" Bradshaw said aloud. "Grady Fletcher."

Al grabbed the phone book. Not much chance the guy would have a phone, but who could tell. There were three Fletchers listed: Mrs. Joseph Fletcher. Richard Fletcher. And a Z. Fletcher. No Grady Fletcher. He slammed the phone book shut.

Wait a minute—a cop Al knew was familiar with most of the private dicks in town.

In a moment he had Carl Wilson on the line. "I'm trying to locate a shamus name of Grady Fletcher, Carl. Ever hear of him?"

Wilson paused. "Sure. I heard of him." Al sensed an edge in Carl's voice. "Whaddya want him for?"

"A few questions. Nothing serious."

Again a pause. "The guy's trouble, Al. An alky. A mean bastard. Stay away from him."

"Carl, do you know where I can find him?"

"Won't take my advice, huh? Okay. Last I heard, about a month ago, Fletcher was working for Arco."

"Thanks, Carl."

Al flipped through the A's and found the listing. Still holding the phone, Al impatiently banged the bar to get the operator.

"Call, please."

It rang a couple of times. Al lit a cigarette—his last one. He threw away the crumpled pack of Camels.

"Arco Detective Agency." The girl's voice was brittle.

"Grady Fletcher, please."

"Mr. Fletcher is no longer with Arco."

"Is there somewhere I can call him?"

"Who is this, please?"

"A friend of Mr. Fletcher's."

"May I have your name?"

"Sure. My name is Ralph Smith. Mr. Fletcher and I went to high school together."

"May I have a number where you can be reached, Mr. Smith?"

"No, I'm sorry. I'm staying with my maiden aunt and she doesn't have a phone."

"If Mr. Fletcher calls in, I'll tell him you called."

Within half an hour Al Bradshaw was walking through the Arco Detective Agency's front door. The girl he had talked with was a cute blond in her early twenties. She was running the switchboard and serving as secretary for the small, rather seedy operation.

Her hair was bobbed in the popular flapper fashion, and she wore heavy makeup. Up close Al saw that her complexion was bad. But she had wide eyes, and her décolletté revealed a healthy set of smooth-skinned breasts. Her dress was pink, and she wore a pink ribbon in her hair.

She brightened when she saw Al. "Hi," she chimed, "can I help you?"

"Yeah," said Al. "I'm Ralph Smith. I called about a half-hour ago."

She hardened. She had met too many men named Smith. "I'm sorry. We don't give out any information on our ex-employees. Besides," she said suspiciously, "I thought you said you and Grady Fletcher went to high school together. He's old enough to be your father."

"No, you misunderstood," said Al. "I said we went to the same high school back east."

"St. Louis, huh?" She smiled.

"That's right." He smiled back.

Her smile disappeared. "You're all wet. Fletcher's from New York and I'll lay my last dollar he never even went to high school."

"You got me," Al said, throwing up his hands and sitting on the edge of her desk. "Okay honey, I'll level with you. The bum owes me forty bucks."

"You'll never see it again. He's drunk it all by now."

"You're right, I'll bet. But I'd sure like to lay my hands on him." He winked at her. "Come on, whaddya say?"

She was softening. "Well, he's probably not at the address we have anyway. He left here about a month ago."

"I've got nothing to do this afternoon. If I could

wring the dough out of him, maybe you and I could have dinner sometime."

"I don't think my boyfriend would like that." She tittered.

"Well, we won't take him along," said Al, cocking an eyebrow.

She giggled, swiveled in her chair, and opened a drawer containing file cards. She flipped through the F's. "I can't tell you anything, but if you was to glance over my shoulder while I was fixin' my stocking . . ."

Al read the card as the girl exposed a shapely leg and smoothed an imaginary wrinkle in her hose. The card read: "Grady Fletcher, 1183 South 7th Street."

First Al stopped at Vera's to borrow twenty dollars. Then he went directly to the Palm. "Harry, I need a bottle," he told the bartender.

"Kid, you know I don't like stuff to leave the place."

"I know, but this is an emergency!"

"Two bucks," Harry said, putting a pint on the counter.

"Gift-wrap it, will ya?"

"Sure." He stuffed the bottle in a plain brown paper bag.

Al was familiar with South 7th Street. Fletcher must really be down on his luck. The address was smack in the middle of the skid-row area of Los Angeles, a hell's kitchen block consisting of dilapidated rooming houses, fleabag hotels, and a mission.

The streets were strewn with garbage, and 1183 South 7th was even seedier than Al had expected. The building was pathetically run-down. The sign over the door read: "25¢ a Night."

Bradshaw slowly opened the screen door and cautiously stepped into a musty, filthy hallway.

"Yeah?" whined a voice. The proprietor was a toothless old geezer with eyes like a rat's. He knew immediately that Al wasn't a prospective customer. "Whaddya want?" He sneered rudely.

"Grady Fletcher."

"You a bill collector?"

"No."

"Waddya want Fletcher for?"

"It's my business." Al reached in his pocket and dug out a quarter. "Here."

"One flight up, last room on the left. Number ten."

Al walked down the hallway and climbed the creaky stairs, which had once been painted yellow. The stench of urine was nauseating, almost overpowering, and Bradshaw had to hold his nose.

The second landing was a dark tunnel. Al the end of it Al found a door with the number ten crudely painted in yellow. Bradshaw knocked. No answer. He knocked louder. Then he banged heavily with his fist.

"Yeahhhhh?" The sound was like a deep, croaking moan from a rhinoceros. Al heard heavy, shuffling footsteps. The door opened a crack. A bloodshot eye peered out.

"Grady Fletcher?" asked Al warily.

"Who wants ta know?"

Al held up the paper bag, the neck of the bottle seductively exposed. "A friend."

A hulking, tough, fifty-year-old warhorse, with eyes so swollen they looked like Ping-Pong balls, swung open the door and stood staring at Al. His gray hair was matted with dirt and sweat. The man wore a dirty, torn undershirt. His trousers were wrinkled and stained. Fletcher wore no shoes. His big toes stuck out of filthy black socks. And the former detective's reddened, bulbous nose was a sorry and disgusting advertisement of his alcoholism.

For a moment it passed through Al's mind that he should have bought cheap wine instead of cheap liquor; this stuff might kill Fletcher.

But even though Fletcher was almost thirty years Al's senior, and under the influence, Al sensed the man was still a physically powerful and dangerous character.

"What's your game, kid?"

"Talk. Got any clean glasses?"

Grady Fletcher shuffled to the dresser and fetched two cheap cups with broken handles. He blew in them to clear out the dust. "Okay?" he asked, a mock smile on his face.

The room was little more than a hole, with an odor worse than in the hallway. "Mind if I open a window?" asked Al, stifling his nausea.

"It's your liquor," replied Fletcher.

By the time Bradshaw had forced open the crooked window, Fletcher had already consumed a cup of rotgut. His hands were clutching at his stomach. "Sorry I didn't wait for you, kid," he croaked. "I *needed* that." He began to cough violently. Al stood by helplessly until the coughing spasm finally subsided.

In spite of the depressing surroundings and Fletcher's appearance, once the man was settled into a crumbling armchair in the center of the room, he assumed some dignity and humanity.

There were no other chairs. Al was about to sit on the bed, but reconsidered. He settled opposite Fletcher on a rickety wooden box, and came right to the point. "Look, I'm a reporter. I'm doing a feature story on Hearst and I need some background. I won't quote you. I won't use your name. If you can help me, I can give you a ten-spot."

Grady Fletcher laughed. "Generous of you!" Al was afraid the man would start coughing again. He didn't.

"Sure, I'll talk about the old fart. Why not? What the hell could he do to me now that I would care about? The Big Cheese had no right to fire *me*. Not after all I did for him. . . ."

Al learned that Grady Fletcher first met William Randolph Hearst back in 1914 when Fletcher was one of the stellar plainclothes detectives on the New York police force.

"Hearst was in his sugar-daddy period then, dating

one showgirl after another," recalled Fletcher. "Our paths crossed about the time Hearst was beginning to shack up with Marion Davies."

Grady was dating a beauty of his own at the time. "I didn't always look like this, kid," he told Al. Peaches, his girlfriend, was a gorgeous brunette who was a pal of Marion's, one of her fellow chorines in *Stop! Look! Listen!* These were the days when Marion's steady beau was Paul Block.

Grady's information filled out details of the same story Frank Fairfield had begun relating last night. According to Fletcher, while Block was squiring Marion, Hearst was paying court to another beauty in the chorus, Justine Johnson.

Then one night the four of them went to a party at Frank Crowninshield's apartment. At the end of the evening, Marion went into the bedroom to fetch her cloak. Hearst followed her.

"I'd like to see you again soon," Hearst told her, handing Marion a gift that glittered in the semidarkness. He pressed her hand around it. "I hope you like this."

Just then Block called Marion and came looking for her in the bedroom. She had no opportunity to look at the bauble Hearst had given her or even to stuff it into her purse. All the way home she was afraid of opening her hand, not wanting Block to spot the trinket.

Finally, when she was alone in her room, she studied the present. It was a magnificent diamond watch from Tiffany's, far tastier than anything Block had ever given her.

Although Marion was accustomed to receiving expensive gifts, she later confided to Peaches that in this case she was a bit wary. "I hope Paul and Mr. Hearst haven't m-m-made some kind of deal concerning me," she said.

Before Marion had a chance to see Hearst and find out, or drop him a thank-you note, the entire *Stop! Look! Listen!* company was taken to Boston. While frolicking down a snow-filled Boston Street, Peaches and Marion had a snowball fight. Later that afternoon, Marion gasped: "Peaches! M-m-my watch, it's g-g-gone!" It had obviously fallen off her wrist and into a snowbank.

The girls retraced their steps, to no avail. When they returned to the hotel, Peaches had a practical suggestion: "Call up the old man and get another watch."

"I couldn't do that," Marion said. "I h-haven't even thanked him for it!"

"Listen honey, if you don't call him and tell him you lost it, I will. What the hell does it mean to him? He could buy you a million watches."

"That's n-n-not the point. What'll he think of me?"

"Don't be a ninny. He'll wonder where the watch is when you're not wearing it the next time he sees you."

After further prodding from Peaches, Marion made the call. Within twenty-four hours a special messenger arrived at Marion's Boston hotel with another watch. "It's beautiful," Marion said. "But it's not as pretty as the first," she noted with disappointment.

Al Bradshaw was listening to Fletcher's story intently. He didn't want to break the mood, but he couldn't help remarking: "Jesus, what gall! Calling up and asking for a second watch!"

"Why the hell not?" Fletcher snorted. "To him it was only pin money!"

He related how he found himself permanently assigned to the theatrical beat. Hearst had taken a liking to Fletcher, and since the mayor of New York did anything Hearst wanted him to do, Grady soon found himself permanently assigned to "theater row." And it wasn't long before Hearst lured Fletcher into leaving the force completely and joining Hearst enterprises, ostensibly as Marion's bodyguard but in reality as Hearst's spy. Through Grady Fletcher, the old man would keep constant tabs on Marion's whereabouts. "Hearst," noted Fletcher, "is insanely jealous."

To illustrate Hearst's possessiveness, Fletcher related another colorful yarn, one worthy of Hearst's own *Cosmopolitan* magazine.

In the winter of 1916, heralded by an incredible fanfare of publicity, the handsome, eligible young Prince of Wales came to America to try to rally Americans to join the war on the British side. General Vanderbilt was planning a spectacular party for Prince Edward. Marion, of course, and other top beauties were on the guest list.

The prince adored beautiful women. Hearst was frantic. He had no doubt the royal heir would be mad for Marion, just as he was, and didn't want her to attend the gala. But he could hardly prevent her and certainly wouldn't threaten her. He knew the only ploy that might dissuade her from going would be to buy her off.

It was snowing on the afternoon he picked her up at the theater after a matinee. The soiree for the prince was scheduled for that evening.

"Where are we going?" she bubbled, the car chugging up Fifth Avenue. "This isn't the way home."

The limousine stopped in front of Cartier's. "Stay here," he told Marion. "I'll be right back."

Marion was excited. What had Daddy planned? Hearst emerged in a few moments carrying a large square black velvet box. "Drive on," he said to the chauffeur.

In the cozy interior of the automobile, Hearst casually asked, "Are you going to General Vanderbilt's party tonight?"

"Oh y-y-yes," she said breathlessly. Her stutter gave her a perennial damsel-in-distress quality. "I'm so excited about it!" She was already wondering if the gift awaiting her in Hearst's hand would go with the gown she was planning to wear.

"Well," he said, "would you rather go to the party or would you rather have this?" He opened the case.

Resting on the white satin lining was a magnificent black-pearl necklace and matching pearl-and-diamond ring. "If you don't go to the party," said Hearst, "you can have these."

Marion was slightly aghast. This was the first time he had ever bargained with her. She deliberated.

"A bird in the hand," he persisted.

"Daddy, they're so *beautiful*!" She kissed him on the cheek and took the jewels.

"Look! Look! Look!" she squealed, bursting in to the Dourases' Riverside Drive apartment. Her mother and sisters were accustomed to Marion returning with beautiful gifts. But even they were impressed with the pearls.

"What'd you have to do for these?" Ethel laughed.

"It's what I'm *not* supposed to do!" Marion said, suddenly serious.

"What does that mean?" said Reine, admiring the necklace, touching the pearls delicately with her fingers, lifting the necklace off its satin bed and holding it to her throat.

"W.R.'s afraid that if I go to the party tonight, the P-P-Prince of Wales may take a liking to me."

"You mean now you're not going to the party?"

"Of course I'm going," Marion smiled. "W.R.'ll never know. And if he finds out, he'll forgive me."

Mama Rose didn't approve. "Oh, no," she said, taking the necklace from Reine and replacing it in its box. "If you're going to accept these for not going to the party," she told Marion firmly, "then you're not going. You can't double-cross old Hearst like that."

"Oh, Mama," said Marion. "It's not a double cross. It's . . . it's a l-l-little wh-wh-white lie."

"Black pearls for a white lie?" mused Ethel. "Sounds like one of Hearst's headlines."

"Marion," said Mama Rose sharply. "If you're going to keep these pearls, you keep your promise. You cannot go to the party. Or go to the party if you like, but give the pearls back."

"Look," Reine pointed out. "You've got a big fish on the hook. Don't louse things up."

Mama Rose and Reine were allied in their belief that Marion must not go the party if she intended keeping the jewels. But Marion, Ethel, and sister Rose thought she could have her cake and eat it too. They helped her dress, and Marion selected a white lace gown to properly set off the new pearls. She wore no other jewelry except the matching pearl-and-diamond ring.

The beautiful young blond spent almost an hour painting her face. When she was ready to leave, Marion surveyed her reflection in a full-length mirror. She looked radiantly beautiful.

Reine stepped into the room. "You're making a mistake," she said. "We're *all* going to regret this."

"That's y-y-your opinion," said Marion, placing a white lace mantilla over her golden hair. "He'll never know."

"That's what you think. Take a look outside," advised Reine.

Marion went to the window. On the street below were two men, walking up and down in front of the building.

"Wh-Wh-Who are they?" asked Marion, suspecting the worst.

"I would assume they're in the employ of Mr. Hearst, my dear. He will obviously be *very* upset if you go to that party and have the nerve to think him such a sucker that you will keep the pearls too."

"Damn!" said Marion. "Damn damn *damn.*"

"It was a cold fucking night, too," recalled Fletcher. "We hadda walk up and down in front of that goddamn building until three in the morning. But Davies musta wanted those pearls pretty bad, because she never left the house. None of 'em did."

Al shifted his position on the wooden box. He hadn't touched his own cup of whiskey, but Fletcher was half-way through the bottle. Bradshaw stared at the ex-cop intently. Fletcher drank in huge, noisy gulps, grimacing as the liquor burned down through his gullet, then relaxing as the alcohol was absorbed into his blood-stream.

It frightened Al to think that a man as obviously ar-ticulate and intelligent as Grady Fletcher had sunk this low. Bradshaw tried to keep his eyes from betraying the distaste and pity he was feeling. But Fletcher seemed to read Al's mind.

"It wasn't always like this, kid." Fletcher motioned disgustedly at the pathetic surroundings and the cheap liquor.

Al kept silent.

"I used to drink the best Napoleon brandy," he boasted. "One Christmas Eddie Cantor sent me a whole case." Fletcher saw the disbelief in Al's eyes. "That's right, kid, Eddie Cantor. He was one of my pals. Cantor, Will Rogers, and me used to have a lotta laughs back when they were doin' the Follies.

"Those were the years. They don't make shows like that anymore. The Follies of 1916 was the best ever! Rogers, Cantor, and real beauties like Mae Murray, Billie Dove, Dorothy MacKail. Peaches. Marion. I'll never forget that big number . . ."

Al was startled when, in a loud vouce, Fletcher be-gan croaking: "The girl I lo-o-ve . . . is on a mag-a-zine co-verrrr . . ." His attempt at warbling triggered another violent coughing spasm. But when Bradshaw attempted to come to his aid, Fletcher angrily waved him back down into his seat. "I'm all right . . . I'm okay . . ." he choked between coughs.

"Chri-i-ist," moaned Fletcher, when the spasm had subsided. He continued, undaunted. "I'll never forget that show's finale. Justine Johnson was wrapped up in an American flag—Justine was the most beautiful Columbia we'd ever seen. I saw the Follies every night in New York. Best seats in the house. Wanna know why?" Fletcher laughed loudly. "Because Hearst was jealous of Flo Ziegfeld! Sure, Ziegfeld took Marion out a couple of times. He took out *all* his showgirls. But I don't think Ziggy really screwed any of 'em. It was all just show for Ziegfeld.

"Anyway," he said, resuming his story, "after a couple of months, the show moved up to Boston. Hearst sent me up there to keep tabs on Marion. I thought I was gonna have an easy time," recalled Grady. "From the hotel to the theater and back again. What was there to watch? But boy was I wrong." Fletcher shook his head. "Old man Hearst knew more about his little Marion than I did. Suddenly there was this handsome young stage-door johnny on the scene. A college boy from Harvard. He gave Marion the rush. He sends her flowers, candy. The race is on. They begin seein' each other every day and night.

"They kept me chasin' all over the goddamn state! Canoeing on the Charles River. Sightseeing. Going out to dinner. They were nuts about each other. They hit every bar and nightclub in Boston. They could stay out all night because they could both sleep all morning.

"But *I* hadda get up at seven, after having been out all night keeping tabs on them, because Hearst wanted detailed information on the Harvard kid.

"This Harvard guy was a nice-enough kid. Yeah, he was okay. Came from a good Boston family. But then I found out he was already engaged to some society dame off at finishing school! Hearst calmed down when he found *that* out.

" 'Well, let's let Marion have her fun, then,' Hearst told me. 'She'll see the light.' "

But Grady remembered that the Douras family also knew that Marion was on the verge of dumping Hearst. "So her sister Reine Lederer comes up to see her while we're still in Boston. Jesus," recalled Grady, "you could hear the hollerin' and fightin' loud and clear."

Fletcher painted a vivid portrait of the confrontation.

"Johnny's young, and good-looking, and he loves me. I'm sick of old men, goddammit. I want a little fun out of life," Marion screamed at Reine.

"Lower your voice, you're sounding like Ethel now," retorted Reine. "You're not a baby. You think I've worked all these years so you could throw it all down the drain for a quick lay?"

"I'm only sixteen, Reine. He's gonna marry me."

"That's what they all say. Get the wedding license first and then talk about love."

Marion lashed back at her. "You're just bitter because your life has been so miserable. You never loved George!"

"I loved *you*, and Mama, and Ethel, and Rose enough to marry him so he could take care of all of us!"

"L-l-leave me alone, Reine. I love him. I know what I'm doin'. When I'm in bed with him, I feel *alive*."

"Poor Marion," reflected Grady. "Reine and Hearst are both seasoned pros. They knew the Harvard kid was takin' Marion for a ride. But she was in love with him. I found out they were plannin' to elope. So I called Hearst in a panic. 'Sit tight,' he says. 'Keep me informed.'

"Well, first Marion and the guy have a big night on the town. Then he sleeps over. He sneaks out of the hotel about six in the mornin'.

" 'I'll be back at noon, princess. Be packed and ready,' he tells her. I felt like crackin' his jaw. At noon she was all packed and ready. Looked like a china doll, all dressed up in blue. Even her suitcase was blue.

"By three, the Harvard creep still didn't show. Marion became crazy. She tried telephoning him and found out he'd left for Maine with his family—and the little society skirt he was going to marry! Then she really flew off the handle.

"What else could the kid do? She phones Reine, and her sister comes runnin'. They fell into each other's arms and both of 'em began bawlin' like babies. 'I love him, I still love him,' Marion kept telling her sister. And she told her, 'I know, baby, I know. But let the old man take care of you.'

"So," Grady concluded, "Marion came back to New York. That's when she finally let Hearst set her up in her own apartment in the Beaux Arts Hotel. He used the excuse that she'd have a place of her own when pressures at home were too much for her. She could be alone there.

"Hah! What a laugh," Fletcher added. "Marion hates being alone. She always keeps herself surrounded with people."

"Did she only use the place at the Beaux Arts to meet Hearst?" asked Al.

"Yeah. Except for Tuesday nights. That sort of became girls' night out, if you know what I mean. She'd meet Norma and Constance Talmadge and that cute tiny little dame, Anita Loos. They'd sit around and gossip. Joe Schenck, Norma's husband, was even more jealous about Norma than Hearst was about Marion. So I used to pick up a few extra bucks sending him a report on Norma's activities on those nights," Fletcher chuckled.

He remembered that Hearst began sending Marion poems and love notes, along with a steady stream of jewelry from Cartier and Tiffany. And Marion was receiving so much coverage in Hearst's papers that her career was really booming. She quickly graduated from showgirl to featured actress in musical comedy.

"I enjoyed hangin' around the theaters," Grady reminisced. I was nuts about Peaches. We had great times together."

"No major trouble between Hearst and Marion?" Al asked.

"Yeah, there was one big blowup. When Marion got a good part in a show called *Oh Boy!*, Hearst's wife started giving him a hard time about 'the little blond trollop.' I suppose it was because it looked like Marion

might become a star. The Hearst marriage was gettin'
sticky anyway. I think the only thing that kept 'em together was America entering the war."

"How the hell do you figure that?" queried Al,
puzzled.

"People wanted to cut Hearst's balls off because he
was rootin' for the krauts! So it wasn't no time for the
old man to have his personal life splashed across
the front pages. He got back together with his wife,
took the whole family here to California for the duration
of the war. Marion musta been pretty pissed when he
did that, because she took up again with Paul Block. I
guess it was a risk on her part, but it worked.

"To get her back and to keep her happy, Hearst put
Marion on the Hearst Corporation payroll. And those
were the heydays for *me*," Fletcher continued.

"Following her around was a hell of a lot of fun. She
had a chauffeured car and I had an unlimited expense
account. She was bored, though, and when she was between shows, she'd take classes. She went to some art
school for drawing lessons. She even went to acting
school, which seemed kind of dumb to me, since she
was already on the stage. But I suppose she hadda
have *something* to do.

"She started pestering the old man about marrying
her. I remember I was in the car once when she
snapped at him, 'You don't think I'm good enough to
be Mrs. Hearst, is that it?' The Chief turned redder
than a valentine. Marion told 'im, 'Your wife was nothing but a tap dancer, W.R. I'm a featured actress now!
I love you and I want to get married.'

"Boy, when Marion told Hearst she loved him, the
old man's eyes lit up. 'We'll see what can be done,' he
says to her. 'We'll see what can be done.'

"But, hell he wasn't about to do anything," Fletcher
remarked. "Some say Mrs. Hearst wouldn't give him
a divorce, but I don't buy that bull. I think he wants
that relationship kept just as it is. Any tries to divorce
his wife are strictly for lip service."

Fletcher lapsed into silence. His eyes drooped. Then his head began nodding until his chin rested on his chest. He sat so still that Al wondered if the man had fallen asleep. But then Fletcher slowly raised his head. "I'll tell ya, kid. It's a strange relationship, Marion and the old man. Sometimes they don't see each other for months. But they always talk on the phone. In fact, there's a special operator at the switchboard of the Hearst building whose only job is to know where each of 'em is so they can reach each other anytime of the day or night.

"Yeah, he loves Marion and he'll give 'er the world. But in a way, he treats her like all the rest of us. Whatever she gets, she gets because he wants to give it to 'er. I'll tell you a little story that people don't know. He didn't want to put her in movies! Everyone thinks that was his idea. Hah! It was hers. I guess she figured if he wouldn't marry her, at least he could make her a movie star."

Fletcher proceeded to sketch a detailed picture of the tactics Marion employed to maneuver Hearst into becoming her film benefactor.

"Norma and Connie are makin' m-m-movies, why can't I?" she badgered Hearst.

"I only make serials and newsreels, you know that."

"So start makin' longer pictures!"

Hearst kept stalling. Marion and Reine were not to be deterred. They came up with an alternative. If Hearst wouldn't put her in the movies, they'd go to someone who would. Although Reine was divorced from George Lederer, they had two children and George was still close with the entire Douras family. He'd produced some movies and owned the Ardsley Art Film Company.

"I'll see what I can do for Marion," Lederer promised Reine. Shrewdly, he called on Paul Block for financing, and the publisher came through. *Runaway Romany*, the story of a runaway girl, was Marion's first attempt at cinema acting. Although the film was only a modest success, it served Reine and Marion's purposes. They proved to Hearst that even though he might not have confidence in Marion's talent, others did.

Naturally, Hearst was furious when he learned that it was Paul Block, his old rival, who was now taking credit for Marion's success. The Hearst corporation had meanwhile entered film production with Alma Rubens as its top star. So now W.R. decided that he would also produce Marion's pictures.

Marion's salary jumped from seventy-five dollars a week, in her last Broadway show, to five hundred dollars a week as a Cosmopolitan Pictures star. Hearst employed Marion's relatives at the studio as well.

The Douras family moved into a white marble townhouse at 331 Riverside Drive. Hearst's generosity knew no bounds. He gave Marion's mother, and each of her sisters, unlimited cash to decorate their own rooms.

There was still the problem of Marion's father. Bernard Douras had been separated from his wife and children for years, but they were still quite friendly. So as an added token of affection for Marion, William Randolph Hearst instructed the mayor of New York to appoint Douras a municipal-court judge, with the modest salary of eight thousand dollars a year.

Marion began making movies in earnest. Hearst's ego was such that since Marion was the girl he had chosen, he wanted the whole world to worship at her feet. *He* would mold her into a greater star then even Mary Pickford. Her career was launched with a barrage of publicity in Hearst's journals.

When Adolph Zukor saw that Marion's pictures were actually making money, he negotiated with Hearst for Cosmopolitan Productions to be distributed through Paramount.

And now for the first time, with Marion's prestige growing, Hearst, to the chagrin of his wife, permitted himself to be photographed with the blond actress.

While it appeared that Marion had been successful

at emotionally blackmailing Hearst into granting her career wishes, what she had done in effect was relinquish control of her own life. Hearst's maniacal possessiveness now invaded every aspect of her existence. To the outside world she was the girl who had everything: youth, beauty, a film career, a wealthy admirer.

But Marion's disastrous affair with the Harvard youth—and the fact that she had settled for Hearst's "arrangement"—had apparently undermined her basic happiness. She began tippling gin, and her taste for liquor accelerated just as the Volstead Act—Prohibition—was to go into effect on January 16, 1920.

"But she's one dame who can hold her liquor," Grady said admiringly. "She's gotta sneak her snorts, though. The old man don't like her to have more than one drink a day. But Marion's got a bottle hidden in every toilet tank in 'er house! She's a feisty little dame. Stands up to 'im. I remember the first time he brought her out here to California. Her mother and sister Ethel came with them.

"Hearst set them up at the Hollywood Hotel. Then he and Marion went for a kind of honeymoon up to a little town about two hundred miles from here. At first he figured he could keep her away from the Hollywood wolves. But she hates bein' alone. She couldn't stand being isolated. So she packed her bags and left for New York. She and the old man had a nasty fight at the train station, and he sent me back to New York to keep tabs on her."

Grady snickered at the recollection. "Marion was really pissed, I guess, 'cause he still wouldn't divorce his wife. When Marion left for New York that time, it really must have scared him." Grady's tone of voice revealed his admiration for Marion Davies. Obviously she was the only person Fletcher had ever encountered who'd defied the Chief.

"The old man even went out and hired detectives to follow his wife," Fletcher continued. "I guess he was hopin' to catch her at something. Hell, she didn't fool around. And they were never gonna pin anything on her. Millie's too smart for that." Grady reflected for a few seconds. "Marion's just gonna have to settle for a sugar daddy." Grady chortled. "The way I see it, Marion ain't got nothin' to complain about, though. The Chief sure threw himself into her movie career. When he does something, he does it big."

Fletcher reaffirmed that it had cost several million dollars to build Marion into a big star, but that Hearst probably would have spent twice that, and willingly, to accomplish his goal.

Al worked the names of other people who had been on the cruise into the conversation. The only name that elicited a vociferous response from Fletcher was that of Hearst's entertainment writer.

"Louella Parsons!" he exclaimed. "There's a bitch who's as shrewd as they come. Hearst was impressed with her because even when she didn't work for him, she wrote that Marion was a terrific actress. Naturally the Chief wanted to put Parsons on the payroll after that. She agreed, but Louella's no dummy. She demanded a contract and two hundred and fifty smackers a week. At first Hearst said no dice. But then a couple of weeks later he figured Parsons must be worth what she's askin', and hired her—on her terms.

"Some people say it's because she sold Hearst on the idea that everybody but him, her, and Marion is a liar, or a thief, or worse."

Grady paused and belched. "But I'll tell you why she *really* got that job. Because the old man had something special in mind. Sure, she's a reporter for his papers. But the other half of her job is spyin' on Marion."

Was that what Parsons was doing on the cruise? wondered Al. Was she keeping tabs on Marion? And had she caught Marion fooling around with Ince? Al's attention returned to Fletcher, whose contempt for the Parsons woman was evident.

"The old man made a good choice." Fletcher spit out the words. "That Parsons dame is a natural-born stoolie and likes snoopin' around and spillin' the beans on everybody. But she sure tries to keep her own private life real private. She's Jewish, did you know that? Maiden name was Oettinger. Keeps that quiet, lemme tell you.

"She's a ball-breaker, all right. First husband ditched her. Her second husband, the riverboat captain, is nuts about her. But she's cheatin' on him—she has a boyfriend, a big shot back east."

Al vaguely remembered reading something about him. But he really wanted to learn more about Parsons being a spy for Hearst. "So she keeps tabs on Marion for the old man, huh?"

"Yeah. I guess he figures she can hang around Marion *all* the time, and there's nothin' Marion can do about it."

"When did you come out here?"

"We all came out last year. After Hearst's Harlem studio burned down. Now the old man travels back and forth across the country the way you and I go to the can."

Fletcher was very weary, very drunk. One important question remained. "Does Hearst keep guns around?" asked Al.

"Sure," confirmed Fletcher. "But he ain't really a violent type. He only gets steamed up when it has somethin' to do with Marion."

"Jealous rages?"

"Sometimes. Sometimes, though, he tries to get to her by makin' her laugh. Like sendin' her a silly poem or a present. I remember once he knew she was foolin' around with some guy out here, while he was back in New York, so he sent her Al Jolson's record. The song about the guy who's bought his girlfriend everything she owns—diamond bracelets and all that shit . . ." Fletcher's cracked voice tackled the lyric. "I gave her tha-at. . . . I gave her thaaat. . . . I-I-I ga-a-ave her that. . . ."

Al quickly interrupted. "Everybody in Hollywood says Davies sleeps around a lot. Then it's true?"

Grady's eyes were closing. He jerked awake. "Whaa . . . What'd you say, kid?"

"Does Davies fool around? Do you know if she was screwing with Tom Ince?"

Fletcher yawned. "Let's put it this way. You can never tell with her. She's got a sweet thing going with Hearst. But when she gets pissed at him she takes up with the next guy that strikes her . . ."

Fletcher's voice trailed off and his head again dropped to his chest. For a moment the room was quiet. Then Fletcher began snoring loudly. Bradshaw considered waking him but decided it wasn't worth it.

Al headed for the door and was startled when Fletcher's voice boomed out, "Heyyyyyy . . . how about that ten-spot?"

Al had forgotten. He walked back and handed Fletcher the money. "Take care of yourself," he said. "You'll be here if I want to talk to you again?"

"Sure, kid." He belched. "My house is your house. Come around anytime."

Grady Fletcher remained motionless, sunken in his armchair, as Al closed the door. But the old detective was neither as drunk nor as sleepy as Al Bradshaw thought.

Fletcher rose lumbrously. He knew this kid wanted to know more than he was letting on, and obviously had dough to pay for information.

Grady stuffed Al's sawbuck into his pants pocket. Then he staggered over to the dresser, spilled water from a cracked pitcher into a filthy porcelain bowl, and splashed his face. He took a couple of nickels lying on the dresser. There were some calls to make.

Saturday, November 22

By nine A.M. Bradshaw was having coffee at Vera's, going over his notes. His next step seemed obvious: track down Diane Enright. Al glanced at his watch. He'd better wait a few minutes more to be sure the switchboard would be open.

When he reached the Personnel Department at the Ince Studios a short while later, Al was told they had no one named Diane Enright employed there. "But this is the Hall of Records in Sacramento," Bradshaw lied. "It's very important that we locate Miss Enright."

"I'm sorry, sir. I told you we have no Diane Enright listed on our payroll records. If you'll leave your name, we can investigate further and call back. That was the Sacramento Hall of Records, you said?"

Al hung up.

"Look," said Vera, passing with a tray of dishes. "If this dame you're looking for is an actress, why don't you go up to some of those studios on Sunset Boulevard? Just ask around. You might have better luck that way."

"Good idea," Al said, kissing her. "I shoulda thought of that myself."

Saturdays in Hollywood were regular working days. It wasn't unusual to spot crews filming right on the streets. Along Sunset and Hollywood boulevards, near Vine and Gower streets, were a bunch of small-time operations. These were the poverty-row studios—tiny offices in front, with open-air backlots used for filming.

med to know a girl named Diane En-

as about to leave, a waiter called him
I did hear that name, mister. Some
dal down at the Grove a few weeks
ed him effusively.

Grove, at the Ambassador Hotel on
vard, was the leading Hollywood night
gathering place for tinseltown's ever-
olloi. It was close to noon when Al ar-
pty nightclub seemed like a deserted
ng for actors to bring it to life.

way through the immense room, past
d palms that gave the club its name.
-backed chairs were piled on top of
es. Bradshaw caught sight of a black
the finishing touches to a gleaming wax
e floor.

Is the headwaiter here?"

kept on waxing. "Bruno's in the office,
ere," she said, without looking up.

the manager's office was open, and Al
a balding man in his mid-forties be-

nocked on the open door, startling the

you later, Fritz." Bruno dismissed the
he asked gruffly.

dshaw, sir. Los Angeles *Tribune*." He
ss card.

n abrupt change in Bruno's attitude. He
is "professional" personality. "Ah, a
he press. What can we do for you?" he
roadly.

for a girl named Diane Enright. Do

ry. I've never heard of her."

tinued Al, not quite believing the man,
don't know her by name. I understand

Al knew that actors who worked as extras in films often gathered around this area, hoping for a day's work.

Bradshaw joined groups at random, asking, "Does anyone here know an actress named Diane Enright?" No one did. One young woman, incongruously dressed as a dowager, told Al to try the rooming houses up on Franklin Avenue. "A lot of young actresses live there."

He followed her advice. His first two stops yielded no information. Rooming House for Photoplay Players and Hollywood Horizons were practically empty. But at Mrs. Pangborn's—Young Ladies Only, business was booming. There were young women of various ages, all obviously anxious to break into films, but probably practicing other, less lofty professions in the interim.

Al was amused at the attempts of some of them to emulate current favorites. The Mae Murray influence predominated at Mrs. Pangborn's. Most of the girls had curly bleached-blond hair and ruby-red bee-stung lips. Erstwhile Colleen Moores and Barbara Lamarrs abounded too, and Al couldn't help but ogle the dozens of bouncy, braless bodies lolling about the premises.

"Hi ya, handsome, lookin' for someone?" The question came from the bee-stung lips of a young, voluptuous redhead, furiously clicking her chewing gum.

"Well, yes, I am," said Al, smiling and winking. Her low-cut dress revealed a healthy cleavage. Thick mascara frosted her lashes, her face was heavily powdered, and a shiny black sequin was pasted on her right cheek.

"Could it be me?" she said slyly, winking back, patting her chest, then pinching his cheek.

"Well, yes, if your name is Diane Enright."

She was disappointed. "Uh-uh. My name's Gilda Grubstetter."

Al couldn't stifle a chuckle.

"It ain't meant to be funny," she said, insulted. "What's *your* name?"

"Al Bradshaw."

She liked Al's looks, and her pleasant manner returned. "Ya know"—she tapped her forehead—"I *did* know an Enright dame once. It wasn't Diane—let's see, Mary, Melba . . . *Martha* Enright. That was it, Martha Enright. But that was back in New York."

"Oh, you're from New York?"

"Yeah, I was making movies there, but somebody suggested I try my luck out here."

Al tried a long shot. "Did you ever make a movie with Marion Davies?"

"Yeahhh!" she squealed. "You saw it, huh? I was in a lot of scenes in *Beauty's Worth*. But only two of 'em got on the screen. The rest ended up on the cutting-room floor, dammit."

"Oh, I'm sorry," said Al. "Did you get a chance to know Marion Davies?"

"Oh, sure!" she said sarcastically. "She wouldn't go anywhere without me. Are you kidding, honey? You couldn't get within ten feet of that dame. Her sugar daddy kept her surrounded by *his* people. She doesn't really like to work, ya know, but she was workin' like a dog. It was *hot* under them lights. 'Do it again, do it again, do it again,' the director would keep sayin'. Not that any of us really minded. I worked longer and made more money on that movie than on any other. But nothing was ever good enough for her old goat, though. 'Shoot it again, shoot it again,' he'd say, and they would shoot it again."

Gilda became annoyed when Al's eyes wandered to a gorgeous brunette climbing the stairs. "Hey, you listenin' to me or what? I could be doin' other things, y'know."

Al apologized. "Look, I'm sorry. I gotta run. I've gotta find this Diane Enright."

She shrugged as Al drove off.

He headed toward the Studio Club, the next stop on his list. Suddenly he remembered that was where

Mona Petersen—Da[v...]
probably knew the En[...]

"Miss Petersen? O[...]
the over-madeup, mat[...]
the desk at the club.[...]

"What? When did [...]
Marion Davies' new pi[...]

"Mona got a wonnn[...]
I believe. She's gone ea[...]

"Do you know a girl[...]

"Diane Enright . . . [...]
At last!

"She lived here two [...]
keep a file on all our gir[...]

The woman leafed thr[...]
funny," she said, perp[...]
name." She leafed thro[...]
"There does[n']t seem to b[...]

"B[ut] you do rememb[...]
like?"

"I remember the name[...]
est, so many girls come [...]
many look so much alik[...]
their makeup, you know ho[...]

"Thank you anyway," A[...]

"I wish I could help. Yo[...]

Al left his name and [...]
you remember anyone wh[...]
Enright."

He drove toward the w[...]
Hollywood Boulevard, the [...]

No one there admitted k[...]

This is insane, thought [...]
was being kept by Thomas [...]
Did he get her name wro[...]
possibly be lying?

Bradshaw decided to m[...]
only a few blocks to the M[...]

too, no one s[...]
right.

Just as Al [...]
over. "Seems[...]
hushed-up sc[...]
back." Al tha[...]

The Coco[...]
Wilshire Bo[...]
spot, the to[...]
changing ho[...]
rived. The [...]
movie set w[...]

Al made [...]
the huge p[...]
Countless [...]
scores of t[...]
woman put[...]
job on the [...]

"Excuse [...]

The wo[...]
mister, bac[...]

The do[...]
saw and [...]
rating a w[...]

Bradsha[...]
two men.

"I'll ta[...]
waiter. "Y[...]

"I'm A[...]
held up hi[...]

There [...]
slipped [...]
gentlema[...]
said, grin[...]

"I'm l[...]
you know[...]

"No, [...]

"Well,[...]

"perhaps[...]

she created quite a disturbance here a few weeks back."

Bruno still wore a blank expression.

"Over Thomas Ince," said Al pointedly.

"Oh . . . oh, yes," Bruno answered, his eyes narrowing to a cagey stare. "A very unpleasant affair."

Bruno was reluctant at first to discuss the matter. "After all, the man is dead, Mr. Bradshaw," he said solemnly. "There are his wife and children to consider."

Al convinced Bruno their conversation would be strictly off the record. Perhaps a ten-dollar bill would further assure Bruno of Al's sincerity? The maitre d' suavely pocketed the bill, and adroitly reconstructed the evening's events.

It had been a slow midweek night, like any other. The cavernous Grove, dimly lit, was only half-full. It was late, and the band was playing softly. Suddenly the romantic mood was shattered when a boisterous group, led by Tom Ince, burst onto the scene. Ince was unusually rowdy. The people in his party tried to quiet him down.

"Don't tell *me* to shhhhhhhh!" said Ince loudly. "My God, let's put some life into this place! It's not a morgue, is it?" he demanded.

"Tom, dear, please," pleaded the pretty dark-haired girl clinging to his left arm. But he ignored her, and she seethed with anger when he began paying attention to a shapely blond in their party. The blond flirted outrageously with Ince, batting her eyes, squealing delightedly at his jokes. At one point she stood on tiptoes to peck Ince's cheek and neck. When he whispered in her ear she giggled. Occasionally they'd both erupt into gales of laughter.

No sooner had the maitre d' and waiters hastily rearranged several tables for the Ince party than the band began playing a romantic foxtrot.

"Let's dance," proposed the blond.

Ince staggered up from his chair. "Let's!" he boomed out.

The brunette grabbed his arm. "You're not going to dance with that little tramp!" Her eyes flashed anger.

The director spoke to her in a low but distinctly audible voice. "Mind your own business, Diane. We're not married, my dear."

Diane Enright sat enraged as Ince led the blond onto the dance floor. Finally Diane could no longer contain her jealous anger. She picked up her glass of champagne and strode over to Ince. "This is for you," she said, tapping him on the shoulder. She hurled the wine in his face.

He was speechless. The liquid dripped down his neck and onto his suit. The blond was shocked. In an instant, Diane was at her throat. The women began pulling at each other's hair, scratching at each other's faces, rolling on the dance floor.

"It's a fight! It's a fight!" yelled patrons, gathering around as though at a prizefight.

Waiters swiftly ran over and tired to separate the girls.

Ince waved them all away. He even held back men from his own party who were anxious to stop the brawl.

"You don't want this kind of publicity!" warned a associate.

"Leave 'em alone!" Ince screamed, waving him away. He continued laughing uproariously, and noted: "Too bad we aren't photographing this!"

His laughter was so infectious that others began laughing too, goading the two women on: "Come on, blondie, scratch her eyes out!" "Pull her hair out, brown eyes!" "A hundred dollars on the brunette!"

Suddenly, simultaneously, the two combatants realized they were making fools of themselves. Exhausted, they separated, sat up, and staggered to their feet.

The blond was humiliated. She burst into tears and

ing. His phone began ringing. He wasn't aware of it until the third ring. "Bradshaw," he answered absently, still fingering through the pamphlet. There seemed to be nothing new here.

"Still interested in Ince's death?" asked the sultry voice.

Al snapped to attention. It was her. "I'm still interested," he said, trying not to betray his excitement.

"I hear you're a good-lookin' guy," purred the voice. "You should talk to Sammy Balenkoff. He'll tell you more than anyone else." The caller hung up before Al could ask anything further.

Balenkoff. Al vaguely knew the man was in show business. He flipped back to the *Times* story that ran two days ago. Samuel Balenkoff had been on the cruise. Al flipped through the *Examiner* and the *Tribune* to check who was at the funeral yesterday. Balenkoff wasn't listed. That didn't mean he wasn't there though. In that crush, reporters covering the funeral could have easily missed him.

Al raced to the entertainment editor's desk. "Hey, Robbie. Who's Samuel Balenkoff?"

Robbie D'Angelis was a gruff, masculine man with a long, thin face that made him resemble a thoroughbred. He was entertainment editor because he was immune to press agents' oversell. Robbie reminded Al of his father. So it was totally incongruous when, in answer to Al's question, D'Angelis stood up, pinkies pointed up, and executed a clumsy pirouette.

Al was baffled.

"He's a ballet maestro, kid."

Al laughed.

"He's talented. Works for the movie studios, but he also has a dance studio here in town."

"You think he'll talk to me?"

"He may wanna do more than that!" D'Angelis winked derisively.

"Oh, Christ," said Al. "That's all I need now."

* * *

Bradshaw rushed back to his apartment. This was an encounter that would require some ingenuity. Balenkoff certainly wouldn't be seeing any reporters. And if he knew as much as the voice on the phone claimed, he'd be wary of talking to anyone at all about the cruise.

Al ripped off his clothes and shuffled through his closet. He finally selected an old, conservative, out-of-style suit. He rummaged through his dresser, picking out an old-fashioned pin-striped, collarless shirt, obviously unworn in a couple of years. He looked through another drawer and came up with a vintage starched collar.

He dressed quickly and studied his reflection in the full-length mirror glued onto the back of his closet door. He had gained weight since he had last worn the suit, but so what? It was a better effect. But incomplete.

His hair was wrong. He took some hair oil, rubbed it into his palms and onto his scalp, brushed his hair forward, parted it in the middle, and slicked it down. He decided he needed glasses, and proceeded to knock out the lenses from a pair of old sunglasses, until only the wire frames remained.

Ah, that was better—the "glasses" finished the effect. They gave him a studious air, a Midwest-college look.

Great! He even looked a little like Harold Lloyd. To complete the hick outfit he put on white socks and oxfords.

Within ten minutes Bradshaw was at Balenkoff's Dance Studio, which was located only a few blocks from the *Tribune*. The studio took up the entire second floor of a clean, pleasant commercial building. The walls of the stairwell leading to the studio were hung with portrait photos of the stars, personally inscribed. "To Sammy, With Love. Mary." "To a *genius*. Barbara Lamarr." "What a naughty, but talented boy! Norma." "I Adore You. Connie." And many more.

Entering the reception area at the top of the second

landing, Al was greeted by an empty desk. A cup of half-finished coffee was resting on its smooth mahogany surface.

The walls here, too, were lined with autographed photos. Behind the desk was a plate-glass window through which Al could see into the large studio. Mirrors and a ballet barre ran the length of one wall. A harried pianist was banging out a version of *Swan Lake* as a dozen young girls in their early teens clumped through their dance exercises.

"May I help you?" It sounded like a rich, deep female voice, but when Al turned, he was face to face with Julian, a slim, bearded, fortyish man wearing black leotards.

"Why, yes," answered Al, sounding remarkably hicklike. "I'd like to see Mr. Balenkoff, please."

"A lot of people would like to see Mr. Balenkoff," replied the man haughtily. "Might I ask what this is in reference to?"

"Why, sure," said Al, repressing an urge to punch this arrogant person in the mouth. "I'm a professor from Iowa College. I'm doing a series of articles on the dance for the college paper, and everyone throughout the whole country knows that Mr. Balenkoff is the world's greatest expert."

Julian had noticed that Al, despite his wide-eyed "gee-whiz" exterior, was handsome and masculine.

"My name is Julian Falk," he purred, becoming much more friendly. "Mr. Balenkoff will be in in about half an hour. Where are you staying in Los Angeles?"

"With my sister," Al answered quickly.

"Oh, my goodness," said Julian, smirking. "How inconvenient that must be."

"Oh, it's quite convenient." said Al.

"A trip to Hollywood must be quite exciting to someone from Iowa," Julian said. "There are so many wonderful-looking people out here."

Al thought he'd better change the subject. "Gee, I hope Mr. Balenkoff gets here soon."

"*I* can give you any information you might need on the dance," said Julian. "I have worked very closely with Mr. Balenkoff *and* the stars."

The man obviously was going to be a nuisance. Al feared the afternoon would prove worthless, and was about to leave. Suddenly a human cyclone burst through the front door. The small figure was wearing a long cape. He raced past Al and stopped dramatically in the center of the reception area. Eyes flashing, hands flailing, he screamed, "That Barbara Lamarr will drive me craaa-a-a-a-a-zy!"

He flew on into the large studio, his sudden appearance there throwing the students into frenzies of "Oh, Maestro!" and "Oh, Mr. Balenkoff, would you look at . . ."

"Continue, continue!" he told them all angrily, as the erstwhile ballerinas flitted around like tipsy birds. Balenkoff vanished into his office at the far end of the studio.

Al, feigning wide-eyed wonder, turned to Julian. "Mr. Balenkoff?"

"That is correct," answered Julian. "Obviously he's much too upset to see anyone today."

But as swiftly as the masestro had vanished, he reappeared in the reception area to give Al the once-over. "Hel-lo," he said, extending his hand. "I'm Samuel Balenkoff. What can I do for you?"

Julian interjected quickly. "I can take care of this gentleman, Mr. Balenkoff."

"I'm sure you can, Julian," said Balenkoff, arching an eyebrow, then returning his attention to Al.

"I'm Albin Bradshaw." Al smiled, offering his hand. Christ, he thought, I haven't used that name since the second grade! He pressed on. "I'm a professor from Iowa College, and I'd like just a few minutes of your time."

Balenkoff shook Al's hand lightly but then held on to it firmly. "Ah, a member of the academic community. I *always* have time for someone who teaches young people and enables them to make their way in life." He continued to clasp Bradshaw's hand.

Al blushed. If this, thought Al, was a prelude to the rest of the afternoon, things weren't going to be easy. He managed to gently disengage his hand from Balenkoff's.

"Mr. Bradshaw and his wife are visiting his sister from Iowa," said Julian.

"Oh, I'm not married," said Al. "Golly no. Not on my salary."

Suddenly a shout came from inside the studio: "Maestro Balenkoff!"

Balenkoff remained unruffled. "Julian, take care of that, will you?" he ordered, pointing to the studio without looking away from Al.

Julian, displeased, nonetheless did as he was told.

"Won't you come into my private office?" invited Balenkoff. "Follow me."

As Al and Balenkoff walked throught the dance studio, the maestro dramatically gestured "continue, continue" to his adoring students.

The office was a far cry from the austere studio and reception area. It was one of the plushest rooms Al had ever seen. Deep carpeting. Overstuffed furniture. Vivid colors. It was what Al imagined a room in a very elegant cathouse would look like.

"Have a seat," said Balenkoff, beckoning toward a long white sofa. "Champagne?"

"Gee, we don't drink champagne back in Iowa. I might get a bit tipsy."

"Tut, tut," Balenkoff chuckled. "A little effervescent grape juice. That's all champagne is."

Al, uncomfortable in his tight collar, felt that the collar button was about to burst. Balenkofff noticed his discomfort. "Why don't you take off your tie and jacket and make yourself comfortable?" he suggested.

As Al stood and removed his jacket, Balenkoff inquired, "What is it you teach?" He handed Bradshaw a glass of champagne.

"Well, actually. . . ." Al was totally winging it now. "It's such a small college, I teach everything from poetry to physical education."

"Ummmmm," said Balenkoff, definitely intrigued. "And what can *I* do for you?"

"I'll be honest with you," Al said, playing his trump card. "I'm in town visiting my sister, and I always wanted to meet you. I've heard so much about you and read so much about you. Some friends in Iowa said you'd be snooty, but I said, 'No, I'll bet he's just a regular guy like the rest of us.' And I bet them I could get an interview with you for our school paper."

"I like you," said Balenkoff, perching on the edge of the couch. "I admire resourcefulness. I shall grant you your interview, Albin."

There was a knock on the door.

"Yes?" Balenkoff was annoyed at the intrusion.

"Your car is here, Mr. Balenkoff," Julian said, a little too loudly, from outside the door.

"Oh, damn," said Balenkoff. "I forgot. I'm invited to Doug and Mary's for a small dinner. An impromptu last-minute thing. I have so much to do. Listen, I have an idea." The maestro bounded up. "We can do the interview en route. Ride with me to my home."

Driving to Beverly Hills in Balenkoff's chauffeured black Pierce Arrow sedan, Al sustained the role of wide-eyed, star-struck Midwesterner. Balenkoff happily played to his captive audience, dropping so many star names Al had to stifle a laugh. At one point Balenkoff leaned over and said, "I'll tell you something no one has *ever* known about Billie Dove, but this *isn't* for your students!" After the bawdy anecdote, Al chuckled inwardly at Balenkoff's revelation. He had heard a much more graphic version of the story last week at the Palm.

As they pulled up to Balenkoff's stately home, Al felt disappointed. Balenkoff was certainly loaded with gossip, but not about the Ince affair. The maestro caught Al's look of disappointment and tapped the young man on the shoulder. "Come in, come in, dear boy. I'll give you an autographed photo for your friends back in Iowa."

Bradshaw wasn't certain he could carry things much further. But Balenkoff seemed harmless enough.

An Oriental houseboy swung open the heavy mahogany front door. "Show Mr. Bradshaw to the study," Balenkoff told him, "and get him some champagne." He turned back to Al. "I'll be down in a minute, dear boy."

Al was impressed with the house. Who wouldn't be? he thought. These Hollywood people sure knew how to live! From the huge picture window in the study Al could survey the rolling lawns and reflecting pool.

A few minutes later, Balenkoff, in an embroidered and monogrammed red silk robe, whirled into the room. "Dear boy, it's so refreshing to speak with someone who isn't involved in show business. I had an *awful* day at the studio today. Have you any plans for the evening?"

"Why, no," said Al.

"Why don't you stay then? We'll take all the time you need. Chatting."

"I thought you were going out to dinner."

"Just a *boring* evening at Doug and Mary's with the King of Siam or someone. I'll take care of that right now." He walked to a gold-plated telephone on a marble-topped painted Bombay chest. Al was aware that the ensuing scene was being played for his benefit. Balenkoff was soon on the line with America's Sweetheart.

"Mary daaa-a-a-a-rling, how are you? No, I'm *not* feeling well at all, dear, what with the yachting party, Ince's death, the funeral and all—it's been such a *frightful* week." Balenkoff looked over and winked at Al.

"Mary, would you forgive me for not coming tonight? Darling, I simply can't, *belie-e-eve me*. What? No, dear. You're an a-a-a-angel. My best to Doug."

When Balenkoff hung up, he turned back to Al. "Of course, she *won't* forgive me. Not for a while. Actually, tonight we were all supposed to go to a costume ball. But Marion had to cancel it. I do hope she reschedules. I have the most fabulous outfit."

"Marion?"

"Marion Davies, of course."

Al followed up quickly. "Gee, do you know Marion Davies? I'll bet you knew Thomas Ince too."

"Ince only slightly. But let's not talk about him. It's too, too dreadful and depressing."

Balenkoff poured himself more champagne. "Drink up, drink up," he said to Al, who had seated himself in a wing chair across the room. Balenkoff motioned for Al to join him on the sofa: "It'll be much easier to talk here." He leered, patting the cushions next to him.

Al was angry. Not at Balenkoff, but at himself. He hated the fact that he was leading this old bird on. But he needed this information.

"Gee, you really know Marion Davies?" Al asked as he walked slowly across the room.

Balenkoff ignored the question. The maestro's eyes expertly surveyed the muscular body that was straining under Al's tight clothes.

"Is Marion one of your favorites?" asked Balenkoff.

"Oh, yes," Al answered.

"Well," Balenkoff conceded, "God knows Marion would like *you*." He drained his glass of champagne, went over to the bar, and switched to brandy.

"God also knows," he said grandly, "Marion Davies would be *nothing* without *me*."

After more liquor and inconsequential gossip, Al managed to turn the conversation back to Davies.

He learned that Balenkoff had first met "the stuttering golden girl" when she was an adolescent. Marion and her sister Reine had been enrolled in his ballet school in Manhattan. "The bills were paid with Lederer's money, of course," Balenkoff said, referring to Reine's husband, George Lederer. "But it wasn't wasted cash. Reine sensed little Marion had that something special, and she was right. Marion was nothing special as a dancer, but when she was onstage, in a group, no matter, you looked at *her*. . . ."

After four brandies, Balenkoff was beginning to slur some of his words. "At firsht Marion was so shy, poor dear. She had no grace at *all*. It was up to *me* to put her over, and I did. I taught her how to stand, to walk, to do everything. One of the girls in her class was Marilyn Miller, and one day Marion said to me, 'I c-c-can't dance like M-M-Marilyn.' I said, 'Stop stuttering, Marion, you have as much to offer as Marilyn, but in a different way.' "

Balenkoff was pleased with that recollection. He smiled. "Of course," he added, "Marion would never have been able to be a headliner on Broadway the way Marilyn is. Marion doesn't have *that* kind of talent. Films are *perfect* for Marion. Reine knew that. And so does Hearst."

Al purposely screwed up his face into a puzzled expression at the mention of Hearst. "Hearst," Balenkoff explained, "is the man who produces her pictures, dear boy. William Randolph Hearst. Surely you've heard of him, even in Iowa!"

Balenkoff had strong opinions concerning the Hearst-Davies relationship. According to him, when Marion finally became a big star she became very independent. She could stand on her own financially. She began referring to Hearst as "the old bastard," though not to his face. Often, she openly defied him.

Balenkoff offered a gossipy firsthand recollection of a typical Davies-Hearst showdown.

"I can't *staaa-and* these dinner parties, darling," Barbara Lamarr whispered in Samuel Balenkoff's ear. "Everybody's trying to gauge old Hearst's mood." The dark-haired beauty was seated next to the ballet maestro, and both were bored with the forced gaiety of the evening.

Marion, gorgeously gowned, was playing the grand hostess. Despite Hearst's glowering disapproval, she had consumed quite a bit of wine with dinner.

On this evening, Hearst's mood was not particularly convivial. At dinner he had engaged in quiet and somber talks with his executives and aides. And afterward, in the palatial drawing room, the party seemed to split into two camps. Marion, surrounded by her show-business friends, reclined on a settee and began quietly sipping gin.

Hearst sat himself in a thronelike wing chair across the room and continued discussing business with several of his executives. Marion became increasingly annoyed. Finally she had had enough.

"Hey, you!" she screamed across the room.

There was sudden silence. Finally Hearst replied: "Are you referring to me?"

"Yes, you," she said. "Come here," she commanded, staring him down, never taking her blue eyes from his.

Hearst's staff literally backed away from his chair, leaving the emperor alone on his throne. They observed Hearst's expression harden, his lips tighten. The only sound was the tapping of his fingers on the arm of his chair.

The guests stood transfixed.

After a long and tense pause, Hearst suddenly stood up. "Well, I suppose I shall have to go," he said rather clownishly, walking over to her. "What does my Lady want?" he inquired, trying to be lighthearted.

Marion remained serious. Disdainfully she said, "Do your business downtown, not in my house. My guests are waiting for a drink. Go get them one, and hurry up."

The fifty guests stood in stunned silence. All were shocked when the Chief obediently moved behind the bar and began mixing drinks.

Arthur Brisbane, Hearst's top executive, turned to an aide and hissed, "Look how he lets that little tramp embarrass him. I don't know why the Chief stands for it."   *   *   *

"Of course," declared Balenkoff grandly, "all that is just part of a game Marion and the old man play with each other. We all know that she only gets away with exactly what he lets her get away with."

"Do you think they'll ever get married?" asked Al.

"She wants him to marry her, of course, but he'll never divorce Millicent."

Balenkoff now astounded Al Bradshaw with an incredible statement: "W.R. is a latent homosexual, you know." Al was speechless. "Doesn't take a genius to figure *that* out," continued the dance maestro. "Have you ever noticed that Marion masquerades as a boy in many scenes in her films? Hearst loves to see her as a boy!" Balenkoff tittered. "Once I heard her tell him, 'Jesus, I'm s-s-sick of playing b-b-boys in my pictures!' "

But at this moment Al wasn't particularly concerned with William Randolph Hearst's sexuality. Innocent and wide-eyed, Bradshaw asked, "Have you ever been on Mr. Hearst's yacht?"

Balenkoff was approaching a state of stupor. "Ma-a-a-any times, dear boy."

"It's a shame about Ince dying on the yacht."

"Yes, we were all shocked." Balenkoff nodded. Al could hardly contain himself: *Ince had died on the yacht.* Not on the train back to Los Angeles or at his home in Benedict Canyon, as the Hearst papers reported. Here was the first real piece of hard information—no conjecturing, no bullshit!

What else did Balenkoff know? Al wanted to shake the information out of him. But the reporter knew he had to proceed cautiously, gently. "Gee," said Al quietly, "tell me more about the yacht. I've never been on a yacht."

Balenkoff continued to babble. Al had to piece the story together, but a crystal-clear sequence of that evening emerged.

The elaborately set dinner table aboard the *Oneida* had thirteen settings. "Thirteen! Marion, dear God, that's bad luck!" exclaimed Elinor Glyn.

Conspicuously absent from the dinner table were wineglasses. Hearst was on one of his teetotaling kicks, and liquor was not being served.

"Not even wine with dinner?" asked Diane Enright. "Tom always has a few drinks before eating."

"D-d-don't worry," confided Marion. "When the old bastard goes to bed I'll have them bring up champagne, gin, and Scotch."

"At least champagne, darling. After all, this *is* a birthday party," declared Elinor Glyn.

"Where's Tom, the birthday boy?" inquired Balenkoff.

"He's in with W.R. and Dr. Goodman discussing business," whined Louella Parsons.

"Business, b-b-business. This is supposed to be a *party*. Doesn't anybody know how to have f-f-*fun*?" moaned Marion.

In Hearst's office, Thomas Ince and the Chief were going over contractual details regarding Ince taking over Marion's career. Cosmopolitan Pictures would move over to Ince's Culver City studio, and Ince would personally direct Marion's pictures. Distribution arrangements were being finalized. Ince had underestimated Hearst's acumen when it came to the picture business. He had assumed Hearst was content just to display his girlfriend onscreen. But Ince was surprised to learn that the old man had an extraordinary grasp of production and indeed knew as much about the industry as anyone in Hollywood.

"I simply don't believe it, W.R.," Ince was saying, patting his host on the back as they emerged from Hearst's office and entered the dining salon. "Those are some of the best distribution ideas I've heard in ten years."

Louella cornered Tom Ince. "Tell, tell," she begged Ince. She wanted the details for tomorrow's column.

"Oh, for God's sake, this is a p-p-party," interrupted Marion cheerfully. "Can't all that wait until later? Let's not talk about business now."

When all the guests had assembled and were finally seated at the dinner table, Tom Ince reached for his glass. "I'd like to propose a toast—"

"Wait!" screeched Elinor Glyn. "Don't drink it in water. It's bad luck."

"Oh, Elinor," intoned Dr. Goodman. "How silly."

During dinner, the chatter was light and gay. Chaplin was on Marion's left, Ince on her right. She flirted with each of them. At the other end of the table Louella Parsons animatedly chattered with Hearst about details of the new merger. Dr. Goodman entertained Diane Enright in light conversation, while Samuel Balenkoff and Elinor Glyn concentrated on studying a new burly, black-haired young waiter.

"He's got *it*," Elinor told Balenkoff.

"I noticed you noticed." The ballet maestro smirked.

When dinner was over, the guests lingered at the table. Hearst finally excused himself and went to bed. She waited a few minutes and then Marion, giggling, motioned to one of the stewards. Shortly, everyone was guzzling the best French champagne, the finest Canadian Scotch and British gin.

The reveling grew. "Shhh," said Louella Parsons. "We must keep our voices down."

"Oh, banana oil," said Marion comtemptuously. "Don't be a flat tire."

"But"—Louella pouted—"if W.R. finds out we're drinking liquor, he'll be very angry."

"So what? If one of us is going to lose a job over it," Marion exclaimed laughingly, "it won't be me!"

The guests roared.

But suddenly, from outside, came Hearst's high-pitched voice. "Maaaaarion," he whined, "Maaarion."

Marion rolled her eyes heavenward. She feigned a yawn. "G-g-good night, kids, s-s-see you in the morning." But she winked at them over her shoulder as she left the dining salon.

It was too early for the others to turn in. The party continued on for another hour. It became obvious, however, that Marion was unable to escape Hearst and rejoin them. And so members of the group either paired off or individually made their way to staterooms—but not necessarily their own.

Hours later, everyone was roused from bed and summoned into the main salon. The guests were confused, annoyed, half-awake. They were used to unusual happenings on Hearst's yachting parties, but this was something new.

"What's this all about?"

"What's up?"

"It's the middle of the night, for Christ's sake!"

"Good God, what is going on? Is the boat sinking?"

Then came the stunning news. Dr. Goodman informed the group that there had been a terrible tragedy. Tom Ince was dead.

Everybody was immediately shocked into silence. Then, after a moment, each guest burst into dozens of questions.

"Dead! Tom Ince . . . is dead?" "Where's Marion?" "Where's the Chief?" "Where's Diane? Does she know?" "Jesus Christ, how did he die? He was with us just an hour ago!"

"Please, please, we must keep our heads," implored Goodman, trying to quiet them all. "Diane became hysterical," Goodman replied. "We had to put her under sedation."

"But how did Tom die?" demanded Elinor Glyn.

"He was complaining of stomach pains," Goodman explained. "It could have been food poisoning."

"How could it be food poisoning?" argued Elinor. "None of the rest of us are ill, and we all ate the same thing!"

"We haven't yet determined the cause of death," said Goodman coolly. "We all know Tom had a bad heart. He *was* drinking heavily."

"Where's Marion?" Balenkoff persisted.

"Where's W.R.?" asked Louella again.

"Please, please, ladies and gentlemen, we must all

remain calm. You mustn't worry. Everything's being taken care of. Tom's body will be brought to Los Angeles as quickly as possible."

"I can't believe it," declared Elinor. "I simply can't believe it." All the others echoed her reaction.

Goodman waited until the group quieted down. When he had their complete attention, he addressed them somberly: "As you can understand, this is a very delicate situation. Any hint that there is liquor on board might precipitate a federal investigation. The captain has already sworn the crew to complete secrecy. And Mr. Hearst has asked me to ask all of you to please remain absolutely silent about the events here tonight. This has been a terrible shock, but we must remain calm. We must avoid a scandal at all costs. Please remember, *we* will handle everything. Mr. Hearst will be most grateful to each and every one of you if you remain absolutely silent."

"Ohhhhh!" gasped Elinor, caught by the drama of the situation. "We must *all* be sworn to secrecy!"

"Exactly," Goodman noted.

He asked each of the guests in turn to give his word of honor that he would not discuss this cruise with anyone. Some agreed with a quiet "Yes" or "Of course." Others just nodded assent.

"Now, if you will all return to your rooms," Goodman concluded, "we will dock in the morning. There will be limousines to take us all back to Los Angeles." Goodman turned to Louella Parsons. "Louella, W.R. would like to see you alone in his study."

As the guests returned to their staterooms, there was little conversation. But everyone eyed each other suspiciously. Tom Ince had died, suddenly and mysteriously, and each person aboard the *Oneida* suspected the others knew more than they were telling.

A sworn-to-secrecy pact! Wow, thought Al, a sense of excitement surging through him, this story gets wilder every minute. At last the pieces of the puzzle were beginning to fit. There were people who would talk.

But with all this valuable information, the one piece of evidence Samuel Balenkoff could not provide was the actual cause of death. None of the guests had seen the body.

Bradshaw was so engrossed in his thoughts that he had forgotten his host's intentions. The liquor had released the maestro's final inhibition. Balenkoff leaned over and placed his hand on Al's thigh. "Loooook," he said intimately, squeezing gently. "It's getting late. Why don't we—?"

Bradshaw bounded up. "Gee," he said, "it *is* getting late. Uh . . . my sister. My poor sister is waiting for me." Al darted for the telephone. It would take ten or fifteen minutes for a cab to arrive, and Al was wondering if he should wait outside. But that would be unnecessary. When Bradshaw looked over to the couch, Balenkoff had already passed out. Poor guy, thought Al.

While Bradshaw was waiting for the taxi, he considered going through Balenkoff's desk. But almost as if anticipating Bradshaw's thoughts, the Oriental houseboy appeared. "Mr. Balenkoff, he asleep," he said softly. "I let him sleep here, I think. May call you cab?"

"I've already done that, thank you."

The loyal houseboy remained in the room. It was an uncomfortable ten minutes for the reporter until the taxi arrived.

The cab deposited Al in front of the Tribune Building. Al had given Grady Fletcher his last cent. He had to borrow a dollar from the night watchman to pay the cab fare. Bradshaw rushed upstairs to reread the story the *Trib* had carried on the Ince shooting. Now that Balenkoff had confirmed Ince died on the yacht, the story might contain an important clue or detail which Al had overlooked.

Five minutes later Al was dashing across the street

to Vera's. He caught her as she was closing for the night.

"Do you have that copy of Thursday's *Trib*?"

She laughed. "Are you kidding? This is Saturday."

"Please look!" pleaded Al. They went out to the garbage cans at the rear of the store. Al sifted through the waste. "Dammit, dammit," he kept muttering. "Wait, here's a page! Here's a page!" But it wasn't *the* page.

"When you *want* them to pick up the garbage, it lays around for four days," lamented Vera.

Back in the diner, they both washed their hands. Vera eyed him closely. Al had ripped off his stiff collar. His hair was stringy. His shirt was damp with sweat.

"You look like hell," Vera observed. "And what the hell are you doing in that ridiculous outfit?"

"I feel like hell," Al said wearily.

"You need a *rest*."

"I can't rest, Vera. Don't you understand?"

"Have you had anything to eat?"

"I don't remember. I know I've had too much to drink."

"Come on upstairs. Lemme make you something."

As Vera scrambled eggs, Al paced about nervously.

"Oh, God, Al. Sit down and relax, for heaven's sake."

He leaned up against the arch of the kitchen door. To cheer him up, Vera suggested, "Maybe after you eat we can check some of the other garbage cans in the neighborhood. A lot of people save papers to wrap garbage in."

"I'm a step ahead of you, baby. I thought of that too. But I went down to dispatching and found out that *that whole entire issue* of the *Tribune* was never shipped!"

Vera was surprised. "Isn't that unusual?"

"That's not the word for it. Seems half an hour after the stringer called in the story he called back and said the story was all wrong. So as the issue was coming off the presses, it was destroyed."

"But I saw it! I read it over your shoulder. How did *you* get it, then?"

"I obviously got one of the only goddamn copies that left that building. And now it's gone. I can't find one copy of that edition that says Ince was shot. In all the years I've been at the *Trib,* I've never known an entire edition to disappear. Casey told me the edition was yanked because they were afraid of a libel suit. *He* may believe that bull, but I don't. Why is *every* copy missing? They'd at least keep a file copy!"

Vera suddenly remembered. "Vince Lewis called the diner looking for you. He said he'd wait for your call at the Palm."

Al quickly got Vince on the line.

"I'm glad ya called, kid," said Lewis. "I got through to Mack Sennett. He'll see ya tomorrow."

"Great, that's great," said Al. "But listen close, Vince. I've got a lot of important stuff to tell you." The young reporter excitedly related the new information he'd garnered. Both men glowed with the satisfaction that they were on the right track.

Then Al hit Vince with the news that every copy of the *Tribune's* "Ince Shot" story had been destroyed.

"You're not surprised, are ya, kid?" asked Lewis.

"By the time this is all over, I guess nothing will surprise me." Al wound up the conversation as Vera's voice floated in from the kitchen. "Your eggs are getting cold."

Vera had prepared a feast: eggs, sausage, toast, coffee—she had even squeezed orange juice.

But Al picked at the food without enthusiasm. "Dammit, I wish we had found that paper."

"Eat your food," soothed Vera. "I'm gonna soak in the tub for a few minutes."

It had been a rough week for Vera too. She was tired and depressed. She liked to believe she was an individual who had her life in order, that she was a woman who could roll with the punches. But this week Vera had suffered an emotional setback. Eagerly anticipating Al's visit on Thursday afternoon, she was thrown into a deep depression when he didn't show.

In the last year her relationship with Bradshaw had fallen into an easy pattern. Although they had never discussed it, there were no commitments. They slept together about once a week. As far as Al knew, it was still all fun and games, no strings attached. But Vera was becoming more deeply involved.

"It ain't goin' nowhere kid," Vera told herself repeatedly. But her other half wasn't listening. She knew that any day now he might walk in and tell her he was taking a job in San Francisco or marrying some college girl. She'd have to wish him luck. They'd have a couple of laughs on his last night in town. . . .

She also told herself: "You always fall for the same type. Some wide-eyed boy scout out to burn up the world. So wrapped up in his job that half the time he doesn't know you're in the room!"

But there was no use trying to be reasonable. Vera wanted to be with him. She needed him. And as long as he needed and wanted her, she'd be there.

As Vera emerged from her bathroom, she saw that Al had already switched off all the lights and slipped into bed.

The room was softly illuminated by light filtering up from the streetlamps below. Vera went over to her phonograph, wound it, and put the needle down on her new Columbia disc: "Gimme a Little Kiss, Will Ya, Huh?" The romantic strains of the song played scratchily but softly.

She slipped into bed with Al and ran her fingers over his bare shoulder

When he didn't respond to her light touches, she was puzzled. She had been genuinely hurt about Thursday, and was hoping he'd make up for it now. But she smiled and laughed to herself at her romantic illusions. Al was sound asleep.

Sunday, November 23

The disarray of the bedclothes spoke of the passionate encounter that had taken place early that morning.

As Al dressed, he heard Vera whistling happily, doing the breakfast dishes. He came up behind her and slipped his arms around her waist. She turned, threw him a dazzling smile, and growled in a soft voice: "Honey, if this is the kind of mornings-after we can have, you can just come home exhausted every night!"

They both laughed. Al kissed her again, but his thoughts were somewhere else. "Geez, Vera, this friggin' story will drive me nuts."

"What happens next?"

Al glanced at his watch. "Vince set up a meeting between me and Mack Sennett at noon." It was 11:30.

"Watch out for those bathing beauties!" she admonished.

A bucket of cold water was poured over Al's head.

"Want another bucket, kid?"

"Sure!"

"Two more buckets," Mack Sennett ordered. "Nothing like a good steam," the veteran director said. "Cleans out your pores. Best thing for a hangover."

They were in the steam room of the Los Angeles Athletic Club.

Sennett was of medium height, had brown hair, and was not particularly distinguished-looking or handsome. Certainly not with sweat pouring down his brow, his hair wringing wet, and his body wrapped in a Turkish towel. Nor did he appear to be the cocksman he was reputed to be.

But when Sennett spoke, even though he was obviously hung over, the lustiness of his personality came through.

Sennett occasionally lived at the Athletic Club, as had many other major motion-picture names—Valentino, John Gilbert, even Chaplin.

"This place is great when we wanna get away from it all," explained Sennett. "Or when someone's between wives!" He chuckled.

"You know," Al remarked, "when I came out to Hollywood the first place I went was out to Glendale to see your Keystone Studios. I grew up on the Keystone Kops."

"You and a few million others, kid." Sennett laughed, slapping Al on the shoulder. "It used to be real fun in those days. Now, we're all in *business*."

"A couple of weeks ago I saw *Down to the Sea in Shoes*," said Al. The film was Sennett's parody of the popular movie *Down to the Sea in Ships*, which had introduced a new flapper, Clara Bow, to the screen.

"Yeah, we had fun making that," Sennett recalled.

Al enjoyed the fact that Sennett, though he was one of the moguls, hadn't lost his ability to poke fun at the pomposity of the industry that had made his fortune. Sennett's films were brilliant, satirical, and irreverent. The underlying theme of his comedies was to make farce of false dignity and to undermine stuffy authority.

"We're shooting a hilarious one now," Sennett told Bradshaw. "*The Sea Squawk*."

Al laughed. It would obviously be a takeoff on the Milton Sills-First National adventure hit, *The Sea Hawk*.

"And after that," Sennett related, "we're doing *The Shriek of Araby!*" Slapping his thighs, Sennett exploded into laughter at his own creative genius. "That'll be a beaut!"

Then Mack Sennett turned serious. "Vince Lewis told me you wanted to talk about Ince."

"That's right," said Al, mopping the sweat off his face with a nubby towel. "Him and a dame named Diane Enright."

"Was Tom foolin' around with Diane?" There was a note of surprise in Sennett's voice.

"You know her?"

"Sure, if it's the same Diane Enright that was one of my bathing beauties a couple of years back. A hot little number. Figures, now that you mention it. Ince always went for that type."

"Do you know where she is?"

"Are you kidding? This town is filled with flappers who'll pull up their skirts for a smile. Who's gonna keep tabs on any one of them?"

The attendant arrived with more buckets of cold water. A few other men drifted in and out of the steam room. It was relatively empty on this early Sunday morning. For the most part, Bradshaw and Sennett were alone.

After fifteen more minutes of chatter about dames, sex, and more sex, Al felt Sennett liked him. The young reporter was confident enough to try his ploy. "Say I heard about that *special* feature at Ince's house!"

Sennett arched an eyebrow. Then a slow, leering smile began spreading over his face. "Oh, you heard about that, huh, kid?" The director laughed heartily. "That was some fun, lemme tell you. We used to go up on that catwalk and see the most popular asses in town grinding away."

Al pretended to know what Sennett was talking about. He nodded and smiled in agreement.

"Leave it to Ince," remarked Sennett admiringly, "to have something like that put in his house. Everybody figured he was the best pal in town, best food, best booze, best bedrooms for the weekend. He was the softest touch around. Who would've guessed that Tom had those peepholes in the ceilings and those sliding doors in the walls! I guess people like us who make movies get bored with your average kind of entertainment," Sennett philosophized. "We need something really special to interest us." He laughed vigorously.

Al played all his cards at once. "I heard Ince was shot. You think anybody found out about those peepholes and was pissed enough to shoot him?"

Sennett's mood changed abruptly. He was suddenly serious, sober, and unfriendly. "Look, buddy," he said harshly, "I wouldn't go around saying stupid things like that if I were you. Ince had a bad heart. And ulcers." Sennett's mood changed again. In a friendly manner, slapping Al on the back, he said, "You know this business, kid. Have fun while you can. And don't believe anything you hear, and only half of what you see. Hey, Charlie," he called out. "Get us more buckets!"

The streets of Los Angeles were almost deserted on this sleepy Sunday. Al drove through Hollywood toward Beverly Hills. After the startling information provided by Sennett, Bradshaw was anxious to view Ince's house.

As he entered magnificent Benedict Canyon, the smell of pine was almost intoxicating. The incredibly lush, verdant hills were an astonishingly beautiful sight.

The multiacre Ince ranch was awesome. This was the way one imagined a millionaire film magnate would live. Tranquillity enveloped the place. There were hundreds of avocado trees and persimmons, a walnut grove and shaded lawns. Hammocks were strung between giant oak trees. Off to one side Al could see a swimming pool, a rippling fountain in the center of it.

The main house was a huge, sprawling affair with awning-covered patios. Al knew the ranch was called Días Dorados—Golden Days. Well, thought Al, they surely were for Ince—until now.

Días Dorados hardly looked like a setting for weekend orgies. Al's eyes scanned the house for some sign of the catwalk-peephole area. Nothing like that, of course, could be seen. Al reasoned the passageways must be hidden in interior walls.

Bradshaw realized it was unlikely that Nell Ince would see him. Even if she did, what would she tell him? But Al drove up to the front door and rang the bell.

A butler opened the small iron-grilled window on the heavy wooden door. "Yes?"

Al identified himself and asked to see Mrs. Ince. The butler was genuinely shocked. "Mrs. Ince is seeing no one."

"I'd just like to—"

"Please have the decency to leave," said the butler, cutting him short. "Any questions you may have can be answered by the press-relations department at the studio." He slammed the small window shut.

Al, hands in his pockets, felt like a reprimanded child. He shuffled back to his car. As he was getting into the Chevy, he noticed two short men at the far end of the driveway. He recognized them as Oriental gardeners. They might be able to tell him something. But by the time Al reached the spot, they had silently disappeared into the walnut grove.

As long as I'm out here, thought Al, I might as well try to see Chaplin. Fat chance. He laughed. Bradshaw knew he'd have as much luck with Chaplin as with Nell Ince. But at least he'd be satisfied that he had tried to get through to everyone concerned.

Chaplin had attended Ince's funeral, but the famed idol hadn't publicly admitted to being on the cruise. He hadn't been listed in newspaper accounts as being a member of the yachting party, and when Al had telephoned the Chaplin Studios, they wouldn't give out an official statement either way. Al had only the word of Mona Petersen, the girl at United Artists. And, of course, Balenkoff's drunken recollections that Chaplin and Louella Parsons had been aboard.

Charles Chaplin's present home on Cove Way was

three stories high, an enormous square-shaped, Georgian-style stucco affair. It had a tiled roof and huge, stately windows. There were many railed terraces. The grounds were magificently landscaped. Sculptured lawns and rosebushes abounded.

The Chaplin butler was even less friendly than Ince's. "You're a little late, aren't you?" asked the man. "The rest of the press was here hours ago." Al learned that Chaplin, his Japanese manservant, Kono, and an entourage had already left for Mexico, where Chaplin was marrying Lita Grey. That obviously, would be tomorrow's headline.

Next on Al's list: Elinor Glyn, the fabulous Leopard Lady herself.

The sun was setting by the time he arrived at her imposing Beverly Hills mansion. She used to have a suite of rooms at the Hollywood Hotel, but now she, too, had purchased an estate. The big house was set back among giant evergreen trees, with a sweeping cobblestone driveway leading up to the front door.

Glyn's Oriental houseboy delivered Al's message— he wanted just a few minutes of her valuable time.

While pacing around outside, Al didn't notice curtains part at an upstairs window as a heavily mascaraed pair of eyes sized him up.

Discouraged after fifteen minutes of waiting, Bradshaw was about to leave when the front door swung open. The Oriental servant motioned him to enter. He ushered Bradshaw through the tiled gallery and into a dimly lit salon. "You wait here, please."

"Thank you," said Al. It took a few moments for the reporter's eyes to adjust to the darkened room. When they focused, he marveled at an assemblage of *objets d'art,* paintings, overstuffed throw pillows, a ten-foot-long couch, all possessing a single motif: leopard. This was like a room out of Glyn's novel *Three Weeks.*

Miss Glyn's preoccupation with the leopard was everywhere. Even the draperies were of a leopard print, and one large cast-iron leopard and one upholstered black velvet jaguar served as footstools for wing chairs. There was even a leopard-skin throw rug in front of the fireplace.

Everything was here but the roaring fire, thought Al. Would she be in a leopard skin too? he wondered. Or would she enter dramatically with a live leopard tied to a leash?

The doors to the room flung open, and there stood an erect, imposing figure. Elinor Glyn wore what seemed to be a diaphanous nightgown, its hem and cuffs trimmed with leopard. Her orange hair practically glowed in the dark. In the dim light it was impossible for Al to determine her age.

"You are from the *Tribune*?" she asked. She spoke with a cultured British accent.

"Yes, ma'am. Al Bradshaw."

"You're not on the entertainment desk." It was a statement, not a question.

"No, ma'am. The city desk."

"And you want to ask me questions? I don't understand," she mused. "Do you want my opinion on a new zoning law?" She motioned him to sit. "Ah, I know!" she exclaimed. "It's about the annexation proposal. I oppose it," she said vehemently. "It's all those real-estate interests in Los Angeles that want to annex Beverly Hills. Now that we—Mary, Doug, Will, Lloyd, Chaplin, Corinne, Valentino, Barrymore, Tom Mix, Fred Niblo, me—now that *we* have made it a fashionable place to live, those small-minded people want to move in and sell lots fifty feet wide!"

Al tried to protest.

Elinor barreled on. "Oh, I know the ploy they're using. We haven't enough water. *They*, the city of Los Angeles, will supply us. Well, darling, we'll get our own water. Does that answer all your questions?"

"Not exactly. I'd like to ask you a few questions about Mr. Ince's death."

Elinor feigned surprise. "My dear boy, the papers have covered all that. A terrible tragedy." She paused.

"Oh, I see," she said, seeming to understand. "This is a human-interest piece." She floated over to a chaise longue and lowered herself onto it, assuming a pose à la Madame Récamier. "A noble idea. Tom Ince contributed *so* much to the industry."

"No, it's not a human-interest piece. There seems to be some question about his death."

"Question? Question? In whose mind? It all seems clear enough to me."

"Well, if his death was a simple heart attack, how come all of you on the yacht were sworn to secrecy?"

Glyn blinked nervously. Quickly and sharply she asked, "Who told you that?" She immediately regretted her tone of voice.

"I can't reveal my sources."

Elinor Glyn rose and crossed the room to a crystal box resting on a lacquered coffee table. She withdrew a cigarette and placed it in a long gold holder. She stood waiting. It took Al a few seconds to realize she was expecting him to light her cigarette.

On his feet quickly, Bradshaw fumbled in his pocket but had no matches. Glyn shot him a disdainful look and pointed to the matching cut-crystal table lighter.

"I've heard that Mr. Ince was dead before he left the yacht," Al commented, lowering the lighter to meet her cigarette. She inhaled deeply, blew the smoke to her left, and turned back to Al.

"Preposterous!" She accompanied the pronouncement with a dramatic gesture of her hand. And then, in a quieter voice, she said, "Actually, young man, I'm glad you're here. If silly rumors such as these have reached the ears of the press, I'm only too happy to squelch them." Then, in an abrupt change of subject: "How old are you?"

"Twenty-one," answered Al. "Why?"

"You're at the very *peak* of your sexuality," she said. Al was appropriately shocked, and Elinor charged on. "Do you realize that a man reaches the peak of his sexuality between the ages of eighteen and thirty?

Whereas a woman"—she puffed on her cigarette
dramatically, blowing smoke in his direction—"is not
equipped for true lovemaking until past the age of
thirty."

Was she kidding? Was this old broad putting the
make on him? "Miss Glyn," said Al, "I've got some
very conflicting information on how Mr. Ince died."

"Tom Ince," mused Elinor. "Now, there was a man
whose sexuality was ageless. He was a great producer,
a great director. But he also could have been a *star,* if
he wanted to. Tom Ince had *it*. Ivor Novello, Norman
Kerry, even John Gilbert, Ramon Novarro. *None* of
them have *it. It* is the quality that sets you apart."

Elinor was building toward something. She narrowed
her heavily made-up eyes and coquettishly tilted her
head. "Have *you* ever thought of going into the
movies?" She coyly fluffed the curls under her head-
band.

Jesus, thought Al. Last night he had had to fend off
Balenkoff, and now this. A middle-aged Hollywood
barracuda was trying to eat him up.

"Miss Glyn, can you tell me what really happened
on the cruise?"

By now she was completely ignoring his questions.
"I may be able to arrange a screen test for you, darling," she purred. "Unfortunately, I have a dinner en-
gagement tonight. Perhaps if you come back tomorrow
night? We'll see if you have any talent?"

She glided over to a fringed sash and rang for her
servant. "Zuki," she said when he entered, "please
show this gentleman out." Then she turned to Al:
"Shall we say tomorrow night at ten?"

Al didn't know what to say. Elinor extended her
hand. He shook it. She laughed. "No, no, dear boy."
She raised her hand again, this time close to his lips.
"You Americans have so much to learn." He took her
hand and awkwardly kissed it.

"Tomorrow at ten?"

Al nodded absently.

As Zuki showed Al to the door, something clicked in the reporter's mind. All the people involved in this cover-up were in show business, but they had another common link. The major clue had been staring Bradshaw in the face all the while! Everyone on the fatal cruise seemed to have Oriental servants—Japanese, Al guessed. He tingled with anticipation. Perhaps the key to the Ince affair could be found in a visit to Little Tokyo.

A section of downtown Los Angeles, bordering Chinatown but distinctly different from it, Little Tokyo consisted of a short block of a dozen or so small, brightly painted wooden buildings. During the day the area had a lively and friendly ethnic charm. But after dark, the atmosphere of Little Tokyo was entirely different—mysterious and foreboding.

The brightly colored lanterns strung across the storefronts cast garish images on the pavement. The few shops and restaurants were practically empty when Bradshaw pulled onto the street.

Al walked past the once-popular Geisha House, probably the only restaurant in Little Tokyo frequented by non-Japanese. Some of Al's reporter pals occasionally still ate lunch there. But Geisha House had fallen out of favor after the Volstead Act. Most Oriental restaurants in Los Angeles suffered a severe economic blow after Prohibition. People liked to eat where they could get a drink. But the Japanese and Chinese dared not serve liquor. It was a federal offense, and they would face possible deportation.

Bradshaw walked past Geisha House and went directly to what appeared to be the door to an upstairs apartment but which actually led to a tiny native restaurant. Since there was a dragon painted in gold leaf on the wooden door, most non-Japanese had come to identify the place as the Golden Dragon.

Al climbed a flight of stairs. At the top of the landing were sliding paper doors. As Al walked into the dimly lit quarters, he was eyed suspiciously. All white intruders always were.

The smell of fish and incense pierced his nostrils. The deathly stillness was broken when a shriveled old Oriental shuffled over to Al and bowed. In broken English, and a practically inaudible voice, he asked, "Help you, please, mister?" Al always found it strange that Japanese could not pronounce the letter *l*, so that it came out: "Herp you, prease, mister?"

"Is Mr. Tishema here?" inquired Al softly.

The old man bowed again and backed away. Al became aware of the presence of someone standing behind him. Bradshaw turned slowly. As though the mention of the name had conjured up the man, there was Hano Tishema.

Al watched the somber and suspicious face of the sixty-four-year-old Tishema slowly blossom into a smile.

"Mister Al-bin," said Tishema, the timbre of his voice like a muffled bell in an ancient temple. "I am so happy to see you. I have not seen you for a long while." He bowed formally.

Al returned the bow, and apologized. "I know, Tishema. I'm sorry. I have not had the opportunity to visit with you."

"You will dine with me."

"I have not the time, dear friend, I regret."

"Ah, just like your father. And just like yourself! Even when you were a small boy, you had 'no time.' Always rushing about. But you are never too busy to help friends. Again, like your father."

Tishema would never forget, and would always be grateful for, Ed Bradshaw's generous aid back in Seattle. The elder Bradshaw had helped the then already wealthy Tishema avoid extortion threats and unjust deportation.

"You will dine with me," repeated Tishema.

Al knew that he could not refuse. *"Domo arigato gozaimasu,"* he said in perfect Japanese. Long ago

Tishema had taught him the Japanese for "thank you" and many other phrases.

As a table was being prepared, the two men sat and talked of Seattle. Al gazed into the face of his old friend. Hano Tishema looked much the same as he had ten years ago—probably even twenty years ago, marveled Al. Large, clear, almond-shaped eyes. Straight black hair, untouched by gray. And, though it was housed in a small, frail frame, his extraordinary strength of character was evident.

Ever since Al had arrived in Los Angeles, he had made it a point to visit Tishema at least twice a year. But Al felt guilty. It always seemed as though these visits occurred when he needed something—spiritual guidance; emotional support; this time, information.

Tishema, who was childless, loved Al as a son. He was always pleased to see the boy, and eager to be of assistance. In the ten years since Tishema had traveled to Los Angeles from Seattle, he had become a powerful force in the Japanese community. His people referred to him as *Ichi Ban*. Number One.

He owned vast real-estate holdings and controlled diversified businesses. But he still comported himself humbly. Few would guess that he was such a leader among his people that his advice and help were often called on by L.A.'s political hierarchy in matters concerning the social and political network of the city.

Though Al was eager for information, in deference to his old friend he could not rush matters.

Nearby, a young Japanese man stoked the coals of a small charcoal stove. He dropped pieces of fish— shrimp, octopus, squid, the Japanese fish tai—into a pan of bubbling fat, swishing the chunks of food around with long metal chopsticks.

Dinner was served. Despite Al's protestations of not being hungry, to Tishema's delight he devoured many of his favorite delicacies.

"The tempura was wonderful. It reminded me of our days in Seattle," reminisced Al.

The elder man was gratified at Al's enjoyment of the meal. When dining was over, an old servant brought finger bowls and washcloths. As they wiped their hands dry, Tishema motioned to the servant. The man brought a wooden tray carrying a delicately beautiful blue porcelain decanter and two tiny, matching cups.

The saki, of course, was of the finest quality. The men had enjoyed the last hour, but Tishema knew there was business at hand. "Tell me," he asked. "Are you in trouble?"

"No, dear friend."

"Permit me to rephrase, then. You are troubled."

"Yes."

"How might I help you?"

Al had barely begun relating the story of Thomas Ince and the suspected murder aboard the *Oneida* when Tishema slowly raised his right hand, motioning him to stop. From his manner and facial expression, it was obvious the Japanese knew the entire story.

"Whatever information I could give to you on this matter," he said solemnly, "would endanger friends close to me."

"I understand, but—"

"More important," interrupted Tishema, "Al-bin, my son—you are endangering your own life."

Al could say nothing in reply.

"If you persist in this investigation," cautioned Tishema, "I will fear greatly for your safety."

"Confirm just one thing for me," beseeched Al. "Ince *was* shot aboard that boat, wasn't he?"

Tishema seemed to withdraw deep inside himself, and he studied Al carefully. After a moment the old man reluctantly nodded in assent.

"Well, then—"

Again Tishema interrupted. He saw Al was going to launch into more questions. The elder man rose. With finality he stated, "I can say no more. Except, it is unfortunate that one man died when the bullet was obviously intended for another."

* * *

Al raced to the Tribune Building. Up in the morgue he dragged out every picture they had of Charlie Chaplin, out of costume—selling war bonds, attending premieres, the races, civic functions. And every picture they had of Ince.

Yes, there was definitely a resemblance. At certain angles, it was more than merely a resemblance. There was a strong similarity—their build, the shape of their heads, their wavy salt-and-pepper hair. In the dark of a yacht's cabin—below deck—especially if a man's back was turned, Al reasoned, anyone might mistake Ince for Chaplin.

As Bradshaw walked swiftly through the city room, Tony Scott, the assistant night editor, called out to him. "You finally get that goddamn call?"

Al slowed down but didn't stop walking. "What call?"

"Somebody's been tryin' to reach you on the phone all day."

Al stopped short. Diane Enright! Dammit, he had missed her call. He wondered what other leads she might have, how much more information she was going to divulge. Now that Al knew she was on the cruise, he had plenty of questions to ask.

Al's silence and the intense expression of his face bewildered Scott. "You all right, kid?"

"Yeah, Tony. Who was it that called?"

"Beats me. All I know is, your phone's been ringing off the hook all day, and everyone in the office was goin' crazy lookin' for you."

"Thanks, Tony." Al whirled and dashed up to telephone switchboard room on the fourth floor. "Hey, Peggy," he shouted.

"Peggy's gone for the night," answered a startled older operator Al had never seen before. No, she said, she hadn't gotten any calls for him in the last half-hour. No, she didn't know who had been calling him all afternoon.

Exasperated, Al grabbed a piece of paper and scribbled down three telephone numbers—his apartment, Vera's place, and the Palm. "Look," said Al. "If anybody else calls for me, please tell them they can get me at one of these numbers."

Bradshaw found Vera and Vince waiting for him at a dimly lit banquette at the far end of the Palm. Al slid onto the seat next to Vera. To cut some of the noise from the speakeasy and assure that no unwanted pals would join them, he pulled the curtain closing their booth off from the main room. The feeling of privacy was equivalent to that of an upper berth in a railroad Pullman.

Al spewed out Tishema's revelatory news.

"Jesus!" exclaimed Vince and Vera. A new question had been raised. Was Ince killed by mistake?

Simultaneously all three began conjecturing on what could have happened on the cruise—what facts they knew, what still had to be discovered, what had *possibly* happened, what had *probably* happened, what was *provable*. Al and Vera began arguing over a minor point.

"Wait a minute, wait a minute," cried Vince, tapping the table with his open hand. "Let's use a little logic here. Let's calm down and see what we've got. And let's lower our voices, for God's sake."

"Okay," said Al in a quiet, intense tone. "This is what I know. They're trying to make it look like Ince didn't die until he got back to Los Angeles, that he died of a heart attack or food poisoning. But Balenkoff confirmed that Ince died on the boat. And Tishema verified that Ince had been shot."

"How does he know Ince was shot?" interjected Vera.

"Through the grapevine. One of the Japanese servants on the yacht must have heard a shot or seen a bullet hole in Ince's body. I know the Japanese well," continued Al. "They're loyal. And discreet. Something really shocking must have happened for one of them to have opened his mouth. They're keeping quiet now, but they know the details of the Ince affair, and they obviously think Ince was shot by mistake. I don't know who shot Ince, I don't know why everyone was sworn to secrecy. But I know Hearst is behind the biggest cover-up since the Teapot Dome." Al slumped back, satisfied he was on the right track but frustrated that most of his information was not provable. Not yet.

"What about Ince's wife?" asked Vera, taking a cigarette from her bag.

"She wasn't on the boat, that I know."

"But the Enright dame was," said Vera, "and I'll bet she's the key to everything."

"How do you figure that?" asked Vince.

Vera leaned forward, elbows on the table and advanced her theory: "This Diane Enright dame is nuts about Tom Ince, and she's got a jealous streak. With him to deal with, she musta had plenty of cause. But she keeps herself in control, 'cause she's got a brain." Vera tapped her forehead. Al and Vince acknowledged Diane Enright had a brain.

"Okay," continued Vera. "She and Ince have a good thing goin'. But old Tom not only has a wife, he has a wanderin' eye, and maybe his glance wanders once too often on this last boat trip. Now, let's say this Enright dame catches him with Marion Davies—or one of the other dames on the cruise—smoochin' in a lifeboat. Enright knows old man Hearst has a habit of shootin' seagulls with his silver pistol. So this time when she catches Ince cheatin' on her, she finds the old man's gun and shoots Ince herself."

Tom and Vince were dubious.

"You can't find the Enright dame, can you?" asked Vera sharply. "I say she probably did shoot Ince, and now she's on the lam."

"I don't buy it," said Al. "Why would she keep calling me? She's called me twice already, and I missed her call today. Why is she goading me to keep up with the story? And why would Hearst cover up for *her*?"

"Now, wait a minute," said Vince, leaning forward himself. "Maybe Vera's theory isn't too far wrong. If this Enright dame did shoot Ince, the scandal would be on every front page for weeks. It would wreck Marion Davies' career, even though she and Hearst didn't commit any crime. Can you imagine the public uproar about such a thing happening on Hearst's yacht? Even if Ince wasn't shot, there's still a lot of juicy material there. Married men traveling with their girlfriends. Unmarried couples sleeping together. A lot of boozing and wild partying going on!

"Could be that's why Ince's wife may be going along with the cover-up. To save what's left of Ince's reputation. Suppose this Enright dame got on the stand and told about Ince's girlfriends. And then told about those peepholes in his house, where he watched his friends get laid! Hot stuff, much *too* hot. So that's why Hearst spirits the Enright girl away."

Vince concluded his conjecturing. "Everybody on the cruise sticks with the food-poisoning–heart-attack story for the sake of Ince's wife and Ince's reputation."

"I don't buy it," said Al. "There's too much evidence that Ince was shot. Maybe he was shot by mistake, maybe not. That's for the D.A. to find out. All I've got to prove is that Ince was shot."

Monday, November 24

A gun was at Al's head, the barrel pressed firmly to his left temple. A high-pitched voice repeated, "Stop looking for any more information, Mr. Bradshaw." From a distance Al could hear another voice. It was Hano Tishema's: "My son, I begged you to stop . . ." Suddenly Al realized the floor was swaying. He was on a ship. A young dark-haired girl approached him. He couldn't see her face. "What did Balenkoff tell you?" she asked. He tried to turn to see who she was, but the gun pressed deeper into his head. He could feel beads of sweat dripping from his armpits. He was transfixed. Why couldn't he move? Why couldn't he strike out? He tensed as he heard the gun's trigger being squeezed. Instead of an explosion, there was a ringing, a constant ringing in his head.

Finally he was able to move. He flailed about, waving his arms wildly. He heard a thud. The ringing stopped. There was silence. He was in a black void. He could discern a faint voice in the distance: "Bradshaw . . . Bradshaw . . ." His arm reached out closer to the voice. He grabbed something and pulled it toward him.

"Bradshaw? Is that you?"

"Yeah . . ." Al groaned. He had knocked over the telephone while shaking himself awake from the nightmare. His hand now clutched the receiver.

For a moment Al Bradshaw could not determine where he was. Then he realized he was in his own bed, in his own apartment, fully clothed. His neck ached. He had fallen asleep in a cramped position.

"Bradshaw? Are you there?"

"Yeah," he muttered, not yet awake. Still groggy, he reached over and grabbed the other end of the telephone. He pulled it toward him. "Yeah, yeah, I'm here."

"This is Grady Fletcher."

". . . Fletcher. Oh . . . Fletcher. . . ."

"Where the hell ya been?" Fletcher barked. "I've been tryin' to reach you for two days. I've got the story of what happened on that yacht."

". . . yacht? . . ." Al was still dazed.

"Wake up, kid. You wanna know who shot Ince?"

Bradshaw popped up to a sitting position. "You know who shot Ince?" he exclaimed, now alert.

"Not so fast, kid, it's gonna cost ya. Five big ones. And I need the dough by noon."

"Noon?" Al thought fast. "How am I going to raise that dough by noon?"

"Won't your paper pay for a story like this?"

"Five hundred's a lot of money."

"My train leaves at one o'clock, kid. I'm blowin' this town."

"What kind of proof will you be able to deliver?"

"It'll be up to you to dig out the proof. But I'll be able to give you the facts—you'll know where to look. After that, it's your baby. Meet me inside the Bradbury Building at noon."

"Five hundred dollars!!" Vera was astonished. Her green eyes widened. "Honey, you are definitely not a run-of-the-mill paperboy. Five hundred!"

"The paper will give the money back to me soon as they break the story," he pleaded.

"What if they don't break the story?"

"If Fletcher's information isn't worth it, I won't give him the dough."

"He's blowin' town," she said. "Maybe it's a double cross."

"Nah. The way I figure it, he's been paid to leave town, and he figures he can pick up a few hundred extra bucks to boot."

"Yeah, but five hundred——"

"He'll take three."

Vera walked to the cash register and lifted out the cash tray. Underneath was a key. She disappeared into the kitchen. In a moment she was back with an envelope. "Talk him down to two. And remember—it's the mortgage money."

"Hey, Bradshaw!"

Casey Clark was waiting when Al stopped in at the *Tribune* to get his daily assignment. Clark angrily motioned the reporter into his office. Al knew from Casey's threatening tone that a confrontation was imminent.

"What's this shit about you investigating a murder plot?" Clark spit the words out through clenched teeth.

Al retained his composure. "Who told you that?" he asked lightly.

"Never mind, wise-ass. You're heading for big trouble."

"Okay," said Al, trying to be reasonable. "I *am* following up Ince's death," he admitted. "I've been accumulating a lot of information. And I've been getting tips on the phone from this dame. I think she was Ince's mistress, Diane Enright. She's got a story to tell. I'm putting it all together, and——"

"I've told you before, and I'm telling you for the last time," interrupted Casey nastily, "stick to the stories you're assigned." Clark rose from behind his desk. Threateningly, he pointed a stubby finger in Al's face. "And stop telling people that the *Tribune* is investigating a murder cover-up."

"But it *is* a murder cover-up, and I'm on the brink——"

"Shut your yap, stupid. You don't have one shred of evidence."

"How do you know that?" demanded Al.

" 'Cause there ain't no evidence, see?" yelled Clark. The editor, suddenly realized people outside were listening. He angrily crossed the room and slammed shut the door to his small office. Several men in the city room were astounded. This was the first time in four years Casey had closed that door.

Casey's attitude changed abruptly. He assumed an almost fatherly tone with Al. "Look, kid, I got a call this morning from old lady Beck." Amanda Beck was the aging matriarch of the family that was holding on to the ownership of the *Tribune*. "She's been getting flack, see? Now, I know what you're doin'. But let's face it, you're not gonna get anyone to give you any real proof. You're just muddying up the water, understand?"

Al stood speechless.

"You're a smart kid," continued Casey. "You know this paper's only hangin' on month by month these days. If they bring any pressure on the Becks, we could fold in a week."

Al was incredulous. "What the hell are you talking about? You mean to tell me that the Becks have been bought off too?"

Casey's temper flared again. "Nobody's been bought off!" he bellowed. "The *Tribune* won't stand for one of its men goin' around sayin' he's assigned to investigate a murder cover-up when the *Tribune* hasn't assigned that story."

Clark strode back to his desk. He grabbed some papers and thrust them toward Al. "Here. *These* are your assignments. If any more news filters down that you're still workin' on that fairy-tale story, you're through. Now, get the hell out of here."

Al stormed out. But in the middle of the city room he stopped short and stood motionless, stifling the urge to go back into Casey Clark's office and punch him in the mouth. Bradshaw tore up the papers Casey had given him and threw them in a trash basket. He stomped out of the *Tribune* suppressing an overwhelming desire to spit at the plaque outside— *All the Truth, All the News.*

"What a load of shit! Even the Becks have been bought off. Or scared off. Well, I don't give a fuck," he muttered. "I'm going to get the goddamn story anyway. If the *Trib* won't print it, I'll take it to the *Times*."

Bradshaw strode around downtown for an hour. He needed to cool off and kill time.

The courtyard of the Bradbury Building, with its tiled floors, wrought-iron grillwork and elevators, beautiful potted greenery, and pretty secretaries bustling about, seemed a distinctly odd meeting place for Fletcher to select. It was a bold contrast to the alcoholic ex-cop's South 7th Street surroundings. Fletcher must be back on his feet, Al thought. He certainly sounded sober on the phone this morning.

Bradshaw didn't expect Fletcher to be on time, but with each minute that ticked past noon, Al's apprehension grew. Be 12:15, Bradshaw knew Grady wasn't going to show. He waited an extra fifteen minutes anyhow, then grabbed a cab and raced to Union Station.

The only train scheduled to depart at one o'clock was the Limited. Ultimate destination: Miami. Al frantically dashed up and down the platform, describing Fletcher to porters and redcaps. No luck. The Limited left on time. Grady Fletcher wasn't on it.

Bradshaw headed toward South 7th Street. "I should have known better," he told himself. "That's the trouble when you're dealing with winos. The bum probably cashed in the train ticket, if he ever really had one, and bought more booze."

At Fletcher's broken-down rooming house, the same toothless old geezer opened the screen door.

"I'm looking for Grady Fletcher," said Al.

"You again, huh? Fletcher's gone. Whatsa matter? Didn't he pay you the money he owed ya?"

"No," said Al. "Did he pay you?"

"Sure did. Gotta admit, I never thought he was good for it. But he paid me all his back rent—twenty-eight bucks."

"Where . . . did he get the dough?"

"Beats me. Leaves here yesterday mornin' lookin' like a bum, comes back last night with a brand-new suit."

"Did he have a train ticket too?" asked Al.

The man was surprised, as though Al were a mind reader. "Yeah," he said. "How'd you know that?"

"A ticket to Miami?"

"Yeahhh! Said he was goin' where there was plenty of sunshine."

"Can I see his room?" asked Al.

"Sure, if you got a quarter."

Al paid, and went upstairs. The room seemed somehow neater now that Grady's clothes and effects were gone. Al looked through the closet and dresser. Both were empty.

The broken-down armchair Grady had sprawled in only two nights previously sat like a deserted, dilapidated throne in the center of the room.

Al kicked it in disgust, and slammed the door as he left.

If it had occurred to Bradshaw to search under the cushion of the armchair, he would have found a canceled bus ticket to San Diego.

Al returned Vera's two hundred dollars. "The mortgage is safe, sweetie pie," he said unhappily. First the confrontation with Casey, and now Fletcher's no-show—Bradshaw's prospects were bleak. "I'm going over to the gin mill," he told Vera. "I need a drink, and I've gotta talk to Vince."

Vince Lewis rushed over to greet Al when he entered the speakeasy. "What did Fletcher have to say?" he asked excitedly. "Did he have any hard facts?"

"No show," Al said wearily, dropping into a chair.

"I'm sorry, kid," consoled Vince, disappointed himself. Patting Al on the back, he added, "But I told you this wasn't going to be easy. Are you gonna give up?"

"Not on your life," answered Al sharply. "I'm not going back to that goddamn office until I have the whole fucking story to throw in Casey's face."

The men rehashed the case and realized there were two alternatives: keep trying to find Diane Enright, or make a trip south to see if any holes could be uncovered in the official story of Ince leaving San Diego alive and stopping off in Del Mar.

"Let's concentrate on finding Diane Enright," Al insisted. "She must have something to tell. Ince was her meal ticket—and the guy she was stuck on. He was bumped off. *She's* the only one who's going to blow the whistle on anybody."

"You already tried to find her," argued Vince. "You see how far you got. Let's forget Enright and head south. Soon. It's our only chance to dig something up before they really cover their tracks. By the way, who called in that story on Ince that you can't find anymore? The one that said he was shot?"

"Jesus, I don't know." Al panicked. "I don't even know if the *Trib* has a regular stringer in San Diego."

"Okay, okay, don't get the jitters, kid. I can find out." Vince went to the phone, and returned shortly, a smile on his face. "We're in luck. The stringer down in San Diego was more than likely Will Greely."

"Do you know him?"

"I know of him. He's a friend of a friend. He strings for a lot of papers. He's a boozer and a carouser. But he's not dumb. If he's the guy who wired that story about Ince being shot, you can bet Ince was shot."

Al and Vince decided they'd leave for San Diego in the early morning. "That long a drive would be too hazardous to tackle tonight," advised Vince. "Let's get a good night's rest. I'm heading home."

Al returned to Vera's diner. He was tired and out of ideas. It was going to be a long night, especially since Vera had to work late. Bradshaw's mind was cluttered with details of the Ince affair and tomorrow's planned trip south. As he sat in his usual booth absently nursing a coffee, his chum Carl Wilson walked in. The off-duty cop was with Roger Frankel, one of the *Tribune*'s police reporters. Al's spirits brightened when he saw them, and he waved for the men to join him.

"Where's my five bucks?" demanded Frankel.

"Oh, Jesus, Rog," said Al, snapping his fingers. "I forgot all about it."

"I told you they'd kill 'em. Boy, isn't that Notre Dame backfield somethin' ?" enthused Frankel, and the men began rehashing the recent Army-Notre Dame football game. "Miller, Stuhldreher, Crowley, and Layden—the Four Horsemen. They're the best," proclaimed Frankel.

"Gimme Grange over all of 'em," retorted Wilson, referring to the Galloping Ghost, Red Grange, of the University of Illinois. "Did ya read about that Michigan game? *Four* touchdown runs. One of 'em was ninety-five yards!"

Vera finally sauntered over. "Hello, strangers." She smiled at the men. "What'll it be?" She joked with the boys awhile after taking their orders, but then left them to their talk of sports and women.

Eventually their conversation turned to business. "I've had one hell of a goddamn tough day," complained Frankel.

"That goes for all of us, buddy," declared Wilson. He turned to Al. "Funny how you don't think of somebody for months, and then a guy's name pops up twice in two days. Remember the other day you asked me about Grady Fletcher?"

Al nodded.

"Well, today some guy down at the precinct mentioned him too." Wilson bit into a slice of rye toast and sipped some coffee. "Funny, isn't it?" he asked, turning to Frankel. "You don't hear a guy's name for months, and then all of a sudden—"

"What'd they say about Fletcher?" interrupted Al anxiously.

"Oh, Nelson said they picked up a couple of dead bums, and one of 'em looked like Grady Fletcher."

"Seen enough?" The white-coated attendant at the Los Angeles morgue was about to wheel away the body.

"Yeah, enough," Al said, swallowing his words, the color drained from his face. It was Grady Fletcher, all right, his face battered and covered with dried blood-stains. Poor son of a bitch, thought Al.

He asked the attendant, "Did they find anything on him?"

"Not a thing. Just the clothes he was wearin'—what was left of 'em. The other bums musta stole his shoes and coat. One funny thing, though," the man added. "His clothes was new. Usually when they pick up these dead bums, they're in rags."

"What was the cause of death?"

"Blow on the head. He probably either fell or was pushed against a brick wall. Maybe he fell in the gutter and hit his head on the curb. Who cares?"

Al cared.

"He was murdered, I know it!"

"You can't be sure of that Al," retorted Vince calmly on the other end of the telephone line. "He was an alky, you said so yourself. He came into some money and got loaded. Maybe he got rolled."

"He had somethin' important to tell me, Vince. He had some hard information, and they got to him."

"Maybe yes, maybe no," replied Vince evenly. "After all, Fletcher wasn't on the yacht. Whatever he had to tell you was only hearsay anyway."

Fletcher's death had triggered in both reporters an awareness that continued investigation into the Ince affair might prove fatal. Up to now their fears had remained unspoken. But now Al, quietly and steadily, said, "I know what you're thinking, Vince. But I'm not laying off now. You can back out. I'll understand if you don't want to make the trip south."

"Forget that crap, kid. I'm in. We go to San Diego tomorrow, as planned."

Al hung up and slowly undressed. He was surprised to spot a bottle of genuine Johnnie Walker Scotch, along with a bottle of ginger ale and two glasses, on the night table beside Vera's bed.

"Where did that come from?" Al asked her.

"I was saving it," said Vera. "For a special occasion. Or an emergency."

"Which is this?" he inquired jokingly.

"A little of both," she answered with a provocative smile. She was happy Al hadn't lost his sense of humor. "I figured you needed a good drink, and I figured it might relax you enough to make tonight an occasion." They both laughed as Al mixed the highballs.

Then they made love. Playfully at first. Then warmly and passionately.

Afterward, they stared up at the ceiling and played the little game which had become an intimate ritual. From the light patterns on the ceilings and walls, they picked out figures—animals, faces—and Al would always joke about new sexual positions.

Vera giggled like an adolescent at Al's bawdiness.

"You're like a little kid when you laugh like that," he whispered, and they made love once more. Then they sat up in bed, lit cigarettes, and finished their highballs.

Suddenly Al remembered his date with Elinor Glyn. "What time is it?"

"A little after ten," replied Vera. "Why?"

"I had a date tonight."

Vera stiffened. She didn't appreciate his honesty. "Oh, yeah?"

"Yeah. She was gonna put me in the movies."

"That's a new line," she scoffed, snuffing out her cigarette.

"I just want you to know what I've given up for you."

"A younger broad, right?"

"As a matter of fact," said Al, grinding out his cigarette and rolling over onto his stomach, "she's about thirty years older than you are."

"Go to sleep," said Vera, cuddling up to his back.

Al affectionately patted her on the thigh.

But as the night crawled on, he couldn't sleep. Every time he'd doze off, he'd wake with a start, remembering Grady Fletcher's grotesquely distorted face.

Tuesday, November 25

They nursed Vince's Oldsmobile down the coast road, stopping only for gas and water. Al and Vince had left before dawn. The drive from Los Angeles to Del Mar took almost four hours, but at least Al was able to catch some sleep.

It was 8:30 when they reached the Stratford Inn. The night clerk, a wan, middle-aged man, was still on duty. He was uncooperative and claimed he knew nothing about last week's events concerning Mr. Ince's stay at the inn.

"You'll have to wait and talk with the day clerk, who comes on at nine-thirty. Sometimes ten."

"Christ, I don't want to waste all that time waiting here!" Al moaned to Vince.

"Tell ya what, kid," Vince offered. "I'll wait to talk with the guy, then take the train down to meet you. You take my car and go on down to San Diego."

By nine, Al was pulling onto Santa Cruz Boulevard. He was in the lower-middle-class section of San Diego's Ocean Beach district, a run-down neighborhood brightened only by a magnificent view of the sea. The only sounds that broke the morning stillness were the cries of seagulls. The entire area had the look of a deserted beach town, and Will Greely's small clapboard house was a dismal affair.

Al knocked loudly on the front door several times. Finally a large German-looking woman, her hair braided and pinned to the top of her head, swung open

184

the door. She was wearing a musty flannel bathrobe and a decidedly unfriendly scowl.

Bradshaw attempted to be pleasant in spite of the woman's foreboding expression. He identified himself. "I'm from the Los Angeles office of the *Tribune*. Is Will Greely here?"

"No," she snarled. She was about to slam the door, but Al's hand flew up and held it open.

"Doesn't he live here?"

"He lives here when he lives here," she snapped. "I ain't seen him for three days."

"Where can I find him?"

"You tell me, sonny."

"Are you Mrs. Greely?"

"Yeah, I'm Mrs. Greely."

"Please, this is very important. Any idea where your husband went?"

"He won't be back until his dough runs out. Then he always comes crawlin' back," she droned. "Judgin' by the wad he had, I figure this time he'll be gone about two weeks."

"He had a wad of money?"

"Yeah, he hit the numbers or the horses or somethin'. Throws me a lousy hundred bucks," she complained, "and then takes off. You newspaper bums are all alike."

This time she succeeded in slamming the door in Al's face. But the reporter had the information he needed. There was no doubt that Will Greely had been paid off. And if Greely had been paid off, others had been too.

It was going to be tough for Al to get any hard information in San Diego, but he hadn't come all this way to give up now.

Bradshaw's footsteps echoed loudly down the marble-floored corridor of the tomblike San Diego City Hall Building. Finally, after passing a dozen offices, he reached the right one. The words were neatly lettered in gold on the frosted-glass, wood-framed door: "Coroner, San Diego County."

Inside, a mustiness permeated the huge office. Throughout the room there were countless rows of drab floor-to-ceiling wooden filing cabinets. A wooden railing separated several workers from the reception area where Al stood. Bradshaw cleared his throat, but no one looked up.

A mousy-looking bespectacled man of indeterminate age was trying to appear totally engrossed in filing a huge stack of papers. He wore a green eyeshade, and there were rubber tips on his fingers. Bradshaw noticed the man sneak a couple of glances in his direction. But Rubber Fingers wouldn't acknowledge Al's presence.

Over in one corner a plumpish man in his mid-fifties was sitting at a desk, struggling with an adding machine and columns of figures. He too ignored Al.

Just on the other side of the railing sat a tweed-suited sallow-complexioned woman, unfriendly and bored. Her dull brown hair was gathered into a neat bun at the nape of her neck. When she finally looked up from her typewriter, she peered at Al through narrow eyes.

"Can I help you?" she asked in an impolite tone.

"My name's Bradshaw. I'm with the L.A. *Tribune*. May I see the coroner, please?"

"Dr. Grant is out of town."

"Who's in charge?"

"Dr. Hall. But he's very busy this morning." She dismissed Al by lowering her eyes and returning to her typing.

"He'll see me. Tell him"—Al chose his words carefull—"tell him it's about Thomas Ince's murder."

Her head jerked up. Al enjoyed the unnerving effect his statement had produced on the prissy, constipated bitch. He allowed himself to smile.

"Wait here," she said coldly as she pushed back her chair and rose.

The other two employees exchanged uneasy glances as Miss Narrow Eyes disappeared into Grant's office.

Within a minute Al was facing a round-faced, ruddy-cheeked, balding man in his early sixties. He had a broad smile and radiated good humor. Hall extended his hand. "Good morning, Mr. Bradshaw. Lawrence Hall. I'm the coroner's assistant. How can I help you, sir?"

Al was somewhat taken aback. Hall's jolly Santa Claus-like demeanor was a startling contrast to the three corpselike employees on his staff. Hall invited Al into his stuffy office, motioned for him to sit down, and offered him a cigar.

"All the way down from Los Angeles to see the coroner, Mr. Bradshaw? I'm sorry he's not here."

"Yes. Well, I think you can help me. I'm investigating the death of Thomas Ince. It seems Will Greely, our *Tribune* stringer here in town—"

"Ah, yes, Will Greely. That poor man will drink himself into his grave."

Al ignored the slur. "It seems Will filed a story that Thomas Ince was shot, and possibly died here in San Diego." Al kept all emotion out of his voice. He studied Hall for the slightest reaction.

"I read nothing like that," countered Hall calmly. "It was my understanding that Mr. Ince had been stricken with a heart attack and died in Los Angeles. I read, of course, in the paper, that he had *been* here in San Diego."

"Some people seem to think he *died* here in San Diego."

"If that happened, Mr. Bradshaw, it was never reported to our office." Hall rose. "I suggest you check the Los Angeles coroner. I'm sure he has a death certificate for Mr. Ince."

Al was ushered swiftly back into the waiting room. "Always glad to talk to the press." Dr. Hall smiled. "Sorry you made the trip for nothing. You could have gotten the information you wanted back in Los Angeles. Good day, now." On the farewell, Hall turned and vanished.

Al stood in the outer office for several moments. There seemed nothing for him to do now but leave. Was he imagining it, or was Rubber Fingers over at the filing cabinets indicating with an almost imperceptible movement of his eyes for Al to wait outside?

Al remained in the outer corridor for two or three minutes. The man didn't appear. "Dammit. It *was* my imagination," he thought. "I'm getting punchy."

He noticed a pay phone at the end of the hall. He called the Stratford Inn, and after haggling with the desk clerk, finally got Vince on the line.

"You just caught me, kid," said Vince. "I finished speaking with the day clerk. Their story is airtight. Seems Ince and Goodman did stop here. Ince was carried in on a stretcher. But I can't find anyone who saw him or talked with him."

"Then he could have been dead!"

"I guess he could have been, you're right," admitted Vince.

"How long were they there?"

"Only a couple of hours. Then a private car came down from Los Angeles for them."

"Wait there," said Al. "I'm driving up. There's no point in your coming down here. It's been a dead end."

As Bradshaw hung up, he spotted Rubber Fingers emerging from the coroner's office, nervously glancing up and down the corridor. "I *was* right." Al beamed. He snapped his fingers and waved to the jumpy little man.

He walked toward Al swiftly. Up close, Bradshaw noticed that Rubber Fingers had close-set, weasellike eyes. Putting a rubber-tipped finger to his lips, the man motioned Al to keep silent. "Follow me," he whispered, and led Al up a stairway. They stopped in the stairwell between floors.

"I gotta make it fast. They think I went to the

bathroom. How much will you pay for an official report saying that Thomas Ince died here in San Diego?"

Al's jaw dropped in astonishment. "You . . . you've got a report?"

"How much will you pay?" he asked, an urgency in his voice.

"I'll give you a hundred bucks."

"Are you kidding? They got *plenty*."

"And they're not splitting it with you, is that it?"

"Those two idiots I work with are too scared to call Hall on it. But I'm not going to let him pocket all that dough."

"Who paid Hall off?"

"How the hell should I know? But it was a bundle."

"I'll give you five hundred."

"I ain't risking it for less than a thousand. And it's gotta be today."

A thousand dollars! That was a *lot* of money. But Bradshaw couldn't allow this bonanza to slip away. "All right," he found himself saying. He reached into his jacket pocket, pulled out a train schedule, and scanned it quickly. "How soon can you get me the report?" asked Al.

"When can you get the money?"

"Meet me in the coffee shop at Union Station at three P.M. I'll have the dough for you."

The man nodded, turned, and scurried back down the stairs.

From a booth in a nearby drugstore, after a harrowing ten minutes with long-distance operators, Al got through to Vera.

Instantly she knew he was in trouble. "Are you all right?" she asked, concerned.

"I need a thousand bucks, and I need it fast."

"A thou . . . Jeez, Al!" Vera only had around eleven hundred in her savings account. This would wipe her out.

"And," continued Al hurriedly, "you've got to make the twelve-o'clock train for San Diego."

The desperation in his voice brought Vera to a quick decision. "Okay," she said. "I'll be on it."

"I love you," he told her.

"I know," she said. "You think I'd be doin' this if you didn't?"

But there wasn't time for sentiment. Al said a fast good-bye, then got Vince back on the phone. "Things are popping down here," he enthused.

"I'll take the next train down."

"No. I can handle things here. Can you get back to L.A. right away?"

"Sure. There's a train outta here in a half-hour, I think. What the hell is going on?"

"Get to the L.A. coroner's office and get a copy of Thomas Ince's death certificate. We can blow this thing wide open. I'll meet you at the Palm around six."

"The seven-oh-three is now arriving from Los Angeles," droned the bored voice over the crackling loudspeakers of San Diego's Union Station.

It was 2:45. The train was late. Al paced nervously up and down the platform, as the express finally came to a halt on the track.

"Vera!" he called, spotting her bright yellow dress. She waved back and began running toward him. He rushed to meet her. They hugged, and breathlessly he asked: "Sweetheart, do you have the money?"

"Of course," she answered, a quizzical expression in her eyes. "Al, what the hell is this all about?"

He took Vera by the elbow and led her to a secluded area away from the mainstream of traffic.

"Where is it?" he asked.

She handed him a manila envelope. "It's in fifties."

He placed the envelope in his inside jacket pocket, then clutched Vera and kissed her long and hard on the mouth.

"I love you too." She grinned broadly. "But at a thousand bucks a kiss, I can't afford it."

Al laughed. Vera turned serious. "Al, what's this dough for? It must be dangerous, whatever it is."

"Don't worry, sweetheart. You know I can take care of myself. And don't worry about the dough. You'll get it all back tomorrow. The *Trib*'ll pay five thousand for what I'm gonna buy with this money."

"What *are* you gonna buy, Al? I'm scared."

It was 2:50. Ten minutes before he was to meet Rubber Fingers.

Al walked Vera to the ticket counter. The Limited was returning to Los Angeles at three o'clock. He fished in his pocket to buy her a return ticket, but came up with only $1.75.

He looked at her sheepishly. "Got five bucks?"

"I bought a round-trip ticket, dear," she stated, annoyed but amused in spite of herself. "What are you rushin' me off for? I can catch a later train. I'm bushed! The diner's closed, and the day's shot anyway."

"Sweetheart, I'm going to be running all over town. There's nothing more you can do, and I don't want you here if there's any trouble. Please go home, sweetie. Gussy up. Tonight we'll do the town like we've never done it before."

As she boarded the train, Vera's eyes met Al's. "Look Al, you know I don't care about the dough. Just take care of yourself."

They kissed again. Neither Al nor Vera had noticed two unobtrusive men at the other end of the platform. They had been keeping a close eye on the couple since Vera's arrival. One of the men opened his palm. In his hand was a small photograph of Bradshaw. "That's him, all right," he said to his companion.

"Who's the dame?" asked the other man.

"Beats me."

"Shall I follow her?"

"Nah, we'll call Los Angeles. In that dress she's wearin', they'll have no trouble pickin' up her trail there. Let's just stay with the guy."

Rubber Fingers sat alone nervously in the station luncheonette, silently dunking a doughnut into a cup of steaming coffee. A large, flat manila envelope rested on the table in front of him. Al walked over and sat down.

"Got the money?"

Al nodded. "But first let's see the report."

Rubber Fingers pushed the envelope to Al.

Bradshaw glanced inside. The document was genuine, all right. A copy, but official. Al had seen enough of them to know. This was certainly devastating enough evidence to demand an official investigation. Bradshaw glowed with self-satisfaction. He'd be a star reporter, knocking the D.A.'s of both Los Angeles and San Diego off their fat asses.

Al hadn't noticed that Rubber Fingers had scooped up the envelope containing the cash and vanished.

In his office at the *Tribune,* Casey Clark had to hold the phone away from his ear as Al Bradshaw's voice boomed out: "I've got it! I've got it!"

"Stop screamin', for chrissake. Where the hell are you, anyway?" Clark asked over the crackling line.

"Down in San Diego. And I'm gonna blow this Ince story wide open."

"Jesus Christ! Are you still on that Ince binge?"

"Didn't ya hear what I said? I've got it. I've got proof. *Proof!*"

"What proof?" snarled Clark, but his voice betrayed his excitement. Casey knew Bradshaw well enough to know that if the kid was putting his ass on the line, he must have dug up some hard evidence.

"Ince was shot, and he died here in San Diego. I've got a signed report from the San Diego coroner's office. That, printed next to a signed death certificate from the Los Angeles county coroner, will make some great front page, won't it? And if the *Trib* is too scared to print it, the *Times* won't be."

"If you've got the proof, kid, we'll print it."

"I've got it right here in my hand. I'm leaving now.

I'm driving right up to L.A. I'll be there in a few hours."

"Bradshaw, wait! Don't be a jerk," cautioned Casey. "If you've got proof, don't walk around with it. Photograph it. Then put the original in a bank vault down there. Bring the copy and get your ass back here."

That made sense. Al picked up a telephone book and located the name of a photographer close to Union Station: Henry B. Hawthorn. His studio was only three blocks away.

"Got a match?" asked a husky male voice. Al closed the phone book and turned around. "Sure, just a minute." He reached into his vest pocket. For an instant Bradshaw was aware of a sudden rush of air behind him, and a heavy, dull pain in the back of his neck. He uttered a startled moan. He had the sensation of falling, but someone caught him.

The extreme shock of the blow lingered. . . . Al was vaguely aware of two men helping him to a vacant bench in the almost-deserted waiting room.

"Take some of this," a distant voice instructed.

"Here, buddy," said another fuzzy voice. A flask was lifted to Al's mouth, and he felt liquid dribble down his chin and onto his shirt.

"Drunk!" a matron uttered disgustedly to her companion as they walked past Al. Bradshaw, legs outstretched, arms dangling, suddenly realized he was sprawled on a long wooden bench. His clothes reeked of alcohol.

Groggily, he shook his head as consciousness returned. What time was it? The station clock read 4:45. In a sickening instant the pit of his stomach told him what had happened. He reached into his jacket pocket—the manila envelope was gone.

Frantically he checked his other pockets. His wallet was still there. His keys. His pocket money. Everything. Except the document.

* * *

"The one with the rubber fingers!" yelled Al into the phone. "The weasellike one. What's his name?"

The woman's response was infuriatingly calm. "You must be referring to Mr. Benton. He hasn't returned from lunch. Call back later, please."

A few moments later Al burst into the coroner's office. It was 5:15. "Where's Benton?" he demanded. The mousy woman, furious at Al's attitude, stood up. "Mr. Benton hasn't returned."

The clamor aroused Dr. Hall. "What's going on here? Oh . . . Mr. Bradshaw. You still here?"

Al's anger had overtaken his reason. At the top of his voice he threatened: "What are you guys trying to pull? Where's Benton? He takes my thousand bucks for the report on Ince's murder, then has me rolled. You won't get away with this!"

It was deathly quiet. The adding machine had stopped abruptly. Miss Narrow Eyes stood motionless, then silently fell back in her chair. Even Dr. Hall momentarily paled.

But the old man swiftly regained his composure. "I haven't the vaguest idea what you're talking about, but I think things are getting out of hand," he said. "You are becoming a nuisance, Mr. Bradshaw, and I demand that you leave. I believe I detect the smell of liquor on your breath. Will you please leave, or shall I summon the police?"

Bradshaw's eyes were burning. "I had it, Casey. I swear to Jesus I had it!" The passion in his voice was painfully sincere.

"Yeah, and we all know President Harding was a crook. But knowin' it and bein' able to prove it are two different things." Casey dismissed Al with a wave of his hand. "Now, will you forget all this shit and get back to work—or get yourself another job."

"Hey, Al," called Johnny from Al's desk. "Phone for you."

Bradshaw's emotions were drained. He had come so

tantalizingly close! He shuffled over to his desk and flopped into his chair. Half-heartedly he picked up the phone. "Bradshaw here."

"I hear you almost had the case solved," breathed the provocative voice.

Al bolted up, as though an electric current had passed through him. "Is this Diane Enright?" he bluntly asked.

There was a tinkling, sad laugh. "No," the woman answered.

"Who is this, then?" As he questioned her, Al feverishly scrawled a note: "Casey, Enright on line . . . get over here . . . listen my phone . . ."

He thrust the note at Johnny, frantically indicating its importance with his eyes and hands.

"It doesn't matter who I am now," she said wistfully.

"Why are they covering up Ince's death?" Al demanded. "He was shot, wasn't he?"

"He was shot," she confirmed.

Why the hell was Casey taking so long to get over here?

"I wanted to tell you you might as well forget it now," the woman lamented. "It's all over."

Casey, chewing angrily on a cigar, finally arrived at Al's desk. "What the hell's goin' on now?" Al thrust the receiver at Clark just as the line clicked dead.

As she replaced the phone on its cradle, an inch-long marquise-shaped diamond flashed multicolored fire from the slender fourth finger of her right hand. She stared at herself in her dressing-table mirror, its beveled edges imprisoning her reflection in rainbows of light. Her expression registered defeat as well as boredom.

Marion Davies ran a brush through her golden hair and then tossed it down carelessly. The heavy brush clattered on the mirrored surface of her vanity.

From a crystal goblet she took another gulp of

champagne. Two empty bottles of Dom Perignon lay discarded on the thick white bedroom carpet

"Maaa-a-a-rion," whined the high-pitched voice as Hearst entered the bedroom. "I've advised you not to drink when you're working on a picture." She didn't answer, but defiantly drained the glass.

Marion closed her eyes and for the thousandth time thought back to last Wednesday. She was in the galley of the *Oneida*. The boat was rocking gently. The night was still. Marion was laughing gaily, sipping champagne, with Tom Ince.

"Maa-a-a-arion." The whining voice interrupted her reverie and brought her back to the present. "Are you listening to me?"

"I'm listening," she answered. But her thoughts were of Tom Ince's handsome, animated face as he was relating a bawdy tale. She smiled as she remembered him reaching across the galley table to clutch her hand.

Neither Marion nor Ince had any way of knowing that the rocking of the boat had awakened Hearst. The old man's hand had groped for Marion's. She wasn't in bed. She wasn't in the loo. Hearst donned his silken bathrobe and stalked the deserted corridors of the *Oneida*. Marion was nowhere to be found. He descended to the galley. There she was, in her chemise, chatting animatedly with . . . Hearst couldn't be sure who he was; the man's back was to him. But who else could it be but . . .?

Marion's eyes widened to the size of saucers when she spotted Hearst in the shadows. She was trapped in the circle of yellow light pouring from the ceiling lamp.

Flashes of light glinted like diamonds off the sides of the silver revolver. "No!" gasped Marion as the gunshot rang through the air.

At the vivid recollection of the horrible moment, Marion knocked over her champagne goblet. It shattered on the glass top of her dresser.

"I'm going to New York tonight," Hearst said impassively. He was addressing her from across her white-and-gold bedroom. There was a chill in his manner. "I advise you to stop drinking and turn your attention back to your career."

Marion simply stared back at him.

"The Ince scandal will blow over soon, my dear," he said. "Time is always on our side if we don't make an issue of things."

"Leave me alone, please, W.R. I'd like to be alone for a while." Her voice had an even, nasty overtone. There was no trace of a stutter when she was drunk.

"Very well," He turned to leave. She stared at his reflection in her dressing-table mirror. "You can't get them all, W.R.," she said.

He pretended not to hear her. She was obviously hallucinating again. He closed the door softly as he left.

Epilogue

The official death certificate stated Thomas Harper Ince died of a heart ailment, "possibly caused by over-indulgence in eating and drinking." Although the death certificate was signed in Los Angeles, rumors persisted that Ince was shot under mysterious circumstances aboard Hearst's yacht, the *Oneida,* while it was moored off the coast of San Diego.

Pressure was brought upon the San Diego authorities to conduct an official investigation. Three weeks after Ince's cremation, an inquiry was held. The case was dismissed with these words:

"We began this investigation because of many rumors brought to my office regarding the case, and have considered them until today in order to definitely dispose of them. There will be no further investigation of stories concerning drinking on board the yacht. If there are to be, then they will have to be in Los Angeles County, where presumably the liquor was secured. People interested in Ince's sudden death have continued with persistent reports, and in order to satisfy them we did conduct an investigation. But after questioning those involved, we are satisfied his death was from ordinary causes."

But although the authorities were satisfied, the issue was not dead and buried. The sudden death of Thomas Ince continued to make news. In 1926, the respected Chicago *Tribune,* one of Hearst's rival newspapers, carried an interview with Chicago District Attorney Robert E. Crowe. One of Crowe's assistants, a man named McSwiggin, had been killed while in the company of known criminals. The Hearst newspapers launched a "Who Killed McSwiggin?" campaign, pressuring Crowe. The district attorney responded with a statement in the *Tribune*: "The police are doing the best they can to find the murderers of McSwiggin. Unless the Hearst press lets up, I think a question which should be raised is, 'Who killed Thomas Ince?' " After Crowe's challenge, the Hearst papers immediately abandoned their McSwiggin crusade.

Though none dared refer to Ince's death as murder, many of Ince's contemporaries continued to echo the sentiments of D. W. Griffith. The legendary director, who had been Ince's friend and partner, often said, "All you have to do to make Hearst turn white is mention Ince's name. We all know what happened, but Hearst is too big to touch."

After the Ince affair, the career of columnist Louella Parsons soared. For decades, with the Hearst papers behind her, she was the most powerful Hollywood columnist. She could not only make or break careers, but she delighted in monitoring the morals of the Hollywood community.

Even after Louella and Marion Davies had a bitter falling-out, Hearst remained loyal to his star columnist. Throughout Louella's career there were allegations that Hearst's unfailing loyalty was due to Miss Parsons' silence concerning the Ince affair.

Though the Ince affair did not terminate the relationship of William Randolph Hearst and Marion Davies, it changed the nature of their union perceptibly. After 1924, Marion seemed trapped in the world of power she had so eagerly and willingly entered. In rebellion, she increased her drinking and decreased her discretion. Her world seemed to be one of synthetic excitement.

Hearst still continued to employ his network of spies, and Marion was aware he knew her every move. But there were no further confrontations regarding her flirtations. Hearst looked the other way when Marion took up with temporary lovers.

Marion Davies and William Randolph Hearst lived together until his death, in 1951, at the age of eighty-eight. Marion lived on another ten years. Although she was fabulously wealthy, by this time she had become a hopeless alcoholic. She died of cancer at the age of sixty-one.

Thomas Harper Ince is acknowledged by film historians as one of the founders of the motion-picture industry, and one of its geniuses. However, to the general public his name is virtually unknown.

Inceville is gone. Ince's films are lost or forgotten. He has a "star" on Hollywood Boulevard, and Ince Boulevard, a street in Culver City, is named for him. But these are hardly ample monuments to a man who once ranked with Griffith, Sennett, and De Mille.

The Culver City studios no longer bear his name. Through the decades the studios have changed hands many times. Their most famous and prestigious owner was David O. Selznick. The Southern-plantation edifice built by Ince became world-famous as the trademark of Selznick-International Pictures.

But when someone today mentions the name of Thomas Ince, the reaction, if any, usually takes the form of a question: "Wasn't he the man who was shot on William Randolph Hearst's yacht?"

About the Authors

Joe Morella and Edward Z. Epstein are co-authors of a number of successful books, including *The "It" Girl: The Incredible Story of Clara Bow*; *Lana: The Public and Private Lives of Miss Turner*; *Brando: The Unauthorized Biography*; *Rebels: The Rebel Hero In Films*; *and Judy: The Films and Career of Judy Garland*.